Net Pucks and Chill

by

Debbie Charles

Texas Tornadoes
Book 2

This is a work of fiction. Names, characters, places, and incidents are either the product of the author's imagination or are used fictitiously, and any resemblance to actual persons living or dead, business establishments, events, or locales, is entirely coincidental.

Net Pucks and Chill
COPYRIGHT © 2025 by Maggie Sims, LLC

All rights reserved. No part of this book may be used or reproduced in any manner whatsoever without written permission of the author except in the case of brief quotations embodied in critical articles or reviews.

No Generative AI Training Use.
For avoidance of doubt, Author reserves all rights, and there are no rights to reproduce and/or otherwise use the Work in any manner for purposes of training artificial intelligence technologies to generate text, including without limitation, technologies that are capable of generating works in the same style or genre as the Work, unless the Author's specific and express permission to do so is given in writing. Nor does anyone have the right to sublicense others to reproduce and/or otherwise use the Work in any manner for purposes of training artificial intelligence technologies to generate text without Author's specific and express permission.

Trade Paperback ISBN 979-8-89044-412-7
Digital ISBN 979-8-89044-413-4
Cover by *Wicked Smart Designs*

She's failing One-Night Stand 101. Hockey has taught him that practice makes perfect. Game on.

"Whatcha looking for?" I ask, bringing my whisky to my lips.

"Just doing what you do. Scanning for prospects."

I choke, sputtering most of my sip back into the glass. Mon dieu, this girl is dangerous to drink around. "What?"

"Hey, it's New Year's Eve. I want to figure out who I'm gonna kiss in a couple hours."

"First, I don't do that when I'm standing right next to a woman."

She scoffs.

Huh. I thought I was more subtle than that. I'm usually focused on flirting with whoever I'm talking to, with only some side-eye for other prospects.

"Second, right here, baby. I'm happy to help you out." Only after I say the words do I think them through. My plan had been to do exactly what she said—scan for prospects, but not for a kiss.

She shares my inner devil's reaction. "Yeah, right. You probably already have your first, second, and third choice lined up, and for all I know, you'll take all three home."

I blink, not sure what I should say.

She sips one of the cosmos and continues, "It's time I started thinking like you hockey players. The world is my oyster, and I'm going to swallow it whole."

Part of me perks up at that idea.

Net Pucks and Chill Playlist

DJ Turn It Up – Dimension
Get Low – Lil Jon and the East Side Boyz
Stronger – Clean Bandit
Bicycle Race – Queen
Winner – Jamie Foxx, featuring T.I. and Justin Timberlake
This is What You Came For – Calvin Harris & Rihanna
Mammas Don't Let Your Babies Grow Up to Be Cowboys – Waylon Jennings & Willie Nelson
I Like the Way You Kiss Me – Artemas
Let You Love Me – Rita Ora
Feeling For You – Milky Chance
Down Bad – Taylor Swift
Symphony – Clean Bandit
Break My Heart – Dua Lipa
Slow It Down – Benson Boone
Lay It All on Me – Rudimental
Yes, And? – Ariana Grande
Stargazing – Myles Smith

~Chapter One~

Nicole

When I'm an hour outside Austin, I punch in my friend Christina Donovan's number on my car's display. She made me promise to call when I got back from Christmas at my family's. We've been friends since attending UT together, so she knows how I feel about trips home and how grueling the drive, coupled with my complex family dynamics, can be. She worries about me, and as part-owner of the new Austin NHL team, the Texas Tornadoes, she has the resources to send help if I need it.

"Hey, are you home?" she asks.

"No, but I'm less than an hour out. I can almost see the skyline."

"How was it?"

"The same." I shrug even though she can't see it. "They barely sat down for the meal before they were out doing ranch chores again."

"I guess that's better than pestering you to help with them."

"True. What are you doing? I'm beat from almost nine hours in the car, but I sure could use some company and a drink."

"Oh, uh, we were going to get Mattie from the airport

in a bit."

My belly flips. Mathieu du Près is the most charming, beautiful man I've seen in a long time on top of being an excellent hockey player. As popular as he is with the ladies, I wouldn't stand a chance with him, but it hasn't stopped me from drooling. I've met him a few times at after-game celebrations at the unofficial team hangout, Chasers. But the last thing I want to do is see him after three days with my family surrounded by two long days of driving. I'm not in a good state of mind, and I probably don't smell all that great, either.

I open my mouth to suggest Christina's boyfriend, Cameron Hill—Prancer to his teammates and starting goalie for the Tornadoes—get his teammate while she comes and drinks with me, but Chris beats me there.

"We could swing by after we get him if you'd like. I'll order snacks for the guys, and we'll bring the drinks. You don't have to do anything."

"You better give me time to shower if you're bringing a single guy to my place."

She laughs. "Ha! It's only Mattie." At my silence, she asks, "Nicole? Are you into Mattie?"

"First, I'd want to shower after this drive for anyone, probably even Cam, now that I think about it. You're willing to deal with me with road grime, but there's no reason to subject others to it. Second, I'm pretty much into any hot single guy about now. It's been a long dry spell. But I also know my place in the world. I'm invisible to someone like him. He sees the exotic fun girls, the ones with legs for miles and honey blonde hair like you, or the spicy tiny dancers like Maria."

For too long, I've been the only one of my friend group focused on finding "the one," hopscotching from one aborted relationship to another. I'm prone to throwing away my priorities to focus on supporting my man, and I'm sick and tired of wondering why they left despite that. This Christmas trip and the long hours with only myself for company made me decide to try something new. I need to enjoy being with me. Not for what I can do for my family or any man.

"Okay. I'm sorry. I know you're beat. We won't stay long. Having the guys there could perk you up or take the pressure off if you don't want to rehash your annoyance at your family just yet…?" She trails off, hopeful. "But I could come alone if you prefer."

It means a lot that she offers. Cam and she had a rocky few months as their secret, supposedly casual, relationship turned into real, long-term love. They've been fused at the hip—as much as hockey travel schedules allow—once they sorted themselves out.

And now that I've wrangled the promise of shower time out of her, the eye candy that is Mattie and the tons of food that comprise hockey player "snacks" sound great.

"Bring 'em. Just no sooner than eight o'clock please."

"Perfect, he doesn't touch down until almost then, and I'll order food to be delivered from the car. Love you!"

"Love you, too." But she's already gone, high on life and love. If I had her looks and money, I would be, too. But I'm the ugly duckling of the group. Not ugly, but not a beauty or unique like any of my close circle, either.

No matter. After this Christmas, I'm determined to start the new year as the new me. I'm going to wear lower cut tops, push-up bras, and more makeup, and I plan to flirt like mad. I'll sleep with whoever strikes my fancy. I'm tired of holding out for someone who wants all of me, and I don't have time for a relationship until I finish my MBA anyway.

Mattie is the perfect practice target, even if he is beyond my reach.

Chapter Two

Mathieu

As the plane touches down in Austin, I recall a similar flight only four months ago when I started for the Texas Tornadoes. New city, new team. Again. You'd think I'd be used to it by now, having played for the Florida Fury before being nabbed by Greg Donovan in the expansion draft. And I am. The first two months of the season are under our belt, and we have some good guys on this team. Great players, too. And because the organization is family run by siblings Greg, Christina, and Amy Donovan, they treat us well.

I also love that more team members are single like me. More opportunities to play. Every city has puck bunnies, but more importantly, my guys here are up for new adventures. If I feel like playing disc golf, I can call someone. If I want to go rock climbing, there's someone up for it. And they don't have to check with their wife or girlfriend to know if they're available.

Austin isn't as hopping as Miami, but at least here, fewer girls are looking for my paycheck as much as my body. And they're less plastic. Women are also more active, which suits me, since I don't sit still well. They go out on a boat to kneeboard or ski or fish, rather than just be boat decorations that want you to "rub sunscreen everywhere."

Despite the ridiculous late December temperature of 18C, I'm happy to be back in my new city. I'd bounced home for a day and a half because we only had a three-day break, and the weather for flights is unpredictable at this time of year.

Ottawa at Christmastime is amazing, although I might be biased. The Rideau Canal is decorated beautifully in readiness for when it opens to skaters next month. And my family home has all the best memories—handmade decorations from my sister's and my childhood art projects, silly holiday sweaters, all of them. Far more important, it has my family. My sister is finishing university this year, so we were both home for a couple weeks this summer. But winter is what Canada does best, and I've missed the colder temperatures and the snow almost as much as I missed Maman's cooking.

We've got practice tomorrow morning, then we fly out to an away game, followed by a home game on December thirtieth and another on New Year's Day.

Prancer and Christina are supposed to pick me up tonight, and I'm starving like usual, so I'm hoping they'll be up for a quick meal before dropping me at home. How the hell Prancer managed to score a part owner of our team as his girlfriend is still a mystery to me, but c'est la vie, and they truly appear smitten.

I turn my phone on, and it lights up. The team texts have been sparse, since almost everyone was focused on family for the holiday, but they'll get going again as we all return.

I skim the ones waiting for me from Christina. Sweet! They're taking me with them to Nicole's apartment from the airport, and Christina will ensure there are snacks.

I've met her friends a couple times, mostly at Chasers, our after-game go-to bar. The accountant one seems like a hardass, and the dancer is a firecracker. But the quiet one, Nicole, shows promise for a no muss, no fuss interlude of fun until I'm bored. We had fun the couple times I'd seen her at Chasers, and the second time, she sought me out.

Half a dozen puck bunnies did as well, and while their asses might have been tighter and their hair silkier, I also like that Nicole seemed to be okay just hanging out with no expectations. I don't have to "be on" or work as hard. If we were to hook up, I wouldn't have to worry about her poking a hole in a condom or hiding a camera. Christina wouldn't be friends with her if she wasn't trustworthy.

Chris is waiting for me at the bottom of the escalator near baggage claim, recognizing me despite my nondescript hoodie and baseball cap pulled low. She expected it, for the same reason she's here and Cam isn't.

"Salut, love. How's our boy?" I greet her with a hug.

"Fantastic, thank you. He found out Dana and the kids are coming back next week, and I swear he's more excited about that than he was about Christmas."

"That may be because he's still nervous having meals with the team owner, even if the guy is your brother. They're setting Zoe up in the dorms then?"

She nods, directing me toward where Cam hovers in his cheap-ass used Honda in the pickup lane.

She drives a Prius so I suppose I should be grateful, but I fucking hate folding myself into small low cars. "Between the two of you and your budgets, I'd hoped someone got a hockey-person sized vehicle for Christmas."

"Whatever. Some of us like breathing clean air. I'll get in the back. I have to order food anyway."

"Thanks." I slide into the front seat and manage a handclasp and half hug with Cam across the console. "Torchy's?"

"Of course." She turns to Cam. "Ha. Told ya. The man has taste. I already have the order in my shopping basket on their site."

Cam shakes his head at us, and I turn to wink at her. "Nicole's in town, huh? So is her family local?"

"No. In fact, she drove all day to get back today, so we can't stay late. But she wanted some company."

"Really? After all that driving?"

"Her relationship with her family is…complicated. But that's her story to tell," Christina said. "I think she liked the idea of *Torchy's*"—emphasized with a glance at the back of Cam's head to reference their ongoing debate over the best tacos in Austin—"and a distraction from the past few days."

How sad. I want everyone to have a super supportive family like mine. And to drive all day to see them and back again when you're not going to enjoy it? That's more commitment than I'd be willing to make. But hey, I can be a distraction with the best of them. I face forward and rub my hands together. "I accept my mission."

"Watching action flicks on the plane again, huh?" Cam says with a snicker.

I snort. Who needs fiction when you're the main character in your own action movie?

Chapter Three

Nicole

Cam's car pulls into visitor parking as I'm looking out of my apartment window. When the doors pop open, my eyes are only on Mattie. He untangles himself from the car and slings off his hoodie. The t-shirt underneath rides up his back as he does, and he doesn't tug it back down until he's free of the sweatshirt and has thrown it into the car.

Holy yumminess. Even from the third floor, the muscles in his back make me salivate. I can only imagine the ones in his ass and thighs and…on his front.

Damn, my dry spell has definitely been too long. My hair is still damp from my shower, and now, that's not the only part of me that's wet.

"You cannot jump your friend's boyfriend's friend. It's like a rule or something." I say it out loud, as though that will help cement the plan in my head. Also, I don't want to jeopardize my opportunity to get free tickets from Christina here and there, since I genuinely enjoy hockey but can't afford NHL prices on my budget.

I make decent money, but I'm saving to help my parents. Work reimburses me for my MBA program based on grades, but I still have the initial outlay for that, and rents here in Austin have skyrocketed since a bunch of big tech companies moved their back office operations here.

The doorbell buzzes. I adjust the girls in the black tank with the built-in bralette, hoping to make them perkier, and go answer it. Showtime—or I guess, dress rehearsal time. Mattie is just practice. It's not even the new year yet, so I have time to warm up.

The food delivery arrives while we all exchange hugs. Yum, hugging NHL players is like hugging a huge block of wood—warm, but hard. We head to the kitchenette and pour drinks while Cam locates the plates and grabs four. Chris's pet peeve is eating food from delivery or takeout containers. Even Chinese; the girl is that weird about it.

"How was your Christmas, Mattie?" I ask as I slide a taco onto my plate and perch on a barstool.

"Fantastic. I have the greatest—" he breaks off, looking stricken.

I shoot Chris a look with pressed lips. "Family? That's great. I'm glad you got to see them. Any fun traditions?"

"Certainement. Réveillon, our Christmas Eve feast, has so many of my favorites. As my parents have gotten older, we've started having it before Midnight Mass, but of course, then we're in a food coma and falling asleep in church. This year, none of us made it. And on Boxing Day we do a family skate."

"Who is we?" I ask, curious about who brings out such warmth in his voice. His accent tends to come and go, as though he turns it on as a charm or pickup tool. Regardless, his flowing pronunciation of French words in the middle of a story turns my insides liquid.

"For Réveillon it varies but is always a party with extended family, neighbors, friends. Family skate is just the four of us—my parents, my sister, and me."

"Older or younger?"

"Younger by four years."

Cam jumps in. "What are your favorite foods, Mattie?"

"Oysters, tourtière, which is a meat pie, pea soup, and sweet potato soufflé with maple syrup. They're all very traditional, nothing unusual. Probably they're my favorites because I associate them with the holiday." I scrunch my nose at "oysters," and Mattie notices. "You don't like oysters, eh?"

"I haven't had them," I admit. "I grew up in the Texas Panhandle where they weren't a thing."

"What is the Texas Panhandle?" he asks with a frown.

"Oh, ha. Sorry. It's the northernmost part of Texas, that square that sticks out of the top of the state. I personally think Nebraska's shape has more of a panhandle, but whatever. No one asked me when they gave it that nickname."

"I've been looking for good cold-water oysters around here. I may have to bring you along for my research."

New year, new me. I'm trying to be more adventurous. I shrug, gratified when his eyes flick to my breasts. *Sorry, buddy, they're too small to bounce from a shrug, but thanks for looking.* "Sure, I'll try them."

Cam asks, "Nicole, would it be okay if we put hockey on, if we keep the sound low or off, please? There's a division rivalry I want to catch because we're playing one of the teams soon."

"Oh sure, you're going to horn in on my friend time with Chris *and* try to expedite your game tape review? I see how it is," I joke.

He laughs. "Hey, I'm trying to give you girls friend time. We'll just be over here quietly minding our own hockey business while you two catch up."

"Nah, that's fine. We can all watch. Chris and I can catch up during the game or in the next few days."

On the way over to the couch, Mattie spies my bookshelf that's stuffed to overflowing. He turns to me with wide eyes. "Have you read all of these?"

"Yes. Some more than once."

He mutters something about reading that many books without being forced, much less multiple times, but I don't catch it all.

We settle in, Mattie and I on the couch while Cam makes Chris squeeze into the matching chair with him. Mattie and I share an eye roll before the puck drops, then the guys are riveted to the screen. I make it through one commercial before the tension of the last few days and the long drive catch up to me. My eyelids flutter shut.

The next thing I know, I'm on my side, my head is jostled off the rock it had been resting on, and I'm scooped up into someone's arms. Mmm, smells like Mattie.

My eyes fly open, and I stare up to find him smiling down at me. "Va bien, mon petit chou?"

I'm guessing the rock I'd been sleeping on was his thigh, and he jostled me awake when he stood to lift me off the couch. I swipe at my face. Did I drool on him? "Did you call me a shoe?"

He throws back his head and laughs, and I sort of want to bite his Adam's apple. "Non. Chou is cabbage, but petit chou is like sweetie or babe. You were quite cuddly in your sleep."

I'm so embarrassed I don't reply. He lowers me to my bed. *OhmygodMattieDuPrèsisinmybedroom.*

Before I can form a coherent thought—*thanks for the pillow?*—he says, "Rest up, Nicole. Cam and Chris left a few minutes ago when the game ended. Will your door lock behind me?" At my nod, he continues. "Sorry we crashed your first night home, and thank you for the hospitality. And the snuggles."

* * * *

With school on Christmas break and the tech company I work for on a holiday shutdown, I'm able to join Chris at the game the day before New Year's Eve. I rideshare to her place since it's closer to the arena, and she has the benefits of owner parking at the stadium. The driver's eyes bug out when she questions if we are at the right place. She drops me off in the circular drive, and I follow the path past the big house to Christina's converted pool-house-turned-cottage. She opens the door and lets out a wolf whistle.

"So it's Chasers after the game, huh?"

I grin. "Unless a hottie takes my interest at the game."

She shoots me a sly grin. "I kinda thought one already had. You literally draped yourself over Mattie the other night."

"I was unconscious! Anyway, I told you, he's out of my league."

She shakes her head. "I hate when you do that. You're gorgeous, and I'm jealous of the fact that you can wear heels without towering over half the men out there."

I scoff as we pile into her Prius, and she aims for the arena. "Not like you need to worry about that anymore.

You found a great one."

"I did, didn't I?" She sighs happily.

Once we're seated, both with brisket nachos and soft drinks, we watch the warmups. Chris only has eyes for Cam humping the ice, but I like watching the whole team. My gaze may stray to number 10 with "DU PRES" over the number more often than other players, especially when they're all on their hands and knees twerking to loosen their hips, but I make sure I don't linger too long, or Chris will notice. She prefers to sit as close to the ice as possible to watch Cam's goaltending, so she's been using his seats. Her brother Greg has a few rinkside seats as well as the owner's box, though, so I figure she will use those.

"What's your plan for when Zoe arrives?" I ask Chris. Cam's stepsister was accepted for a mid-year start at the University of Texas and will move down from Indiana next week.

"For the rest of this year, I'll either come with Zoe, or if she wants to bring a friend, I'll use Greg's. Cam has encouraged her to keep their connection on the down-low for now, so she knows who likes her for her. So I suspect I'll get to enjoy these seats for a lot of games. And they'll spend time together at his house or mine more than down near campus."

"That's a good idea." Okay. Deep breath. I've been hiding something from Chris and the girls for months, and the guilt has started to eat at me. "I can also keep an eye on her some of the time if he wants."

Warmups are over, and we're in a lull before the game starts. She turns to me and frowns. "How would you do that?"

"I enrolled in the MBA program. Work reimburses

me if I make at least B's in my classes. Of course, I'll be there at night rather than during the day when she has classes, but I could probably buy her a meal and see how she's doing here and there."

Chris is staring at me, mouth agape. "You did? You are? How did I not know this? That's fantastic, Nicole! I know you've been looking to score a promotion at work, so hopefully this will help. But seriously, that is a lot."

I nod. "It is. It's why I wasn't available that often to come to games. And I didn't tell anyone until I knew I wanted to see it through. Besides"—I gesture at Cam—"you had your own stuff going on."

"Okay, but I still wish you'd told me. I'm excited for you. You can have first dibs on weekends if you'd like. Well, you and Maria, since she doesn't teach dance Saturday or Sunday nights."

Whereas Lauren and I met Christina at UT during an elective on Women's Studies, Maria met her through competitive ballroom dance before Christina had to quit for health reasons. Maria is still competing and recently opened a studio in Austin.

"Fair enough," I reply. "First semester was okay, but I've heard this one is tough. It's still a lot of core classes but next level, building on what we learned last semester. So more reading, more homework."

"Well, don't worry about Zoe. My schedule is flexible, so I plan to hang with her when and if she's interested, especially when Cam is traveling for games. It'll help me not miss him as much maybe."

I bump her shoulder with mine "You have it so bad. I'm super happy for you both."

The opposing team is introduced, then the Tornadoes' song starts, and our boys come out to raucous applause. After the national anthem, the puck drops, and we're focused on the game until the end of the first period. Chris turns to me as the players file off the ice, eyeing me from head to toe. "So what gives with the new look? It can't be school if that's been going for months."

"New Year's Resolution. New year, new me; I started a few days early. I know you hate when I say this, but y'all each have something special that makes you unique. Even at work, the experts doing the work on each project feed me information on steps and dependencies, management gives their desired outcomes. All I do is put it all into a database and formulate a plan."

"Project management is a unique skill, and one I don't have. You have to know how to layer those interdependencies, but more importantly, you have to inspire people to make their deadlines without being their manager." Chris shudders. "There's no way I could do that. People make me bonkers."

"I suppose."

"That's also far more of a transferable skill than dance." She winks. "But don't tell Maria I said that."

We laugh.

"You should tell the others," she says.

"I will. How about we see if they can come to my place for a pre-party before we go out tomorrow for New Year's?"

"That works, although parking is better at my place, if that's okay?" At my nod, she activates the group chat.

Chapter Four

Mathieu

Christina had offered her pool house and pool for New Year's Eve, but the guys wanted to be somewhere they could find someone to kiss, fuck, whatever they could get, for midnight. So here we are at Chaser's. Yes, it's the same old crowd, but there's something to be said for a sure thing. And we're new enough in town that women are still finding us.

Half the guys are wearing shirts with the team logo on them. The other half think black is the new black. Only a few of us are bold enough to be individuals. I'm in a Ty Cranston signed Ottawa Redblacks jersey. I know him well enough that I can wear it and not frame it. Besides, who knows whose jersey I'll want to wear in a few years? Life is short, and I like to keep my options open.

Some of the bunnier bunnies have asked me if I play for the Redblacks and where they're located. Kind of a lame opening line if you ask me. I mean, Google it already, and then lead in with a question about Ottawa. And a couple did. With potential midnight kiss recipients in mind, I rewarded them with some lighthearted, French-accented flirting.

Winding my way through the crowd, I greet each of my teammates with a one-armed hug and a handclasp.

I've caught up with most during practice and morning skate before our game yesterday, so it's a quick path to the bar where I lean over to kiss Renee's cheek. "Ma petite amie."

"Go on with your bad self, du Près. I'm not a bunny to have my head turned by a few words of French. Bonne Année."

I laugh and squeeze her hand where it rests on the bar. This is a longstanding exchange between me and the lovely fortyish-year-old bar manager. Thankfully, she was open to enough influence to stock my second favorite whisky, since Found North isn't distributed here in Texas. My family and I smuggle bottles in our luggage whenever we can, but not enough to keep me in sips all year round. So Wiser's 18 Year is my go-to, but only for celebrations like wins, assists, goals, and of course, New Year's Eve.

"Wiser's please, ma petite amie."

She rolls her eyes and grabs the bottle and a glass. "How was your Christmas?"

"Excellent. I got two days with my family and managed to make it back here with no flight delays or issues. How was yours?"

"Oh, you know, the usual. Sleeping when I can so I can keep you guys in liquor and bunnies."

I narrow my gaze. Renee never gives us details of her life. I have no idea if she is single or married. With a man or woman. Kids or no kids. Or anything. But tonight is not the night to pursue my curiosity.

When I turn toward the door, Nicole is entering the bar with Lauren right behind her and Maria and Chris bringing up the rear. Cam said Christina was having the girls over to pregame, and I try to figure out how lubricated they are.

Cam has a homing beacon planted in Chris, and he beelines to her and sweeps her into his huge wingspan for a hug. The girls coo.

I roll my eyes but quickly school my features so they—Nicole—doesn't catch me.

She takes off her coat, revealing a sparkly halter top, and while her tits are young and perky, I'm quite certain she isn't wearing a bra under that. There for sure aren't any straps outside the halter neckline.

She turns to drape her coat over a chair, and I'm glad I hadn't picked up my drink because I'd have dropped it. The back of her top doesn't have any sparkles. It doesn't even have fabric. Instead, it's three crisscrosses of strings, with a tie at the bottom.

My mouth goes dry as my airport car ride thoughts of hooking up with her slam into the forefront again. I imagine pulling those ends and having it drop away from her smooth skin, giving me full access. My tongue tracing those delicate shoulder blades. It'll have to happen in front of a mirror so I can enjoy both the front and back of her luscious body.

I turn back to the bar. Geez, what the hell? On any given night, I'm surrounded by beautiful women who rub up against me, and when I choose one to take home, I don't get a boner in the middle of the bar. And from all things, her back. Cleavage, a great ass, even pouty lips I could understand. I'm like some Victorian dude who caught a glimpse of an ankle.

Shaking it off—okay, not literally—I gulp my whisky and gesture to Renee for another to be delivered to the girls' table. Then I head over to do what I do best— flirt. My conscience is telling me I should stick with bunnies, since Nicole and I share a tightknit group of friends. But flirting never hurt anyone.

Maria is wearing some corset thing that gives her tiny dancer's body an hourglass shape, and Lauren is with the undertaker half of the team in a LBD, a term I only know because I have a younger sister.

But as I greet them, my eyes are drawn back to the shimmy and flow of Nicole's top, ice blue one minute, aqua-y-silver the next. "You ladies look fabulous tonight."

Lauren, the eternal ball-buster, answers, "What, don't we always?"

"Ahh…"

Maria bursts into giggles at my deer-in-headlights expression. "She's just poking at you."

But I'm too busy worrying she's going to come out of the corset top with her jiggling—I mean, giggling—to answer either of them.

Nicole links her arm around mine and leans in. "Thank you. I think that's what they meant to say."

I turn my head to grin at her. "You're welcome. That color highlights your eyes."

"Thank you again. Want to come with me to the bar? I'm getting first round. You can help me carry." She leans on me more, and I recall the pre-party plan. Looks like she's already tipsy.

I wrap an arm around her shoulders to help stabilize her and steer her toward Renee. My hand meets bare skin, and I wish for scissors to cut my jersey's sleeve off so I can feel more of her. It's satin smooth and warm and my thumb brushes over the top twice before we squeeze our way into an empty spot at the bar and I'm forced to drop my hand. While we wait for the three cosmos, she scans the room.

"Whatcha looking for?" I ask, bringing my whisky to my lips.

"Just doing what you do. Scanning for prospects."

I choke, sputtering most of my sip back into the glass. Mon dieu, this girl is dangerous to drink around. "What?"

"Hey, it's New Year's Eve. I want to figure out who I'm gonna kiss in a couple hours."

"First, I don't do that when I'm standing right next to a woman."

She scoffs.

Huh. I thought I was more subtle than that. I'm usually focused on flirting with whoever I'm talking to, with only some side-eye for other prospects.

"Second, right here, baby. I'm happy to help you out." Only after I say the words do I think them through. My plan had been to do exactly what she said—scan for prospects, but for a fuck, not a kiss.

She shares my inner devil's reaction. "Yeah, right. You probably already have your first, second, and third choice lined up, and for all I know, you'll take all three home."

I blink, not sure what I should say.

She sips one of the cosmos and continues, "It's time I started thinking like you hockey players. The world is my oyster, and I'm going to swallow it whole."

My stupid cock reacts to that, of course.

She's not done. "This year is gonna be my slutty year."

"Hey." My voice is sharp enough to make her blink and stand straighter as she brings her gaze to mine. "I don't like that word. I mean there are a couple guys on the team who take things to a whole new level, but any of us who are single have the right to do who we please, when and how often we please, without being called names. Our bodies, our choices. That goes for girls as well as guys. My sister would have my head if I allowed anyone to use that term, especially about a nice girl in a room full of hockey players."

Nicole snickered at my "who we please," but now, her baby blues are soft, like she's going to get weepy.

Oh boy.

She lays a hand on my arm. "Mattie, that is super sweet. I didn't realize you were a feminist. You and Lauren might have a beautiful future ahead of you."

My eyes widen in alarm.

She hiccups and bends double, laughing. Through giggles she says, "Oh my gosh, you should see your face! Lauren's a nice person. Stop looking like that."

Disgruntled, I pass her two drinks to take back to the table, and say, "My last feminist comment—you may want to consider going easy on the drinks. Any self-respecting guy isn't going to give you more than a peck if you're drunk. And you should beware of the ones who don't give a shit."

"Aww. I can't wait until Lauren hears this," she says with a snort.

* * * *

After dropping the girls' drinks off, I escape to make the rounds. The clock edges closer to midnight, but I still haven't been able to settle on someone to pound in the New Year with. I've had a few offers, but none appeal.

Instead, my eyes are drawn to that strap-crossed spine time and again. Ever since the idea of a fling with her crossed my mind on my first night back from Ottawa, it's been simmering in the back of my thoughts. That top has brought it to a full boil, and I'm ready to eat. But only if she's sober enough to consent.

With that in mind, I circle closer. When Christina excuses herself from the table, I slide into the chair next to Nicole. At her sidelong look, I raise a brow and reach for her cosmo. I sip and promptly sputter most of it onto the table and back in the glass.

"Gross," she says, taking her glass back. "I thought you were smoother than that, hockey boy."

"Gross is right. What the hell?"

She arches a brow, mimicking my earlier expression. The other two women lose interest in my reaction and return to their conversation. She leans in. "Grapefruit flavored sparkling water. It was the only thing that looked like a cosmo. And yeah, it's gross."

"Good girl," I say.

Her pupils blow wide.

"What is that expression about?"

"You clearly don't read romance novels."

"Um, yeah, that would be a big no. But now, I'm curious."

"'Good girl' is a thing in romances. It's called a praise kink."

"Are you telling me you're kinky, blondie?" I rub my hands together. "This night is looking up."

She laughs, shaking her head at me. Then tilts it and bites her lower lip. "Maybe. What if I was?"

This pixie may be new to the flirting game, but she's a fast learner. My cock is hard as a rock, and I scoot my chair in farther.

"Then maybe you'd have found yourself a New Year's Eve partner."

Christina returns and grabs the girls. "We need to dance!"

Nicole rolls her eyes at Chris.

"Not *my* dancing, silly. Just shaking our thang."

Lauren says, "Ugh, does that mean you and Cam are going to get down and dirty on the dance floor?"

"*Maybe*," Christina drawls. "Now, let's go."

Nicole flicks a glance at me.

"Go get your groove on, blondie. I'm going to watch you shake your thangs. Especially in that pretty top." I wiggle my eyebrows. Her eyes widen, and she smooths her top self-consciously, which highlights her small high breasts. I swallow hard and add, "Go on, good girl. If you do, you'll get a reward."

She slow blinks, and since I know she's not drunk, I can only surmise she's as turned on as I am. Excellent. Now, if only my hard-on will deflate enough to get her out to my car and headed toward a bed.

Chapter Five

Nicole

I'm hyperventilating as I dance with my girlfriends. Ohmigod, Mattie du Près might be my first one-night stand. Little does he know it will be my first ever. I was never confident enough to pull that off and was always looking for the softer feelings.

Way to set the bar high for the year, dumbass. How are you going to top this one?

I don't care. Not everyone gets to see a professional hockey player naked, and I plan to make the most of this opportunity.

The last of the vodka sizzles through me, just enough to keep me warm while remaining clearheaded.

Suddenly, everyone is counting down to midnight. I hadn't realized it was that close.

Cam stills with Christina in his arms and whispers something in her ear, making her smile wide enough I think she might sprain her face.

A hard chest presses against my bare back before thighs and a delicious-sized package follow, nestling against my butt. That better be Mattie.

I catch Maria's never-discreet thumbs up as I turn, and by "two," his lips are descending toward mine.

I don't hear the rest of the countdown because the buzzing in my ears echoes in my clit. Surprisingly soft lips settle against mine. His tongue glides along my lower lip as though asking for permission to enter.

I greet it with a touch of my own, withdrawing and inviting him to follow. We continue to slow dance against the chorus of Auld Lang Syne without moving anything but our mouths. It's like his kiss is touching my pussy. I'm as wet as if he licked my clit. His hips move, and I almost straddle his quads of steel, wanting to ride his thigh shamelessly.

What they say about Frenchmen knowing how to kiss definitely applies to French-Canadian men, too.

He pulls back an inch, and my eyes flicker open. His gaze is heavy-lidded when he says, "Bonne Année, mon petit chou. You ready to get out of here?"

I nod, too busy savoring the echo of his taste to form words.

The rideshare takes five minutes to come, and when it arrives, I realize why. He requested the luxury level, so we climb into the back of an SUV with tinted windows.

He tugs me onto his lap. Sideways, sadly, so I can't grind a quickie out. But the unparalleled kissing continues, making me begin to worry about leaving a wet spot on his pants.

All too soon, we're pulling up to a high-rise apartment building in downtown Austin, where the cool kids live and party. Certainly far out of my price range.

He hustles me inside and into an elevator, where he backs me into a corner and finally, finally, shoves a knee between my legs. I hold onto his shoulders for dear life while he kisses the breath from me and allows me to twist and turn and align and hump.

The elevator dings, and he simply lifts me and carries

me to his door with my legs around his waist.

The darkened apartment whizzes by, all shadows and dark mounds of furniture and a hallway with framed photos and awards. Then I'm falling backward, my legs not quite fast enough to catch me. His bed is high, though, and I land softly, my shoes plunking to the carpet.

He reaches behind his head and yanks off the jersey, followed by the t-shirt he wore beneath it. Without hesitation, he grabs my hand and pulls me up and into the bathroom where he flips on the light. I'm standing in front of the vanity—an enviable double vanity in granite. One day, I'll be able to afford luxuries like this.

I'm facing him, my back to the mirror. We're standing there looking at each other, and already the electricity is palpable. I need to savor every inch of this man. He peers over my shoulder, tilts his head, and spins me to face the mirror as he runs a hand against my shoulder blades. His gaze flicks between my back and my mirrored front, and he nods.

I smirk. *He likes my top. Win.*

He finds the ends of the two thin cords at my lower back and holds them out to the sides. Flashing a grin at me in the mirror, he pulls them outward, slow and steady, his eyes dropping to my lower spine.

My answering smile is full of satisfaction. This is the exact scenario I pictured when I bought this top, although I never dreamed it would be him holding the ties.

When the bow is untied, he tugs on the little loops that hold the cords on each side. One set, and I feel air above my belly button. Second set, and the fabric falls away from my lower breasts, tightening my nipples. Third set is at the back of my neck at the narrow halter top.

He loosens that enough to whip the top over my head and drop it somewhere behind us as his big hands cup my breasts, covering them.

"Peau de porcelaine," he mutters while staring at us in the mirror.

I raise my hands to his wrists but don't stop him. Self-conscious, I avert my gaze from the whole of us and instead watch our hands and my breasts. I've never experienced something this hot before.

"Good girl," he says.

I swear flames shoot through me at his words. Turning, I go on tiptoe to fuse my lips to his, my hands on the fly of his jeans. Shoving them down, I palm his length through his boxer briefs. And oh boy, I do mean length. My hand does not cover his shaft.

Yes, please.

He lifts me, hands on the back of my thighs encouraging me to wrap them around him again, and casts a lingering last glance at my back in the mirror before whisking me back to the bed.

My dark skinny jeans have never come off so easily as when Mattie hooks his hands in and yanks them down, taking my lacy boy shorts with them.

He skims off his own boxer briefs, and I have a moment of regret because the room is too dark to enjoy him. I vaguely register the sound of a nightstand drawer being pulled open before his weight hits the bed beside me. A muscular leg nudges mine open to nestle between them, and his chest is hot against my side. Dropping a condom to the other pillow, he props himself on an elbow.

"Mattie, please. I can't take much more. I need you."

Smiling, he shakes his head. "Then I get a second round. I don't like to be rushed."

"Yeah, okay, sure. Whatever you want, just please." I'm tugging at him as though I could actually move his weight over me.

He skims a hand down my body—shoulder, breast, belly, then core. Dipping his fingers between my pussy lips, he smiles. "You do need me. You're soaked."

When he flicks my clit once, I jolt and cry out from the pleasure and the pain. He rolls the condom on and hovers over me once more on his elbows.

A sigh of relief escapes me, but I shout a short scream when he glides in. I'm so fucking close already. Dry spell or not, I swear this wouldn't happen with anyone else. It for sure never has. Shoving at his hips, I grit out, "Ohmygod, *move*."

He chuckles but obliges me. Sliding out, he repeats the long slow motion.

I grip his hips with my legs and rise to meet him, hoping to hasten the climb. But he's not having it. After a few tries, I give up and lie back. My eyes have finally adjusted, so I run them over him. Shoulders and biceps bunch as he skates in and out of me. I skim my hands down his back to enjoy the flexing of his delicious hockey ass.

He shifts up to his hands, arching his back to change the angle, and it's game over. His cock must have found my G-spot. His pubis is hitting my swollen needy clit just enough, and I'm in a maelstrom of pleasure, swirling outward from where we meet.

My nails dig into his shoulders, and I strain upward, yelling his name. He thrusts faster and faster, extending my orgasm as he closes in on his. His cock bucks inside me as he groans and stills, collapsing to his elbows but careful to keep the weight of his upper half off me.

He rolls us so he's on his back with me nestled in that sweet spot between his shoulder and chest. "Bonne Année, mon petit chou."

"Happy New Year, Mattie. Thanks for ringing it in with me."

We giggle before he reaches toward the nightstand for a tissue to take care of the condom. I excuse myself to clean up. I'm not sure I have round two in me, but I promised him. When I pad back to the bed, still naked, he's on his stomach, his breath gusting out in long, even, *sleeping* bursts.

I remember he has a game tomorrow—make that today—and anyway, I need to start how I intend to go on. A well-mannered one-night stand wouldn't linger hoping for breakfast or round two. She got what she came for and would make herself scarce.

With that in mind, I grab my clothes, tiptoe out of the room, and dress in the front entryway. I'd love to peruse the pictures on his wall, but I remind myself those aren't something a one-night stand would care about.

Calling a rideshare, I check the time. Nearly two o'clock, hopefully long enough after midnight that it won't be an hour wait. It isn't, even for the cheaper option I choose.

High bar or not, this was a fucking fantastic way to start the new year.

Chapter Six

Mathieu

The opening chords to Queen's *Bicycle Race*, my usual alarm chosen to get me to the gym, drag me from a dreamless sleep. The two whiskies I drank linger as fuzz on my tongue, but I can't detect any other lasting effects of last night. Memory kicks in, and one desired effect rises when I replay my first hours of the year with Nicole.

My eyes pop open, and I grab my phone. I don't remember setting an alarm, and today is a game day, meaning I have to get to morning skate.

Silencing the alarm, I check the clock to see if we have enough time for that round two she promised. We do, but that's not going to happen because the other side of the bed is empty and cold. She's long gone.

Merde.

I frown at my instinctive reaction. Always before, I've been grateful when my play partner understood the rules, or insistent on helping them learn them if they were still in my bed. Nicole is part of our friends group, so I might be gentler about it with her, but that should make me more appreciative of her respect of one-night stand etiquette.

After a moment of discomfort, I shrug and chalk it up to the fact that I didn't get the second round she promised me.

More awake now, I spy a note under where my phone was.

Mattie ~ I wasn't sure what time you'd need to get up, but I knew it was game day. Sorry if I set this too early. Happy New Year ~ N

I've never had a one and done who was so considerate. While I make my breakfast, I grin. She said she wanted to turn over a new leaf and act like a hockey player this year, but she might need some practice. Slipping out in the dark of night after sex is certainly on brand for many players, including myself in the past. Without the niceties of setting an alarm and leaving a note.

Since I'm up, I head to the rink early and cycle off the last of the whisky, tired of my circling thoughts.

Morning skate flies by, but back at my apartment, I can't nap. The sheets smell of something pretty and sweet, like Nicole did last night. Instead, I rest with my eyes closed, wondering if she'll be in the stands with Christina today.

Would it be weird if I texted her and asked? *Mon dieu, Mathieu, just because she's acting like a hockey player doesn't mean you have to act like the girl in this scenario.*

My sister's voice kicks in, chastising me for that sexist thought.

Nicole left before I was ready for her to leave. Zut, the fact that she left rather than me leaving or kicking her out is a first. So these feelings are probably hurt pride. That must be it. I sure as hell don't want a relationship or to give a woman any ideas about one. I'm having way too much fun at this stage in my life to settle down.

Fed up with the internal voices, I run hockey drills in my head instead, getting into game mode.

* * * *

As they have been since our first pre-season game, every seat is filled this afternoon. Austin has embraced us with their whole heart, although there will never be as much purple as burnt orange in this town. UT and football are long traditions here, and we're not looking to replace them. We can coexist and offer an alternative for sports fans who prefer cooler temps to some of Austin's football days.

Skating onto the ice for warm-ups, I can't stop myself from checking the seats Cam secured for Christina. Sure enough, Nicole's pixie face and blonde tendrils peek out from her toque.

I head over to where Cam is doing his usual "hump the ice" routine and get down to pigeon pose next to him, albeit nowhere near as low as he goes. When he's got his legs at ninety degrees on the ice, I try to imitate that and twerk a few times.

He side-eyes me. "What the fuck, du Près?"

"Just cuz I usually do my stretches out there with the guys doesn't mean I can't mix it up with you occasionally."

"Didn't you leave with Nicole last night?" His change of subject catches me off-guard.

"I don't kiss and tell."

"Well, you better not fuck and duck either with one of Chris's friends. Don't shit where you eat, Mattie."

"Worked out okay for you, didn't it?" I throw out and skate off, ready to smash some pucks at his goalie mask. Of all people, he in the most fragile glass house of all should not be throwing stones. It doesn't matter that I told myself the same thing before that backless top fried my brain cells.

I flash a look at Nicole. Chris is making googly eyes at Cam, and Nicole is staring hard at me, a flush on her cheeks. I skate along the glass and throw her a wink when I pass, but in no time, I put her out of my head to focus on the game. I'm all about winning, and it'll take every ounce of concentration to do that.

When the puck drops, I'm on fire at left wing. There are zero lingering effects of whisky and all the residual happy hormones—I never remember their names—from my orgasm and knowing the girl who made it happen is in the stands with her eyes on me.

I'm in the zone, whirling and twirling and mixing it up with the Minnesota Wildcats offense and defense alike. As I whiz by after a second puck steal, Buzz comments, "You're killing it tonight, Mattie."

After a rapid-fire pass that results in a goal at the buzzer for the second period, I glance to my left. We're at the end where Cam's seats are. Nicole is on her feet, jumping in place with the rest of the crowd. Her hair has a little static, and she's clutching her hat like it's a cheerleader's pom-pom.

As we clomp off the ice for intermission, I try to figure out when I started thinking fly-away hair was cute.

Chapter Seven

Nicole

"Do you feel okay?" Chris asks when she turns during the first intermission.

"Yeah…why?"

"You're flushed, like you have a fever or something."

She's right that I'm running hotter than normal. Usually, I'm sipping hot chocolate and fighting to stay warm at Tornadoes games. Tonight, I have to take off my pom-pommed hat, and when I touch my cheeks, they're warm to my ungloved hands.

No wonder she's worried I'm fighting the flu; however, the image of Mattie du Près's body underneath his hockey gear is prompting this hot flash. That and watching the elegance of his races up and down the ice, his twirls to steal the puck from Minnesota, and his cheeky grin when he spies someone open to pass the puck.

If I didn't know how expensive rinkside seats were, I'd be contemplating getting my own pair. Cam had gotten seats in the Tornadoes zone, given that he's the goalie. I'd want seats on the more popular end for home games, where the Tornadoes score two out of three periods.

Although, watching Mattie sprinting away is as

much fun as watching him speeding toward me.

Chris asks, "So, was it my imagination, or did you and Mattie leave together last night?"

"Yep."

"Guess you weren't as invisible to him as you thought, huh?" She sips her hot chocolate with a smile.

"I told him my New Year's Resolution—to be sluttier." I jump back when Chris spews her hot chocolate. "He ever so generously offered to help me kickstart it."

She's staring at me wide-eyed. "I don't even know where to start with all that. First, you said he could have anyone he wanted, and he chose you, so I don't want to hear the self-deprecating crap. Second, that's not the way you described it to me. And third, are you sure you're up for this? You've always been a relationship girlie like me."

"All part and parcel of the new me. With adding night classes around work, I don't have time for a relationship. My past attempts haven't been successful anyway, so I'm tired of being the goodie two shoes and missing the fun."

She narrows her eyes. "You sure about this?"

I throw my arms wide. "Look. I already had one successful round with Mattie. I didn't stay the night; I didn't check my phone every five minutes the next morning. And here I am, ready to look for the next hookup at Chasers tonight."

She stares at me for a long moment, as though she can tell I did check my stupid phone every hour until I put it in a separate room. "I did wonder about the tighter sweater with the deep V. All right, I'll be your wingman. This'll be fun."

When the second period starts, I force myself to watch the other players. Making it a game, I evaluate their attributes as potential next conquests. Every single one comes up short against Mattie's skills, personality, and physique. Ugh.

Running through the team for one-night stands would be a terrible idea, anyway. I'm going to spend time with this group whether I want to or not, given Christina and Cam's connection. And I'm already making a mess of that with lingering thoughts of Mattie. Fuck, I suck at this.

Practice makes perfect. Who needs to bang a hockey player? Anyone with a nice enough smile and a teeny bit of skill could turn me on. I'll see if there are any interesting looking fans in Chasers tonight.

Right now, I'm here to watch a game. No one need know if I warm myself up by ogling the hottie who is number ten.

They're tied 1-1 in the second period, and Cam has his brooding look on. Chris says he was pissed at himself for allowing the goal. The puck has gone back and forth a shit ton of times. Even with line changes, I have no idea how these guys can keep this up for sixty minutes of play. And there seems to be a lot more slamming into the boards tonight, but that may be my new appreciation for Mattie's body and a desire to keep it bruise-free.

He comes flying down the left side of the ice, his gaze fierce when it flips between the defensemen and the path to the goal. Gabriel St. John is controlling the puck on the other wing, and Drew "Buzz" Busbee is in the center. Saint sets up to receive a pass to the right of their goalie, blocking his view of Buzz. Mattie zooms in between two defenders as Buzz slaps the puck to him, and he one-times it right over the goalie's shoulder into the corner of the net.

The light flashes and we're all on our feet. Just before the giants—or okay, anyone, given my height—in front of me stand. Mattie is doing that celebration thing players do, pumping his fist at waist height as he goes down on one knee, sliding along the ice on one skate before effortlessly rising to two blades again.

My mouth goes dry at the thought of his thigh and butt muscles tightening to pull that off. This is ridiculous. My dry spell before New Year's Eve was almost a year long. Now, I've had a fantastic orgasm I didn't have to give myself, and less than twenty-four hours later, I'm gagging for it again.

The guys do a quick celebration, and Mattie swings by and taps the glass with his stick and winks at us while we stand and clap. Would he do that if I wasn't here? Maybe he's sucking up to Chris as an owner. Maybe there are hot chicks behind us he's inviting to the bar. *Ahhh!*

The third period flies by while I give and receive a stern internal lecture, reminding myself I'm trying to do things differently this year, *casual* rather than obsessing over every wink and tap. No more catching feelings from the first kiss—or even the first fuck.

We head to the friends and family lounge down on the players' level, where I graze on hummus and carrots from the buffet, so I won't pig out on bar food. It's uncomfortable when everyone else but me is a WAG or direct relation to a player, so I lurk in Christina's shadow as she chats to players' families, ever the hostess.

Her brother Greg comes in, and the three of us chat for a moment before Chris's attention diverts to the doorway and she lights up like a supernova.

Behind Cam are D-man Jack Landry, Buzz, and a few of the others. Jack comes right over with a hug and a smile. As Cam's roommate, Jack's gotten to know Christina's friends, as have the other guys Cam is closest to on the team.

Slinging his arm around my shoulders, Jack says, "I hear you're partying with us tonight."

"Unless I find someone better." I elbow him in the side. Gently, though, because who knows what bruises lurk under his dress shirt. He did his share of slamming and being slammed tonight.

"Ah, you wound me." He laughs. When Saint comes in, Jack bounds over to him to harangue him about joining us.

Saint ignores him, heading toward Amy Donovan, Christina's sister and the third owner of the team. She shakes her head at his look, then hugs him and seems to comment on the game, making him smile. Saint is a star player and captain because of that and his maturity. He's a team player, always looking to facilitate plays, unworried about whether he gets the points or someone else does. He mentors and inspires the younger players.

Jack heads back to me. His brother and parents fly in for games when they can, but otherwise, he'd be through here and headed to Chasers normally. My guess is that underneath his always-on, fuck boy exterior is a nice guy, and that he's hanging here to keep me company.

I turn to tell him I can ride with him when movement at the doorway catches my eye.

In a heartbeat, Mattie is in front of me, frowning.

"You done with the press, man?" Jack asks, and at Mattie's nod adds his famous on-ice call. "Let's ggooooo! You want a ride, Nicole?"

Pressure from Jack's arm turns me in the direction of the exit, but Mattie grabs my hand and yanks me back, forcing Jack's grip on me to drop. "You're coming out?"

I nod with a frown. I look down at his hand on mine. "Is that a problem?"

"Ride with me," Mattie replies.

"Sure." I shrug. I don't care who I ride with, but his reaction is interesting. If only I believed he was jealous.

In the car, Mattie looks like he is going to say something, but instead he firms his lips and huffs a breath. I keep it light by chatting about the game highlights as I saw them, hoping he won't notice that most of the ones I remember are his plays. By the end of the short drive, he's relaxed and grinning, which likely means my hope was for naught.

At Chasers, he leads me through the bar, his hand searing me through my sweater as though it was as backless as my top from last night.

Jack is at the bar joking with Renee and ordering massive amounts of food.

Renee is kind enough to keep alternate menu items for the players. They're too expensive for the crowd here other nights, and not enough people order them, so she doesn't put them on the standard menu. But she has cauliflower crusts for the pizzas, unbreaded chicken strips, and other substitutions for regular menu items. Now, I'm sort of bummed I grazed in the lounge.

Mattie keeps hold of me, a hand loose on my hip, as he asks me what I want and orders Topo Chicos for us. The game was at five o-clock so it's early yet, but I work the next day, and I'm sure he has practice.

We head over to sit with Jack and other players who

are trickling in. On the way, Mattie leans close and says, "You owe me."

My brows hit my hairline. "For what?"

His lips are near my ear now, his breath making me shiver. "You promised me a second round."

Yes, please. No, wait, I need to keep it casual—one-night stands only. It's too easy for me to start craving dates, cuddles, and monogamy. But my body is already reacting. Liquid warmth pools in my belly, and I'm suddenly aware of my breasts in their lace cups. Unable to help myself, I channel my new self and smirk. "I can't help that you fell asleep."

"You could have stayed, chérie."

"I didn't want to overstay my welcome. I thought it was just a hookup."

He grunts. "Come home with me. We're still within twenty-four hours, so it can count as a hookup, a one-night stand, whatever you want it to be."

A second round with his hot hockey body and Frenchisms? I don't have to think about it. "Okay."

My brain continues to argue with my wanton body. *You'll get attached. You were already pining watching him play. This is a bad idea.*

Fuck me. Literally. Orgasms are worth working through a little attachment, particularly when it was spectacular the first time, yet he's determined it wasn't a good enough showing on his part.

"I need sustenance first, though," he says, waving over one of the pizzas.

"That's cool. I wouldn't want you to fall asleep before you accomplish everything you want," I tease him.

Chapter Eight

Mathieu

Mon dieu, I've never been so glad of a loophole in my one-night stand policy. I've been craving this second round since I woke up this morning.

After half a veggie and buffalo chicken pizza—hey, don't knock it until you try it—I'm refueled and ready to rumble.

Nicole has chatted with a few of the players who stopped by our table, including Cam and Christina. When I tilt my head toward the door, Nicole leans in.

"Look, don't take this the wrong way, but Christina was asking about us leaving together, and I don't want her to get any ideas, so can we leave separately, please?"

Cam's attitude during warm-ups makes me agree. "I don't like the idea of you lingering in the parking lot alone. I'll settle my tab and wait for you at the car, oui?"

"Thank you. You're a very considerate one-night stand," she says with a giggle. Her note showed the same thoughtfulness.

I swear I feel her eyes on my ass as I thread my way through the tables, and I'm grateful once again that genetics and training ensure I'm in peak physical condition. It's all I can do not to sprout a boner anticipating the rest of the night.

Five minutes later, we're in my car headed to my

place. "Thank you for the note and alarm, by the way. I would have had some explaining to do if I missed morning skate. Coach gave us a lecture about partying too hard on New Year's, and I struggle to be on time even with an alarm."

"Happy to help." She turns sideways in her seat and runs her hand down my arm, humming under her breath.

"Hey, no starting without me," I say with a grin.

"I can't help it. You're that sexy."

"Well, then. Please, stroke whatever you can reach."

She laughs and leans in, stroking my chest, down over my abs to cup my cock. Given the loose suit pants, it's managed to find room to expand at her touch within my boxer briefs and is sitting along my left leg. She squeezes it, and my thighs tighten, which makes her hum again.

I daren't look at her, focusing on my surroundings to ensure I don't crash the car as her hand continues to play, fondling and pressing.

Finally, we pull into my parking space, and I rush her up the elevator, crowding her against the back wall and pressing my hips into her stomach while I explore her mouth.

She tastes of honey and flowers, or maybe that's her perfume. The wet warmth makes me want to savor other spots on her, and I grind into her more.

In a repeat of last night, we rush to my apartment where I press her against the wall, having her ride my knee to get her higher. She's such a little thing. I don't want to break her. Or maybe I do. I want to be savage with her, and based on her begging last night, she's up for that.

She claws at my dress shirt, unbuttoning the front but

forgetting the cuffs, so it's caught on my arms. Moving to her own sweater, she drags it up over her head and flings it away to reveal her high, tight, perfect breasts covered in lace.

This view is just as sexy as last night's bare version, and I take a minute to stare. Never would I have imagined this shy pixie would be so fierce when it came to sex. More, she's fun to talk to, surprising me with her words, her crazy workaround for a cosmo, whatever. That thought freaks me out, and I shut it down.

There's no way she'd want a hockey loubard like me, anyway, even if I wanted more. The very idea of trying to meet a woman's expectations makes me shudder, and I push it away.

I'm going to enjoy the feast in front of me. Reaching around her, I pinch the clasp one-handed to open it so I can cup her mounds in my hands.

She moans, rolling her head against the wall. I brush my thumbs over her hardened tips, making her moan again.

Her hands fumble at my waist, undoing my belt, then fly, to reach inside and cup me.

"Yesss. Such a good girl." I say in a rumble, using the phrase ruthlessly to turn her on and ignoring the fact that I wouldn't have this knowledge about a one-night stand.

Her thighs tighten around mine in reward.

"Come on." I slide her down an inch at a time, her eyes drifting open but not fully focused. I take her hand and pull her into my bedroom, tugging her down to sit on the bed. Unfastening my cuffs, I whip my shirt off, shove my pants down, and kneel in front of her.

She stares at me, uncertainty clouding her

expression.

"My turn to play." I pluck her shoes off and tug at her leggings, hooking my fingers in her underwear to take them off as well.

She's naked, leaning back on her elbows on my bed. A sense of rightness, of possession, arrows through me, making my breath catch. Mine.

But no, she only wants tonight, so I best make it memorable.

Leaning in, I part her pussy lips with my thumbs, my big hands spanning the width of her thighs as I hold her open. I nuzzle my nose into her folds, inhaling her scent. She smells of honey here, too, so it's her natural scent.

Somewhere above me, she moans. Hands grab my hair. "Mattie…you don't have to…"

I lick her clit, then lock my lips around it and use gentle suction, continuing to flick it with my tongue.

Her fingers tighten against my scalp, and her words change to, "Oh, God, that's amazing."

My goal is to make her speechless, incoherent with pleasure.

I lick my finger and slide it into her, recapturing her clit to suck and slide in tandem. Her moans teach me what patterns she likes. When her voice goes shrill, I stay on that spot and curl my finger against her front wall.

"Oh!"

Still not incoherent. I slow down.

She squirms. "Mattie, please. I'm begging again."

"Not begging enough, mon chou," I say against her clit. I suck harder and earn a reward when her hips lift and push against my mouth. My finger rubs that little rough patch on her front wall, slowly then faster.

She twists her upper body, keening, but keeps her

pussy against me as though begging me not to stop, not to let up.

Definitely the right spot, given that she's inarticulate. Those keens make me want to abandon this and shove my cock inside her, but no. This is my show, and I'm in control. I think.

Her clit tightens in my mouth, growing firmer. Mon dieu, she's super close, and I can't wait for her to come against my mouth. I bite down on her nub, gently, but with more pressure than my lips. My tongue goes to double time.

Her hips make micro-pulses against me, and her clit throbs and quivers as she explodes. Her pussy clamps down on my finger like it will never let me go. Which doesn't sound bad at all. Tabarnak, what the fuck is wrong with me?

My cock is leaking in my boxers, ready to go off at any moment, but I'm swallowing her essence and loving every second of this. As her clit stills, I lessen my hold on it, kissing it as I might kiss her hello or welcome back. Her hips sag, and I slide my finger out, separating us, so I can suck it clean.

"Holy…no one's ever…"

Still somewhat incoherent. I smile in satisfaction. My work here is done. It's play time. Standing, I grab a condom out of the drawer and roll it on. My bed is this height for a reason. "Now for round two."

"I think you mean three."

"Hmm. Bien sûr, we can count according to your orgasms if you'd like. You okay to continue?" I check in.

"Hell, yeah. I may lie here for a minute while I recover, but you can start without me if you want."

I chuckle and lift her legs to my shoulders. My "Merci," accompanies my cock, gliding into her until my groin settles against hers.

She moans, and her walls ripple around me in an aftershock. I'm determined to make this unforgettable by bringing her to another high.

I slide in and out, holding her shins to my chest. "How are you doing, good girl?"

Her pussy clenches on my cock. Sweet, I'll remember that trick.

Her taste is still on my lips, her breasts are jiggling with every thrust of my hips. So much for control. I'm close to coming when she likely needs more recovery time.

"Mattie." Her eyes are wide and on mine.

"Yes, my good girl?"

"Lean in a little?"

I put one hand on the bed, angling my torso toward her. "Here?"

"Yes. Yes, yes, yes."

Bon, recovery time is over. I place a finger on her nub, and she nearly shoots off the bed. "Come on, mon chou, one more."

A few more thrusts, a couple rubs, and she's flying again, strangling my cock while I watch in wonder. I can't hold back anymore, my spine buzzing with the need to come, and I pound into her still spasming channel until I pour myself into the condom, grinding against her.

I lock my elbows, my arms holding myself up as I sag over her. One at a time, I lower her legs gently to the floor, then shift her so she's lying full length on the bed.

Stepping into the bathroom, I dispose of the condom and get a warm washcloth.

After we've cleaned up a bit, I throw myself down next to her. Even a professional athlete needs a rest after three rounds of great sex, practice, and a hockey game.

"Stay," I mumble, putting a hand on her arm as I give in to my need for rest.

Chapter Nine

Nicole

Needless to say, I don't stay with Mattie. I do have an ounce of self-preservation, and I have work the next day.

The minute my head hits my pillow, I'm out, so the overthinking doesn't start until the morning. Why did I try to stop him from going down on me? That's something I did in *relationships*, trying not to be too needy or too high maintenance. New year, new me, dammit. I should take all the orgasms, all the ways, and all the freaking oral pleasure I can get, and let the guys worry about theirs.

A little voice whispers, *But it's Mattie*. He's so cute and super-sweet, despite his playboy reputation.

Nope. Nopedy-nope-nope-no. There will be no pining. No more repeats. And no more passing on getting head.

The following week, classes start, and I try to get a jumpstart on my reading. I'm only in my apartment to sleep and haven't seen my girl gang or hockey, televised or live. My sleep is disturbed by memories of Mattie's stick and what he can do with it, but I'm determined to ignore that and move on—when I have time to breathe and check dating apps.

Even on these first two January weekends, I'm so

tired I don't plan anything, instead trying to figure out what to do for the marketing project my professor wants us to develop ourselves.

By the third weekend, I'm more under control—other than that independent study thing—and I might have hockey on in the background, but I'm not watching it. I'm struggling to decipher a cash flow statement, although my plan after the first several attempts is to never, ever, need to understand one of those in real life. I'll pay people to do that. Blech.

The game pulls at me, the announcers calling the plays, the points, and the fights. Any time they say du Près, my gaze snaps up before I force myself to refocus on my textbook. And yeah, I do recognize that I might actually learn these financial statements better if I wasn't distracted. But again, I'll pay people.

By that Sunday, I'm so stressed I call Christina. As soon as we exchange niceties, I cut right to the chase. "I need your help, please."

"Of course. What's up?"

"My marketing professor wants us to shadow someone in a relevant department at our employer for a certain number of hours and evaluate how they apply the marketing theories we learn in class, as well as how they are evaluated in each organization. But I spend my day immersed in my tech company managing the development of new software. So I'm bored, but also the head of marketing is a misogynistic pig, and I prefer to avoid asking him for anything, even though the company is sponsoring me in this degree. But most companies' hours would be the same as mine, and I'd have to negotiate for time off." By the end of my explanation, I'm circling my small living room.

"And the team's marketing is sometimes done at offset hours, given game times and the nature of our business, so it could be a fun alternative, am I right?"

"Well, yeah. I hate asking for favors, though." I throw myself on the couch with a sigh.

"Pish. Don't be silly. This is *not* a favor. Don't you think the organization might be interested in seeing the potential of a local MBA candidate to fill future roles here?"

"Wow. Maybe you should be in marketing. Or you've been hanging around Saylet too long."

"Ha. That woman has more energy than any one human should be able to contain. But hey, if you want, I can hook you up with her. She's an amazing PR Director for the team."

I stand to pace again. "Whatever works. Ideally, someone who does some of their stuff on the weekends or evenings. I'll get some leeway from my manager, but my weekdays still have to focus on my job in large part."

"Gotcha. Let me see what and who are the best fit, as well as who might be the most motivated to scope out a potential hire for a year or so from now."

"Thank you." With a promise to catch up soon, we hang up.

I crash hard that night, finally able to sleep with a possible solution to my project. My next marketing class is tomorrow, and I've already outlined the argument I'll make to my professor should the need arise. She should be fine with it.

My relief translates itself into dreams of a certain big hard hockey player I've been trying not to think about. I wake up in the morning refreshed, but horny as hell, as I had for a week after our second night together.

I repeat my new mantra. *The best way to get over one guy is to get under another.*

* * * *

A week later, my project is approved, Christina has found me the right contact, and I've been put to work. Tonight is a Sunday early evening game with a bobblehead doll giveaway, and I've been assigned to help out. My goal is to evaluate how many people indicate an interest in returning to another game when they get the doll, and if there is a difference when the player comes out to sign them after the game. When I showed up, I was super excited, wanting to ask the marketing rep a zillion questions.

One look at the bobblehead threw me. Of course, it's a du Près #10 figure. I exhale a deep sigh, ask my questions, and am now standing behind a table in the outer ring of the mezzanine at the Tornadoes' stadium where various food vendors and sponsors have booths.

The marketing rep said they chose Mattie because his lifetime stats are stronger than Buzz's, and they're saving Saint for end of season games.

The final buzzer sounds, and the scoreboard shows a 3-1 Tornadoes win. Fans start lining up at our table, and the rep informs me that Mattie will be coming out to sign dolls and boxes for season ticket holders who stay for it.

Of course, he will. Because this is my life, and I've never been lucky. I swear if I'd had more one-night stands I was trying to get over, they'd all be here tonight. And since it's an early evening game, there are of course many who want to wait.

Mattie had an assist, but Saint had two goals tonight, so he'll be in the press room, allowing Mattie to head here sooner.

In the next moment, I sense him. He's on the wide concourse ringing the arena, wending his way through the crowd toward us. I can't see him, but sweat breaks out under my arms, and moisture moves from my mouth…south.

The rep mutters about the fans getting restless, and without thinking, I say, "He's here."

She frowns in confusion and scans the hallway.

His milk chocolate hair approaching catches my eye. I can feel his saunter though I can't see it. Then he's there, larger than life, grinning and greeting fans. He does a double take when he sees me, but his smile widens, and he throws me a wink and a twitch of the corner of his mouth.

The marketing rep gives me the side-eye but jumps in with a Sharpie for him to use.

Mattie squats down to talk to children in line with their parents, talking hockey and charming the moms and dads. He nods, his face solemn, while hockey-wanna-be bros tell him what he could have done better. He poses for selfies, even offering to hold the phone with his giant arms. And he flirts outrageously with the ladies in line, whether they're eighty or eighteen. For those in between, he signs almost anything they put in front of him, until…

"Mathieu, could you sign right here, please?" one bleached blonde bunny asks him, tracing her finger along the deep vee of her Tornadoes t-shirt. She pronounces it Matthew, and I grind my teeth. The boldness, when she can't even say his name correctly.

He glances at me.

I can only imagine what he sees on my face. Distaste, jealousy, and hurt war within me. *I have no claim on this man*. I must remember that. And he's a consummate flirt.

And he's here to sell tickets. I grit my teeth and blank my face as best I can, turning away to make an unnecessary check of the empty boxes, since we ran out of dolls ten minutes before the first period ended.

"Ah, chérie, this ink is terrible for your skin. And it'll last longer on your shirt." I'm weak. Instead of focusing on my made-up task, I turn around. He winks at the bunny while giving her his signature grin that could melt off the panties of any female within a ten-mile radius. His hand sweeps the hair off her shoulder, and he leans in close—*get a grip, Nicole*—signing his name as high toward her collarbone as the cut of the shirt allows.

She giggles and leans close, but he's quick, stepping back before she can rub against him.

That was actually pretty smooth. She toddles off, happy, and he avoids any inappropriateness when the hall is filled with cameras.

"Give me a minute, folks." He comes around the table, holding the pen out to the marketing rep. I have my doubts that it's run out, but he's signed a lot of stuff. While the rep swaps the pen out, he turns to me. "You slumming it, or desperate to see me, p'tit chou?"

His timing is intriguing, since he could have asked that at any point but chose to chat with me after the bimbo incident. It's almost as though he's reassuring me. No. I'm worse than the blonde bunny if I let my brain once again read more into a man's actions than there really is. He's a flirtatious NHL player who probably changes women more frequently than he changes socks, given their notorious superstitions. Plus, his comment is conceited. I almost stick my tongue out, feeling bratty, but answer honestly. "Neither. I'm here for a school project, and I didn't know which player was going into doll form."

"School, huh? You'll have to tell me more about that. Chasers after this maybe?"

A thrill goes through me before I tamp it down. No thrills. He's just another member of our friend group now. I attempt a casual shrug, probably looking like I want to chew on a shoulder. "Yeah, Christina and Cam want me to meet them there for a bit, although I have an early meeting tomorrow."

I hand him my bottle of water, so the fans don't wonder why he's taking so long behind the table. Wisps of misplaced jealousy still trail through me. "Your adoring public awaits you."

He heaves a huge sigh, grinning. "Yeah, it's tough being me."

And there's the hockey player I knew was under there.

Another thirty or so fans and we're almost alone in the concrete concourse. The vendors have long since cleaned up and closed their metal rolldowns. It's us, the janitors, and security waiting to lock the doors.

Mattie gives me a one-armed hug and gestures with his thumb over his shoulder. "I'm parked off the players' entrance. Did you drive here?"

I shake my head. "I came with Christina. I told her I'd walk over to Chasers."

"Come with me."

This is another terrible idea. Sitting beside him in a small, enclosed space for the short drive to Chasers will only turn that thrill I'm not supposed to feel into lower belly flutters. Entering Chasers with him could also send the wrong vibes.

I'm not a bunny, I'm not worried about the other

players thinking they'll get a turn. Unless I want them to, of course. But I know myself. I've been a serial monogamist my whole life, and a third night with him will put me into full-on pining for a relationship mode. Which I've sworn not to do, especially with the flirtiest player out there. Jack may be the team slut—or whatever Mattie wants to call him—but Mattie is the team flirt and is a hit-it-and-quit-it kind of guy.

"Tell me about this school thing. I thought you had a job?" Mattie asks, putting his hand on my lower back to lead me through the maze of tunnels behind and under the arena to his car.

His hand burns me, sparks emanating from where he touches me directly to my pussy, giving it ideas counter to my emotional well-being, which requires that I stop lusting after him.

I swear the pulse in my neck beats visibly as though to lure the predator in for the kill. No, that's not fair, he's not a predator. As he said to me, it's nobody's business who he does. Including mine.

Taking a deep cleansing breath before sitting in the Mattie-infused vehicle, I outline the project and my preference to go outside of my company for it. My speech gets faster as I get more excited about what I've learned. "I interviewed the Marketing Director two days ago and learned about their overall strategy with giveaways. This inaugural year, they're also feeling out sponsors to see who's a good fit to work with long-term, including big name companies to be added on the ice."

"Hmm, yeah, it's nice not skating across words like Ford or Amerant Bank." He references two of the Florida team sponsors who paid truckloads of money to have their insignia painted outside the team logo at center ice.

"Yeah, well, I hate to tell you, but this is probably the only year with pristine ice and no corporate logos interrupting the field of play."

"Ah well, c'est la vie. So what have you learned so far?"

"Anything that makes them feel closer to the players generally keeps fans coming back. Signed jerseys, signed photos…you get the idea. Same with the mascot. He or she ventures out to local stores and plays quick lighthearted games with people to win tickets. Hence why they had you come out to sign. It makes it even more personal, for those who didn't have to rush home for dinner or school or work the next day. The pre-signed ones are for the people who can't stay." I finish my spiel as we pull into Chasers parking lot.

"And how will you judge how well it works in bringing fans back?"

"Ah, that is always the crux with marketing. ROI."

"Roi?" He pronounces it "rwah." "A king?"

"What? No. R.O.I. Return on investment."

He chuckles. "Oh, that makes more sense. R-o-i is 'king' in French."

I shrug. "From now on, you can assume I'm not speaking French, since I don't know any, apart from you calling me a cabbage."

Inside, I aim for Christina, determined to avoid him for my remaining time here. He is my kryptonite, and I'm not feeling as strong as Superman.

Chapter Ten

Mathieu

She is partout—everywhere. When I played in Florida, I had an arrangement with a bunny. We weren't exclusive, and we always had the right to say no to a request. But when our moods and schedules fit, we'd have a lot of fun in bed, with no strings attached.

I suspect that Nicole wouldn't be comfortable being a fuck buddy. She might be attempting that, from what I've gleaned in her New Year's Eve remarks. But her eyes hold pain. Chris said something about her trip home being rough. I don't know if it's from that or from a past relationship, but either way, I'm all about the fun, not the drama.

If only she wasn't such a hot pixie and smoking in bed. However, she's in graduate school and I needed tutors to finish secondary school. She threw out "ROI" like I should know it, but dummy that I am, I had to ask. We don't make sense together for anything other than an enjoyable fuck, even if I wanted that.

Inside Chasers, I veer off to Renee and then to Saint to celebrate his goals, along with Petrovsky's. It's a great night, and I love that the early game means we'll all get to bed by midnight. I order one of Renee's healthy pizzas because I'm ready to eat someone's size thirteen shoe if I don't get food soon, after the post-game signing.

When I sit to eat, I grab a spot next to Quasi that gives me a view of the bar, so I can people watch. In no way am I eyeing Nicole while I debate if I can get away with one more round of fun with her without causing issues.

"Coach is here," I say, surprised. He is leaning against the bar chatting with Renee as I had been.

Saint replies, "Yeah, I invited him. He said he didn't want to cramp our style, but also his daughter lives with him after his divorce, so he doesn't like to get home at crazy hours and set a bad example."

I frown. "Does he have more than one kid?"

"I don't know," he says, shaking his head. "He's pretty private and likes to keep that line between coach and team, so I haven't asked outright. Anyway, I convinced him to come tonight, since it's earlier than a lot of our games."

"Cool. How old is the girl? I haven't seen her in the family lounge or owner's box or anything."

"Eighteen or nineteen, I think. She attends UT. And even if she's into hockey, I suspect he keeps her isolated from us since she's close enough to some of the players' ages."

"I can see that. Talk about a career-limiting move. Ouch."

Near Coach at the bar is Kyle Scott, Jack's wingman on the defensive line and often in bars. Kyle, who we call Scottie, is ordering another drink. He's been drinking more recently, and I nod my head at an angle toward him. "Do you know what's going on with Scottie?"

"Nah. I'm trying to make myself available to see if he'll let his guard down a bit. He hasn't been hanging with Jack and the wilder bunch as much recently. Maybe he caught something from a bunny and is regretting things."

"Ha. Maybe." My eyes catch Nicole talking to Scottie, and I lose the thread of the conversation.

She throws her head back and laughs, then nods when he gestures to her empty drink. I clench my fists to stop myself from getting up. I told her on New Year's Eve, if she wants to pick up a guy not to get too buzzed, and to beware of the ones who would enable that behavior. And here she is accepting a drink from a manwhore. But she's not mine to protect. Tabarnak.

Saint is watching me when I turn back.

"What?"

"Why is your jaw clenched?" he asks.

"Just worried about Nicole catching whatever Kyle has. She's a good girl." I unconsciously use the phrase she loves because it fits her so well.

He barks a laugh. "What does Mattie du Près know about good girls?"

I catch myself. Why am I getting into this drama? Live and let live. I sigh and settle into my usual social butterfly persona. Leaning against the chairback, I raise my whisky. "How to ruin them for good boys."

He laughs and drops the subject like I hoped he would.

But I keep one eye on Scottie. He says a few words to Nicole followed by a few to coach. His yet-again empty glass is set down on the counter, and he winds his way toward the exit.

Nicole drops by Chris and Cam's table to say good night and leaves within minutes of Scottie. Clearly, they're going back to one of their places for a private celebration. My hands clench into fists, and I hide them in my lap.

When I turn back, Coach is putting his wallet away and sliding his ticket back across the bar to Renee. He waves to us and gestures that he's heading out, then follows Scottie and Nicole through the door to the parking lot.

Saint is watching me again when I face him. "That pulse is going in your jaw again, Mattie. Don't break a tooth, you should enjoy your teeth while you have them."

Our captain is too perceptive by far. I scan the crowd, but I don't want a hookup. I hadn't yet decided if I wanted Nicole again tonight, but it wasn't cool that Scottie got the jump on me. I force myself to finish my pizza then excuse myself to go home and sulk alone.

* * * *

We have practice the next afternoon, and the first order of business is to watch multiple game tapes. First to evaluate what we did right and wrong, then to study our future opponents so we can strategize our attack plan. We fly out tonight for games in Arizona and Colorado.

I'm still stewing over Nicole choosing Scottie for a hookup last night and only hear half of what Coach points out as their weaknesses. I have zero right to care who she chooses, how many, and when. That doesn't mean I can turn it off. At the very least, I feel like it would have been polite not to choose a teammate and maybe not to choose anyone on a night I drove her to the bar. Maybe I can give her a ride after every home game...

Merde. Coach is wrapping up, and I've missed more than I should have. Thankfully, we're playing Arizona first, and we've already played them and gotten some fantastic pointers from our winger Bergstrom, who used to play with them, so I have time to get up to speed on the rest.

As the team shuffles out of the meeting room with auditorium-style seating, I time my exit with Kyle's. He's yawning despite the coffee in his hand. "Scott, you worn out from last night?"

He freezes, blinking fast. "Uh, what?"

"D'you go home with someone? Is that what has you too tired to practice?"

He casts a furtive glance at Coach, who frowns and slips out of the room past us, head down.

"No-no one. Why?"

"Did you drive yourself home then? Cuz it looked like you were over the limit. You know they want us to keep our noses clean this inaugural year."

"No. I, um, caught a ride." He straightens. "What the fuck, du Près? What's with the inquisition? You're usually the guy saying who we do is no one else's business."

I drop my shoulders, chagrined. "Yeah. You're right. Just—if it was Nicole, be careful, man. She's one of Christina's best friends. You know, one of our team owners?"

He laughs.

I glare.

"Fuck no, it wasn't Nicole."

"What the fuck is so funny about the possibility of taking her home. What, you think she's not hot enough?"

You can't have it both ways, Mattie. Either you want him to choose her or you don't. And try to remember your preferences don't count anyway.

Now his chin is retracted, and he's staring at me like I've grown two heads. "Holy fuck. Are you into Nicole? Dude, I meant no disrespect to her. I laughed because she hadn't been on my radar. Are you two a thing?"

Merde. No, we're not a thing. Neither of us wants a thing. So I need to stop grilling my teammate. He's right, whatever he does on his own time, other than driving drunk, is his own business. "No. Simply looking out for Christina's and Cam's friend."

"Okay, cool. So maybe next time she *will* be on my radar. She's cute."

I growl at him, clenching my fists. After not referring to her as my friend, I have zero excuses for this behavior, and he knows it.

The idiot turns his back on me, assuming he's safe from harm when he's not, and starts down the hall. "Sure, you're not a thing, Mattie."

At the end of practice, we're on opposite scrimmage teams, so we're in each other's grill a lot, fighting for control of the puck. Every time, he chirps at me.

"She's got a tight little body."

"Man, I remember that top from New Year's Eve."

"Absolutely on my radar now."

Until finally, he's up against the boards, and I'm dropping my gloves to hold him by the jersey. "Shut the fuck up, motherfucker."

"Still not a thing, eh?"

The whistle blows, Coach bellows, and I drop my hands and skate backward. He orders me to do extra skating drills, which give me time to recalibrate.

Tabarnak. She didn't leave with him, but she didn't leave with me either. I guess she really has embraced the idea of one-night, or at least two-night stands. I need to get back to doing the same.

Chapter Eleven

Nicole

Tonight is our girls' night out. I arrive late, having updated the status on all deliverables for the next month on the software implementation project I'm managing, so no one questions whether school is interfering with my job. It's all so exhausting, and I ask myself almost daily if this is all worth it. Hopefully, it will earn legitimacy at work.

Then there's my family. Originally, I'd hoped an MBA would put weight behind my recommendations for the ranch. But nothing I say or do seems to change their minds. They know best for the ranch and are waiting for me to outgrow this strange desire to work elsewhere. Calls and visits with them almost always degenerate into them asking when I can come home to help out, why I can't, or the waste of money on rent in a big city and now more schooling. Never mind that my suggestions for improvements would cut their workload or increase their profits.

Whatever. I'm doing this for me. Even if my testosterone-poisoned workplace doesn't appreciate me, I'll have more options. And heck, maybe by then, my parents will at least try one of my ideas.

The girls have been texting about going to Vegas for the All-Star Game. We may not all be able to get into the game, but between the skills competitions and some of our favorite players being there, the weekend will be fun no matter what.

Saint was chosen by the league, no surprise there, and it won't be his first All-Star Game. Then Buzz was selected as a fan favorite, so he'll participate in the skills competition to see if he can earn a spot in the game.

Cam is staying home to spend time with Zoe during the league break, but Mattie is heading to Vegas to support his teammate or hang with Buzz if he doesn't make the final game. Because of course he is. He is everywhere I am these days. Or is it vice versa, given my choice of marketing project? Chris and Greg have a limited number of seats as owners, so I'm not sure who will sit with them. Either way, I don't care. I'll watch them on TV at the hotel bar if I have to. The trip sounds fun and like the break I need, assuming I have no major assignments due the week after.

Tonight's girls night is for planning the trip and getting a final decision on who is going. Part of the reason I updated all those deliverables was to ensure I could take two days off, since we'd go Thursday through Sunday. My budget can barely accommodate it, but I'm determined to take the weekend for fun early in the semester while I can. Maria's already texted that she can't take the time away from her fledgling studio.

Christina's a sucker for fine dining and even finer wine, so she has some site pulled up on her phone, trying to snag reservations when I arrive. She says, "I'm trying to find out what Buzz and Saint want to do after the game Saturday. That's the best night to plan a dinner, given the schedule. So do I make it with them and then change it? I don't want this place to get booked."

Lauren replies, "Make it with them. Unless you think a private room would be better, given all the hockey fans who are likely to be there?"

"Damn, I hadn't thought of that." Christina taps a nail on the table. "I'll make a regular reservation for now and check with them. Now, what else?"

"Gambling and shopping, obviously," Lauren responds.

"Spa?" Maria says. "Just because I can't go doesn't mean I can't live vicariously."

Christina purses her lips at the fact that Maria doesn't feel she can join us. I can understand. Maria's trying to get her dance studio off the ground, and Saturday is a prime day for lessons, many of which she teaches. She's also training for a competition and has a tighter budget than the other two.

As do I. Paying for school upfront and still sending money home to my family to help them, on top of rent, food, books, and clothes, doesn't leave a lot left for local shopping excursions, much less a trip to Vegas, but I'll manage it to enjoy a much-needed dose of self-care. However, a little project management will ensure the trip doesn't go off the rails for me or my finances.

"Let me see the schedule again," I ask.

The others don't try to hide their smirks at having handed over the cat-herding responsibilities to me.

I roll my eyes at them and skim the three-day hockey event list. "We need to figure out what we want to attend for the All-Star events and how late we think we'll be out. Will y'all want to gamble in the evenings?"

"Ohh, late shows," Lauren coos.

No, no, no. I can't do flights, shopping, even a shared hotel room, and a spa visit as well as a show. I'm going for the girl time and to escape the textbooks that stare at me at home. I'd also thought I'd escape the temptation of Mattie du Près, but that didn't work out.

I attempt to rein in the wild ones. "Hmm, that's why I'm asking about the All-Star events. I think between those and dinners, we might miss show times. Those might have to be a separate trip." *Without me.*

"Well, boo. But why do you care about whether we gamble?"

"Because I know you two. It won't be a simple manicure or massage. You'll want a half day bundle. Which means the morning option is out, and the afternoon will run into hockey stuff."

"Ha. Too true!" Lauren admits. "Yeah, maybe we leave that off and do that as part of the spa trip. This one can be shopping and gambling and hockey."

Yeah, and maybe I can afford it if we space it out. A spa visit is way higher on my list than a show. Without guaranteed orgasms like I had with Mattie, I need all the sources of relaxation and rejuvenation I can find.

"Sounds good," Christina says. "Our project manager is on the ball."

Chapter Twelve

Mathieu

We split the road games with one win and one loss and are back on our own ice tonight. Petrovsky is still a hothead, and Coach has been mixing up the lines to find our optimal balance. I personally think he's more of a third line player, a grinder, than Bergstrom or Boulanger.

We'll see how he does in the mix with those two, since they work well together. Bergstrom started using French on-ice with any of us who speak it. It's been genius when there are no French-speaking defensemen on the opposing team.

Whatever differences young Scottie and I had are long forgotten. Even if they weren't, they'd never appear on ice during a game. We're a team with a shared goal, and that's all that matters out here.

When I check the usual spot during warmups, Chris's seat is empty. It's been over a week since I saw Nicole. Maybe she'll accompany Chris tonight, and they'll join the team at Chasers after the game. I'm interested in how her marketing project is going.

My conscience chimes in. *Is that what we're calling it these days?*

Shaking my head, I shut everything except hockey out of my focus.

After Coach's pre-game pep talk, we're back out for

the national anthem and the puck drop. As we get into position, I glance over, allowing myself one last check. Chris has Zoe with her tonight. I stifle my disappointment. Zoe's a good kid. Although I guess she's the age a lot of us were when we started playing professional hockey, so perhaps I shouldn't call her a kid. That feels like forever ago now.

Then it's on. We're up and down the ice, neck and neck with our counterparts. Their defense are big guys who don't hesitate to use their weight to pin us to the boards to steal the puck. But we're faster. After a couple back and forths, Buzz gets tangled up with one of their defensive players, and I slide into the slot. He passes the puck to me right behind a D-man who conveniently screens their goalie. I shoot! I score! A one-timer from me sends the puck under the goalie's elbow into the back of the net.

I check the clock as I head to the bench for a shift change. We're only five minutes into the game. That is motivational and daunting, because now we have to defend that lead for fifty-five minutes while they're going to double down on evening up the score. I can hear the sportscasters now.

"They need to keep the momentum. Yes, Bob, it's early yet, blah blah blah."

I catch my breath, and I'm back in, the desire to quash my imagined sportscasters' annoying drone driving me up the ice at breakneck speed.

For all our efforts and theirs, the first period ends at 1-0, thanks to our stellar defense and Cam in goal. We rally during the intermission, determined to get out there and give ourselves a cushion. Despite my goal, the other team seems focused on Saint and Buzz, maybe because they've been named All-Stars, which I could see might feel threatening.

So we do it again. This time Saint has it, he fakes a pass to Buzz, then drops it to me behind him and angles a sharp right to get out of the way leaving me with only one defender coming at me in a desperate sprint and the goalie hunkering down. Buzz whizzes by me, and I dish it to him, skating forward for the rebound as needed. The defenders are so focused on Buzz and Saint, and their offense is slow. Buzz takes the shot to the goalie's right, away from his glove side, and he deflects it but doesn't control it. I zoom in right as it bounces back and curl it around him into the same corner of the net I hit for the first goal.

The lamp lights, and the two of them are on me celebrating, patting my head and butt as we skate back to the bench.

We're halfway through this game and up by two. We've got this.

In the last minute of the second period, a defender slams into me by the boards, fighting for the puck. I manage to slide it away, but it's grabbed by one of their team and taken down the ice. I catch my breath and race after it. Lucas Kucera and Joon Park are in as defenders, but they aren't Jack and Scottie, and somehow, the other team's center is in the slot and someone passes it to him. In the jostling of Kucera coming in to defend, it bounces off the center's skate and between Cam's legs.

The lamp lights, but we're up in arms, in the ref's face.

"The guy was in motion."

"It was off his skate. That's not a goal."

"We want a review."

The referee hears what Kucera and Cam and the opposition's offense have to say and moves to confer with the linesmen. He then heads over to discuss it with the goal judge. We're on a timeout so I grab some water.

Finally, they call it—in our favor. As the player was in motion, a goal can't be off a skate. While it hadn't been a distinct kicking motion, he'd directed it in with skate movement. Phew. But damn I wish it had happened with more time on the clock before a break because that will mess with the other team's mindset.

We spend intermission icing our knees and sucking down water while Coach reminds us to stay focused and defend our two-goal lead. That's all we have to do to win this.

Our team's superstitious nature means that no one looks too hard at me, offers to help me, or in any way references a hat trick. If it happens, great. But we're here to win the game as a team. And saying it out loud could jinx the whole thing.

Saint stands. "They've been all over Buzz and me like cheap suits."

Coach nods. "That means all the rest of you, do whatever you can to get open or to keep the puck. Defenders, come forward a little more. Take the shot if you have it."

Jack checks in with his roommate, "Prancer, you okay with that?"

Cam gives a sharp nod. "Yeah, man. You're also one of the fastest freakin' D-men in the League, so you've got me covered."

The second and third line get a bit more ice time this period, not because we're up, but because the other team is forced to play more evenly.

At the start of the third period, Coach puts me in with Boulanger and Bergstrom. Perfect, since we all speak French. Bergstrom is such a smooth skater, no one realizes how fast he is, and he's awesome at winning the puck in the corners.

Any other time, we'd probably get yelled at for being lazy, using dump and chases, but with Bergstrom there to catch up to it or win it back, it's perfect for the three of us.

"Laisses-la et chasses!" I yell and smack the shit out of the puck.

Emil and Remi race for the other team's zone as the puck goes flying.

I'm right behind them, and Jack and Scottie are on my heels.

Emil catches the puck, dropping it back to Jack to set up the play. Unfortunately, he's got a defensive player in his face, so he shoots it blindly to where he saw me. I twirl around the player in front of me and get between the goalie and the puck, so he can't see where I'm aiming. I barely get the puck on my stick before shoving it forward as the goalie's legs come down. It snicks between them a second before he's there to block it, and the lamp lights for a goal.

I grin and pump my fist, skating by the bench to give gloved high fives to my teammates.

And the hats come. Mon dieu, I love my home crowd. Austin has been good to all of us, and I'm here for it. Purple and black knit caps rain down on the ice, pom-pommed, skullcaps, you name it. I grab a few of them and do a lap to wave to the crowd while maintenance comes out to clear the ice.

We hold the lead and finish the game on a high, and

it's time for the celebrations to begin. I've kept a hat with an oversized pompom that I'm absolutely wearing to Chasers. Hell, maybe I'll grab a puck bunny to celebrate with.

* * * *

At the bar, I can't buy a drink to save my life. Everyone there wants to congratulate me. Which is awesome, but I can't down whisky and make practice tomorrow, so I decline after the first two.

The guys are hyped. Two team members invited to All-Star weekend plus my second hat trick is a good start to the calendar year and a nice way to go into that break before we push for a playoff berth.

My phone buzzes in my pocket, and I'm more excited than I care to admit that it's from Nicole.

Nicole

<hat emoji> <hat emoji> <hat emoji>!!! Again! Congrats!

Me

Thanks. Celebrating at Chasers - come by.

I take a selfie in the pom-pommed hat and send it to her with the caption, "My prize. Now we match!"

Nicole

Irrational annoyance spikes. Maybe she thinks she's too smart to hang with a hockey player. She's bagged the pro athlete and is now back to her college boys.

In my next breath, I recognize I'm not being fair. This is my own baggage talking. My parents have degrees, and my sister is well on her way to getting hers, at McGill, no less. Since they talk nonstop about how Annabelle is doing in school, I'm pretty sure university is the one thing they wish I'd done before going pro. But hockey was easy and fun, and I knew I could make it work. And they never found out what a struggle high school was for me. If I hadn't had tutors assigned to help the dumb jocks, I might not have finished. Dieu merci for my talent.

Nicole doesn't owe me anything, after all. We both went into those nights with eyes wide open. And it's impressive that she's working and going to school at the same time. I'm sure she works a fuck-ton more hours every week than I do, even if her work isn't as physically draining.

I'll just pick the next lucky girl. I sip my whisky that's now half melted ice and scan the room, looking for someone who appeals. Not a single one makes my pulse jump or my gaze linger.

Buzz appears next to me. "What's going on with

Scottie?"

I frown. "He's drinking too much."

"But why?"

"I dunno. Doesn't Saint usually take folks under his wing?"

"Kyle brushed him off and is back to hanging with Jack, who has the tolerance of an elephant, so that doesn't help. And Jack's not one to babysit."

I snort at that image. Landry is the biggest partier of all. I like to play—sports, games, women, you name it. But he parties *hard*. Scottie, though, isn't going to open up to me after our exchange at practice. "I don't think I'm his favorite person right now."

"Ugh. Okay. I'll keep trying." He turns and leans against the bar next to me. "Scoping out part two of your celebration?"

"Eh. I looked. No one worth doing."

"Dude, are you kidding? I swear they grow 'em prettier here in Texas."

"Maybe than the burbs, but not Miami." I try to play it off, belittling Buzz's prior team's location. Tampa Bay and Miami had a big regional rivalry about all things, including hockey.

"Ha. Whatever. More for me, Jack, and the rest of the team. You were all about the casual celebrations in the beginning of the season. What changed? That chick in Miami?"

"No. She and I had an agreement; we were never dating or exclusive. Nothing changed. I'm not feeling it tonight. Sheesh. Maybe I'm tired because I had to make all our goals."

"Fuck you." Buzz laughs and strolls off to engage a dark-haired bunny.

I sigh in memory. My Miami days were easy. My on-call girl and I knew where we stood and enjoyed ourselves in every moment. In a way, Nicole is like that. No one here can hold a candle to her. She's sexy, fun, and something about her does it for me. Plus, like me, she's busy and not looking for a relationship. I know it's a long shot, but maybe I can float the idea of a similar arrangement. After all, we seem to be friends, so why not add some mutually satisfying benefits, too?

Chapter Thirteen

Nicole

I park in a visitor spot at the arena and head toward the office entrance for my project meeting with the Director of Marketing.

As I'm walking, I check the time on my phone. I'm on time, but I need to ensure this conversation doesn't run long so I get back to my own workplace on time.

"Nicole!"

My head shoots up, and I turn to find Mattie jogging toward me. This must be the parking area for the team entrance, also. Even his jog is graceful, his body a well-oiled machine. I swallow hard at the memory of it against mine.

Here be dragons. I have enough on my plate without catching feelings for a habitual flirt who probably wants another round because I'm in his proximity and he knows I'm available. I need to move on. But no one else has appealed, not at school, the games, the bars, nothing.

He leans in for a hug, and I inhale his tangy, spicy scent. It's not heavy enough for cologne, so I assume it's a body wash or a deodorant spray or something. Whatever it is, it evokes more sensory memories of our nights together, and my pulse quickens.

"Coming to visit? Want to watch me—us—practice?" he asks with a big grin.

"You do know it's not all about you, right?"

"Are you sure? I bet it is." He makes a mock-confused face.

"I'm here to meet with the head of marketing about my project."

"Ha!" He wags his finger. "You see? It is about me. My bobblehead was the first part of your project."

I roll my eyes. "If you say so."

"Come on," he wheedles. "Grab lunch with me after?"

"Can't. I have to get back to work. I'm taking this as my lunch hour."

He pouts.

I pat his arm. "Poor Mattie. I'm sure your playmates—I mean teammates—will eat with you."

"They're not as cute."

I blush but play it off. "I need to go to my meeting."

"Hey, do you have class tonight?"

"No, why?"

"I was thinking we could chill and see if I could give you a different perspective on the marketing stuff…?" he half-says, half-asks.

My mouth flattens. Is it me, or is this a euphemism? The thought makes my pussy pulse with anticipation; my head and heart flash warning signs, though. I shake a finger at him with a smirk. "I know your idea of chill—more like 'net, pucks, and chill.' I think the head of marketing is probably going to cover enough."

He laughs. "Hey, I was serious. You'll never know. Anyway, I thought we were friends. I'm interested in your project. I never took a marketing class."

"Yeah, you probably took Hockey 101, 201, and 301, huh?"

He drops his head to stare at the parking lot pavement, scuffing a sneaker. "I didn't go to uni. Secondary school was as much classroom learning as I could handle."

"Oh, I didn't know that, sorry. But it seems to me you're doing just fine without it, huh?" I smile to try to put him at ease. And my soft heart prompts my next words, "Friends. Okay. I'm free after six. Tell me where to meet you."

We have each others' numbers from group chats with Christina and Cam and the others.

"Cool!" His sultry smile is back, and I worry about the state of my panties for the hours between now and dinner.

"*Not* your apartment. Or mine. Friends," I repeat.

He tips an imaginary hat, and jogs off toward the players' entrance, where others are arriving and entering now.

I make it back to my cubicle and through my workday. When I leave, I force myself not to race home and change clothes, as I wouldn't for any of my other friends. We end up at the north location of True Food Kitchen. I'm familiar with rush hour traffic in this area, but Mattie must not be, since he arrives fifteen minutes late, strolling in without a care in the world. He wraps his arms around me for a squeeze—the second hug for the day. If he wasn't such a risk to my heart, I could get used to this attention. But his lack of apology is a loud and clear warning to keep things casual and friendly. I've been watching the clock for sixteen minutes. If I'd been the one who was late, I would have been falling all over myself asking forgiveness for being tardy.

"No problem." I gesture to the cocktail I grabbed

while I waited. "They don't have any Canadian whisky. I asked. I'm sort of surprised you picked this place."

"They have a lot of tasty healthy options, though, and I don't drink the night before a game, other than New Year's Eve. Let's order because I'm starving—" he laughs when I narrow my eyes, not realizing I'm biting my tongue not to make a sarcastic comment about being on time. "—and I want to hear about marketing."

I'd half-expected the marketing interest to be an excuse for him to get into my pants again, even after my stipulation. But this place is all shiny surfaces and bright lights. Kale salad and quinoa don't lend themselves to seduction.

I outline the principles of marketing and tell him I have to identify which are used and how they're applied in the industry and company I'm reviewing. But the tricky part is evaluating their value. Marketing is often one of the first areas to be on the chopping block for budget cuts or staff reductions because there is not a clear way to measure success.

He frowns. "Are there certain…"

"They're called campaigns."

"Interesting. Like political campaigns."

"Just another form of marketing," I say with a smile. He's cute when he's inquisitive. I'm surprised; I really thought it was an excuse to try to get in my pants.

"Huh, I see that now. Okay, are there certain campaigns that are more profitable? Or at least more measurable?"

"Measurable, yes. For instance, in retail, they use bounce back coupons. When a customer buys something, they get a discount if they come back and buy something within a certain timeframe. The company can measure the success by the coupon being redeemed."

"Huh. Maybe we can do that on apparel," he says, his eyes lighting up.

I love that he's so into this. Given that and how easily he followed my amateur explanation, it's a shame he didn't get to attend university. But I need to redirect him on the clothing idea. I explain, "Unless the discount is for tickets to a future game, I'm not sure it's worth it. You want to channel the customer into buying more of your core product. In the case of hockey, you want them to go from buying single games to multi-game packages to season tickets to better season tickets."

"How do you measure that?"

"Data analysis and interviews, as best as you can. But it's difficult. For instance, the ones who got your signature were all season ticketholders already. I got people's names from the giveaway, but most didn't return my call asking if they plan to attend more games. Of those who did, not all have their next tickets bought yet, so that might be them saying what I want to hear. Maybe if it had been Buzz…" I trail off, teasing.

"Hey! He doesn't even have one hat trick this year."

"True. But a lot of women think he's hot."

"Bah, not hotter than me," he poo-poos the thought, then spoils it by asking, "Right?"

"Ah, hockey boys and their fragile egos."

He goes quiet while he finishes his dinner. "If it would help you, we could run an experiment with me as bait."

I raise my eyebrows. He's willing to participate in some marketing gig to help me? "Why would you want to do that?"

He shrugs and gestures with his fork. "We

established that we're friends. I like to help my friends when I can, and I have a fair amount of free time in my job, unlike some people whose lunch hours are restricted."

Chuckling, I accept it. Help is always appreciated, given my lack of free time.

He adds, "We might have to run it by the Tornadoes first, but I can't see them having an issue with it. It's more publicity for the team."

"Wow. Thank you, Mattie. I'll have to think about that, but I'd love the help, I just can't envision exactly what that experiment would be."

"You know," he drawls almost as well as a native Texan. "I'm always happy to be someone's experiment. For example, if you wanted to go for a three-night stand."

Tempting. But I daren't. "We stipulated friends. Neither of us wants things to be messy when we're hanging out with Cam and Christina and the rest of them. We've done well so far, and I don't want to screw with that."

"You mean, you don't want to screw me." He gives me his famous pout, and I want to bite that damn lower lip so bad.

"My brain says it's a bad idea."

"But that smokin' little body says it's a good one. And my brain and body vote yes, so you're outvoted. Come on," he wheedles.

I sigh. As nice as it feels to have a pro hockey player pleading for another night with me, he would hate the stage-five clinger I'd become. I have enough pride not to disclose that possibility with him, though.

Instead, I stand and put my purse strap on my shoulder. "Thank you for dinner, friend. I'll see you soon, and I'll text you to see when I've thought of a marketing experiment that will work with our schedules."

* * * *

The next week flies by, and I'm swamped at work because my project hits a milestone. Thankfully, that means we'll be starting a new phase of the software development for the two days I'm taking off for the All-Star weekend trip, and I'll have the time to enjoy myself.

I'm still waiting to get approval from the Tornadoes to implement Mattie's offer of help, but that will be after Vegas, so I can let it go for now.

Finally, we're on a plane late Thursday morning, drinking mimosas. Christina had paid for all of us to upgrade to first class. As she doesn't throw her money around much, we have all allowed ourselves to be okay with these occasional splurges.

I couldn't resist searching for Mattie from the minute we got to the airport, but there was no sign of him. Maybe he got tickets with Buzz and Saint. It's just as well. After two mimosas, I'd probably be wondering if we could join the mile-high club, although that has always sounded terribly unsanitary and uncomfortable.

"All right, ladies. What is the first order of business?" Christina asks.

They all look at me.

I groan. "I've been buried in work all week, being paid to herd cats, so I can't remember if I downloaded the Google doc to my phone."

Christina nods. "Lauren is our recorder and secretary. She keeps the spreadsheets. You are our time manager, keeping us on track."

"Okay, okay. Give me a minute to look." Thankfully,

past me was as organized for my personal life as I am for my job. I scan the list I've built from our first planning meeting. "I say we all have an hour by the pool this afternoon, then freshen up and hit the town. We can do happy hour before tonight's event, followed by a late dinner snack after with drinks?"

"Sounds great."

It's a relaxing start to our time off from work. Mattie continues to be absent, lulling me into a false sense of security. The next morning after a leisurely breakfast, we head to the Forum Shops at Caesar's. We'd gotten an excellent room rate at Paris Las Vegas, so we can walk across to Caesar's easily. From there, a tram connects to outside the arena.

Lauren makes better money than I do, so she and Christina are in their element. I'm more of a Marshalls girl myself, but I wander through the designer shops. We all brought clothes for dinner Saturday evening, but they're shopping for something new to wear, something they wouldn't find as easily in Austin.

We all take things into the dressing room, but my selections are more to be social than to purchase. I don't even look at the price tags, especially since I'd already justified a few new tops as part of my resolution to dress sexier.

When I try on a strapless mini-dress I fell in love with through the window, Christina gasps. "Nicole! You have to get that!"

I laugh, trying to keep the laugh light and without bitterness.

"It is perfect for you. It wouldn't be decent on me given my height. Lauren could pull it off, but you know how sensitive she is about her butt."

Lauren nods. "But it gives you the curves you're always wishing for."

The dress is fitted from the waist up and has corset-style boning in lieu of needing a strapless bra. Then it flares out to a bell shape. The whole thing is made of nude tulle with magenta and purple-toned embroidered flowers, some of which are three dimensional.

When I turn and look in the mirror, I agree with them. It's perfect on me. I was drooling in front of the window where it was featured on a mannequin; now I'm speechless. If only I could afford it.

"It's pretty," I say nonchalantly, reaching around for the invisible zipper. "But y'all know I'm on a budget and this trip was my splurge."

Christina presses her lips together. She'd never pressure me to spend money I can't afford. But Lauren pushes. "Nicole. That is a once in a lifetime dress. Treat yourself. You deserve it."

I step out of the dress carefully and pull my own clothes on. Not wanting the sales lady to overhear me, I hiss, "It costs more than I expect to spend on a wedding dress. *That* will be my once in a lifetime dress."

At that moment, Saint's wife Jessica St. John flounces into the communal dressing room. "Oh, hi girls. Are you hoping to find something for Saturday's game, too? I'm not sure they have tall sizes, though."

She makes a fake pout with her lips as though sorry Christina is a giant and therefore undressable.

"Hi, Jessica." Christina ignores the jab.

Ugh, none of us like her. One would think Jessica might have more of a care for her husband's position on the team that Christina owns, but I guess with his captaincy and selection for this weekend by the league, she feels safe. We all clam up, not wanting to talk about our plans for the day in case she invites herself along.

I return to the store and wander around for a bit but feel conspicuous for not buying anything, so I text the other two that I'll be out in front.

Of course, standing out front means I'm face-to-face with my dress again. I stare, mesmerized, picturing myself wearing it with heels in one of the flower colors or maybe black patent. I'd have so much confidence that I could have my pick of men. Or perhaps it would be for a date with someone special.

"That's almost Tornadoes colors. Why don't you try it on?" Mattie's voice is next to me, breaking me out of my dress-induced trance. Because of course he's here.

"I did. It was perfect."

"So buy it! Wear it Saturday."

"That"—I gesture with a grimace—"costs more than my car is worth."

"Oh," he says quietly. "Sorry, I didn't mean to pressure you. I would just love to see you in it. You deserve pretty flowers and dresses."

I give him a one-sided smile and point inside to Christina and Lauren, with Jessica hovering behind them gesturing at a store clerk about various pieces. "Thanks. The others are buying pretty things for Saturday."

He looks. "Hmm. I bet they are."

At his words and tone, I look askance at him.

He glances down at me. "You ladies haven't cornered the market on not being Jessica Rabbit fans."

I laugh at the moniker referencing an iconic 1988 animated movie character. Like the original, this Jessica sees herself as a femme fatale who expects men to fall at her feet. And, like the cartoon, she's immoral and mean.

He hugs me, saying in my ear, "You'll be gorgeous in whatever you wear. I'll see you later, mon chou."

The girls rescue me before I can tear up over the combination of the dress and his unexpected compliment, and we head off to coffee.

Chapter Fourteen

Mathieu

I linger in the center aisle of the mall and wait for the girls to get out of sight. Jessica comes out, and I turn my back, hoping she doesn't notice me. Although she'd probably snub me if she did since I didn't make the All-Star cut.

Once she's sashaying away, I step into the store and ask the sales associate for what I want. Five minutes later, I'm out several thousand dollars but happier than I've been in a while.

I'd been wallowing a bit this week. I have two hat tricks when Saint has none and Buzz has one, something less than a thousand players in NHL history have attained. Yet they're on the roster this weekend and I'm not. In retrospect, I'm questioning why I tortured myself coming here when I wasn't selected, but I wanted to support my fellow forwards.

Yes, we play as a team, and Saint and Buzz made those goals possible for me. They have more assists and more points than I do; mine were simply concentrated in those two games. Nicole would laugh at my ego, and she'd be right to. I want it so badly. This is my thing. I don't have the degree she and my parents do. This has to work, for the rest of my life. It's the only skill I have.

I manage my money carefully, even though I play

hard. Thankfully, I make enough to do both. Christina's assistance and guidance were a big attraction when I got the call from the Tornadoes. So why am I here spending this much money on a single dress for a two-night stand? Okay, a two-night stand who has become a friend, and who I still find hot AF. I shouldn't be thinking about her at all, much less buying her something. I don't want a relationship. Cam and Christina are a cute couple, but Jessica Rabbit is a walking, talking, warning for any self-respecting hockey player, much as I love Saint.

I look at the bag, wondering if I should return it, then shake my head. I'd do the same for one of my close guy friends, although probably not with a dress, ha. I've never had a steady girlfriend, so I have no idea what I'd do for her, but Saint sure lets his wife spend ten times this. Fuck it. I don't need a reason other than it makes me feel good to do something nice for someone I care about.

Buzz appears at my room door only moments after I've tucked the dress bag away in my suitcase. He's offered to teach me blackjack.

We sit at the small round table in the corner with the pack of cards I bought in the hotel gift shop. There's no way I'm wasting my money on a game as I learn it.

He lays out a bunch of hands, each with one card down, one card up. I understand the object is to get closer to twenty-one than the dealer without going over. But when he starts talking about when to hold on a twelve, depending on what the dealer has, I'm lost.

"How do you remember all this?" I asked.

"Well, I read a book, but mostly it's practice. You can play it on your phone when you know you're going to Vegas or somewhere," he says with a shrug. "I tell you what. To keep it simple, if the dealer has a six or less showing, don't hit. They're more likely to bust. But if you have a pair…"

The rest of what he tells me about splitting, doubling down, and whatever else is a blur. I thought blackjack was the easiest game in the casino. Apparently, I should stick to the machines or roulette.

I stop him, saying, "Buzz, I don't think this is for me."

"Aw, come on. I can sit with you and help you. I want a wingman to play with."

"Sorry, man. I hate math, and I was never one for playing by the rules. Remember, I'm the guy who takes as many mulligans as he can and then plays off the best ball when we golf?"

"Ha! Yeah, okay. And I agree, math sucks, but I win enough to keep going. I'll see if Saint is up for hanging at a table tomorrow. Wanna grab lunch before the games?"

Relieved he didn't laugh at me for my idiocy, I nod.

* * * *

After lunch, we head to the rink. Yesterday, Saint and I cheered in the stands when Buzz participated in the skills competition. He hadn't been chosen for those last two fan-voted spots on the team, but it's early days for his career. Hopefully, he and I will play in that game in the next few years. Today, Buzz and I will cheer on Saint.

The games take the afternoon into evening and are awesome, the three-on-three format making them somehow more intense and less so. With only three players moving around the ice, they reserve their energy and aren't skating quite as fast as an intense game. In particular, the defense knowing when to stay back and when to press is something to watch.

Afterward, I head to the restaurant where the girls made reservations. According to the Vegas group chat, Buzz will join us, but Saint won't. He said he wanted to catch up with players he knows from his past; what he didn't say is that he'll probably have to juggle Jessica's demands with that desire.

Everyone is at the hostess stand when I arrive, last as always. I love that not only is this a young team, but we have young owners. Between that and her relationship with Cam, Christina is just another part of our friend group, other than the fact that she'll get the rather substantial check for this dinner. We're closer to Amy and Greg than most teams to their owners as well, although there will always be an invisible line with Greg because he's more involved in team management.

I tease Christina, "How's Cam doing without you for a whole weekend?"

"Oh, never fear. Zoe's keeping an eye on him." Since Zoe is too young for Vegas at nineteen, Cam stayed in Austin to spend a rare weekend during hockey season with her. I miss Annabelle and wish she and my parents lived closer so I could see them more than a couple times a year. Maybe after university, she'll come down to Texas if I can help her find a job. After all, the Donovans have connections with some serious movers and shakers.

Nicole is chatting to Lauren about a celebrity she thinks she saw. When the hostess returns, they pause their conversation, and Nicole turns to follow her to our table. Behind her, I suck in a breath. Once again, her back is almost completely bare. From the front her dress is simple, a mint green with slightly raised polka dots. Spaghetti straps hold the dress up while the rest of it follows the line of her fantastic body. Its raised waist sits right under her breasts, and my eyes can't help but linger there. But when she turns, above the waist there are only straps that form the outline of a bra, basically where the seams would be.

I can't resist. As we are shown to the table, I fall in next to her, placing my hand where the dress stops at her waist.

She starts at my touch and glances up at me.

"You know what happens when you wear something backless."

"There are no mirrors handy to drag me in front of, and I'm sharing a room tonight, so you'll have to behave yourself."

Interesting. Her wording leaves an opening. I push from flirting to full-on "what happens in Vegas stays in Vegas" mode. "I am the sole occupant of my room, milady."

She ignores me.

I lean in. "You're the most beautiful woman in here. And I love this dress."

"Laying it on a bit thick, aren't you, du Près? There must be hundreds of gorgeous women here."

"None that are hotter than you. Or whose back I'm allowed to touch."

"I'm sure I could prove you wrong, but I'm hungry," she retorts, grabbing a chair. I nudge her around it and hold it for her while she sits before taking the one right next to it at the round table.

Talk at the table is about the games, and Buzz's performance the night before.

Christina orders some amazing wines, and I try a little of each, ensuring Nicole gets some as well.

"What did you ladies do this afternoon?" I ask under cover of hockey talk.

Nicole answers, "Laid by the pool. Other than Christina, those of us in apartment buildings with pools don't get a whole lot of down time to lounge by them. Or they're annoyingly crowded. It's nice to work on our tan, particularly in February."

"Hmm." Leaning toward her and lowering my voice further, I wiggle my brows and offer, "I'm happy to apply some après-sun crème to help you preserve that. I'd like to see those tan lines since I missed the bathing suit. I hope it was a bikini."

"Honestly, if this table was all guys, I swear you'd flirt with them. You can't help yourself, can you?" She shakes her head, adding in a whisper, "I thought you were all about the casual, and I'm trying to be. What's with this?"

I love that she's straightforward about it, not wanting to assume anything. Her question also opens an opportunity for me to make my play. "I find I'm not done with you yet, mon petit chou. We can keep it casual for a few more rounds if you are up for it."

She shakes her head. "I'm not sure I can do that. My brain doesn't work that way."

Warning bells go off in my head. My brain *only* works that way. And as she and my conscience and Cam have all pointed out, we can't get away from each other and remain in this circle of friends. But I'm not thinking with that head right now. I give her my most charming smile that almost always drops panties. "Only one way to find out."

"I'll think about it," she grumbles into her glass of wine.

After dinner, the group decides to do some gambling. Most of them want blackjack, and there are enough of us that the casino might open another table if they have the staff.

Nicole says, "I'll watch. I'm a good cheerleader."

Finger to my chin, I cock my head. "Hmm. A good girl with pom poms."

She blushes and bites her lip.

If she wants to play, I'd be willing to try again to learn all the math, so I offer quietly, "If you know how to play, I'll put up the stake, and we could play as a team."

She shakes her head. I didn't think she'd go for it, but I figured I'd offer. I wish she was more confident in her intellect. Make that in herself in general.

I let the group find their spots, divided between two tables already in play. While people order drinks, I turn so my back is to the group and keep my voice low. It's a long shot, but I have to try. "My room? We can get drinks at the bar to take up or enjoy the minibar or skip the drinks for the mirror."

A tremor ripples through her at my words and her nipples peak under her dress. "You know, I am feeling sunburned. Shall we make our excuses?"

I nearly pump my fist with excitement. Apparently, she's thinking with…whatever her equivalent of a little head is, too. "Nah, text whoever you're rooming with after we're upstairs. That way, you can tell them as much or as little as you want. For now, they won't notice we're gone."

My fingers itch to get to her bare back again. She turns away from the bar to the elevators, and I step in, putting my hand between the bra-style straps and the waist and letting my pinky finger slip under the fabric to hover above her tight ass.

As we aim for the elevator bank, I make all kinds of promises to myself. After tonight, I'll be done. Clean slate back in Austin. I just need this last hit, this last fix of my pretty petite blonde.

Chapter Fifteen

Nicole

It's probably good that there weren't spare seats available to watch blackjack because I might have left a wet spot on my dress and the chair.

Mattie is not only hot. He's incendiary, and his flirting turns up the flames. That man could charm a brick. He's charmed me out of my New Year's resolution of not getting involved with anyone. Because I'm most definitely involved, despite my best intentions. Clearly, new Nicole still needs to work on her one-night stand, no-feelings-involved rule. I need to extricate myself, but my getaway weekend is all about indulging, and Vegas is all about vice. I'm giving in one last time.

In the elevator, we stand with the other hotel guests as we're whisked upward. His pinky makes desultory swipes across the base of my spine, making me wetter with each pass. I'm about to start panting when we finally reach our floor.

Stumbling out, I follow him blindly to his room, my entire focus on his hockey bubble butt in what are clearly tailored slim-fit black pants. The purple dress shirt could only be worn by a confident man who plays for the Tornadoes.

In the room, I make fast work of the buttons covering his chest, peeling the shirt back to place my teeth against his pecs. If this is our last night, which it has to be for my sanity, I'm making the most of it.

"Feeling a bit feral, are we, p'tit chou?" he asks from above me as his hands unzip the bottom half of the dress and search for a way to undo the top half.

"Yes." I squirm against his erection before making an inch of space to palm it through his clothes. "Please."

"Okay, then." He pushes me back and says, "For the sake of expedience, you undress you, and I'll undress me. We'll skip the mirror for now, although it makes me sad."

I whip my dress over my head while he undoes his cuffs. He shrugs out of the shirt and reaches for his belt, but stops and stares at me. I turn toward the bed to give him the full picture of me in heels and a thong.

He kicks off his shoes, shoves free of his pants, underwear, and socks, and practically dashes into the bathroom to get a condom out of his wash kit.

I lay on the bed as he rushes back, a willing sacrifice at the altar of Mattie.

Then he's over me, on straightened arms and toes, brushing his body over mine with light sweeps, teasing us both.

"Mattie, please," I beg, unable to form a coherent request. I'm too far gone. I need him in me, taking me over. It's been too long, and he's been flirting every time we're together. It's all been foreplay, and tonight has been hours of building my desire.

His cock catches between my legs when he makes another pass, and we both groan.

I tug him down and bend my legs to cradle his hips against me.

He snaps the thong against my hip and kneels up to

drag it off me. His fingers run through my pussy lips, grazing my clit, and I arch. "Mon dieu, you're so sensitive."

"You've been teasing me all night. I can't take any more." I reach over and grab the condom and hand it to him.

"You're rushing me again. You know what that means," he warns.

Then he's sliding into me, a smooth glide made easy by how eager my body is. My hands roam his chest and back, gripping his hair when he retreats. At every forward surge, my fingers clutch his shoulders to try and hold him in place. I raise my head to press my teeth to his chest muscle again.

"Go ahead, my vicious little cabbage. Mark me if you need to. I'm not rushing this."

Instead, I lick the pad where my teeth pressed and move to the small dusky disc of his nipple. I tease that with my teeth, then soothe it with a lick, and he gasps, his cock pulsing deep inside me.

He holds himself on one elbow and brings his hand to reciprocate, tugging on my nipple.

I arch under him again, my heels digging into the tops of his thighs to push him to a faster cadence.

He ignores me, the jerk, and my pleasure spikes higher like a rope stretched taut that is going to snap if he keeps winding me up.

His fingers pinch the tip of my breast a tiny bit harder, and the rope snaps. I tighten my legs around him and grab him to set my teeth and bite that pec I've been teasing. Chaos erupts in me, that snapped rope of ecstasy recoiling around my body, sparking nerves in every part of me.

He groans, his hips making micro-thrusts under my heels. His cock thickens and pulses over and over in me as his orgasm overtakes him.

I loosen my teeth, arms, and finally my legs. "Oh my god, I'm dead. I've died of pleasure. The best way to go. Highly recommend, ten out of ten."

He chuckles as he raises himself to flip over and deal with the condom, wrapping it in a tissue until one of us can rouse ourselves to vertical.

When I catch my breath, I sit up.

I'm flung back down by a hand on my shoulder yanking me back. He looms over me from my other side, pointing a finger. "Nope. Be a good girl and stay. I'll be right back."

Getting up, he goes into the bathroom and runs the water, ostensibly to get it warm. While he waits, he pokes his head back out to ensure I haven't moved.

I'm entertained. And while that took the edge off, I'm definitely up for round two, even if there is a niggling voice in my head asking what the hell we're doing. I stay, like the good cabbage I am.

He comes back with a hotel-sized bottle of lotion, which he places on the nightstand and a warm washcloth. Cleaning me gently, he turns away. I enjoy the view as he tosses the washcloth in the sink, then grabs two bottles of sparkling water from the mini-bar.

"Cheers." He hands me one and clinks the neck of his against mine, plumping the pillows behind us so we can sit against them.

I raise mine and respond, "To round two."

I finish most of my water in a few gulps and roll the still-cold bottle around Mattie's body. He lays still, pliant, while I explore. When I see goosebumps rise on his leg, I rub them away with my other hand before moving on to his muscled arms.

As I lean in to roll the bottle from nipple to nipple, the opening notes of *Mammas Don't Let Your Babies Grow Up to Be Cowboys* play.

I frown. "What time is it?"

He laughs. "No clue. Vegas hotels don't make knowing the time easy. Why?"

"That's my family's ringtone. I have to get it." I'm already scrambling off the bed to find where I dropped my clutch. Glancing at the screen, I see it's three o'clock in the morning, five o'clock where they are. So yep, about the time my family starts their day on the ranch.

"Hello?"

Chapter Sixteen

Mathieu

Nicole frowns and clutches a pillow to her, sitting with her back to me on the far corner of the bed. Everything about her posture is defensive and makes me realize she hasn't said much about her relationship with her family, other than the "it's strained" Christina gave me on the way from the airport in December.

I get up, ignoring my persistent erection from staring at her naked back, and pour us whiskies. Handing her one, I scooch behind her and grab the small bottle of lotion from the bathroom that will have to do as the après-sun crème I offered at dinner. Warming some in my hands, I rub it along her shoulders, showing her the bottle when she glances around in question.

"Is he okay?" she asks into the phone.

"Uh huh…No. Mom, you know why. I have a job and an apartment here, and I need one to pay for the other."

A long pause. She takes the drink and stands to pace, the pillow and my shoulder rub forgotten.

"No, I can't just come home…Okay, won't. Let's not have this argument again." She sighs. "I'll see what I can spare, and I'll send it Monday"—she shoots me a look and lowers her voice—"once the banks open."

Her family is asking her to come home and/or send

money? What the hell? Parents are supposed to take care of their kids, not the other way around. Unless maybe they're in poor health or something. But no, Christina said they live on a ranch. I guess I should have spent more time asking questions and less time flirting.

Waiting for her to get off the phone, I vow to be a better friend. She won't want to answer questions tonight, but next time, I'll start to learn more about her. Maybe that will help me shift from lust to friendship, which is what she has asked for. As long as there are no commitments or calendars, I'd like to be closer friends. Nicole is possibly more interesting out of bed than she is in it, and that's saying a lot.

We're clearly not going to get back to round two, or four, or however she wants to count them. But I still enjoy watching her pace, her petite frame lean, with a little jiggle where women should have softer parts. I hadn't noticed her earlier in the season until she came to Chasers a couple of times and congratulated me on my game. Why was that? Sure, her hair isn't as long as I usually go for, but it frames her face perfectly, and it's softer than silk. She might not be as busty as my past hookups, but those tits are perky and often braless, which makes them fantastic.

"And you're sure he won't go to a doctor?…All right, let me know how he's doing each day, please." She hangs up and tosses back the drink.

"Come here," I tell her, scooting back from the edge of the bed and patting the space between my thighs. When she perches, I hand her my whisky and resume my lotion application and massage. She's so tiny, my hand covers her from neck to arm, and my thumbs are the length of her shoulder blades. I squeeze gently, pulling my thumbs upward.

She gusts out a sigh, and her muscles loosen. She raises the glass and sips.

"Want to talk about— Hey, that's mine," I teasingly protest.

"You gave it to me." Her voice is innocent, but I can see in the reflection from the TV across from the bed that her expression isn't.

"Minx."

"No, I don't right now. But thank you for offering to listen."

"Fair enough. Finish my drink and come here." I stand after her and tug her around to the side of the bed where I lay us down and spoon her. I resume her backrub one handed, less about relieving muscle tension and more about soothing.

This feels weird. I specified keeping it casual, and she was down with that, but here I am snuggling like I'm six months into a relationship and wondering when I can learn more about her childhood. The guys would tell me my vagina hurts, although my sister would kill them and me if she knew.

But I like this girl. Not only her backless top torture or her eagerness in bed, but her brain. Now what? The idea of a relationship still gives me hives.

* * * *

Nicole jumped on my offer to be a guinea pig for her project, saying her marketing professor would love that. The Tornadoes Marketing Director identified which planned events would work best for this, so today, I'm supposed to help sell tickets at a local retail spot for part of the day. The Marketing and PR Department had to be talked off the ledge from posting my presence all over social media because that would skew the results. In the end, I had to remind them that this wasn't a contractual appearance, and I was under no obligation, so they couldn't use my name. Annoying, when I only got involved to help Nicole, not to get sucked into some PR campaign again.

After a couple hours with me there, the table will be staffed by her and the Tornadoes' mascot. Then she'll compare sales.

She said twelve to two pm, so when some of the guys invited me to Topgolf to hit some balls and hang out at ten this morning, I figured I had plenty of time.

Of course, we immediately form teams and entered into a mostly friendly competition. After a couple of games, I check my phone, since I'll need a shower before I met up with Nicole.

Holy shit, it's 11:45. Her sales booth is nearby so I could go sweaty, but I don't want to meet fans and maybe take selfies with them like that. It'll be fine if I show up a little late. I head home, shower and change into a purple Tornadoes polo and cargo shorts. Finding parking in the outdoor mall is beyond challenging, and I nearly cancel the whole thing because I'm so frustrated. But Nicole will kill me, so I persevere. When I check my phone again as I approach the table, it's almost one o'clock. Oops. I probably should have texted. She's more time conscious than I am.

Nicole's jaw is clenched. Her gaze flicks to me as I'm walking up then drops to the table.

I slap the mascot's proffered paw in greeting and try to catch her eye to no avail. Okay then. Miss schedule-my-life-hour-by-hour doesn't like tardiness. Whatever. "Where do you want me?"

The muscle in her cheek pulses.

"And, uh, sorry I'm late," I try. "Had to finish a game."

Her lips purse.

The mascot gestures to the end of the table, so he and I flank it with Nicole behind it between us.

Nicole stands and murmurs something to the mascot and starts to walk away. Since no fans have recognized me yet, I step after her, catching her arm.

"Good morning," I try with the most winning smile I can manage.

"It's afternoon. By like an hour." The last words are said through clenched teeth.

"Yeah, sorry." I shrug one shoulder.

"Are you, though? You had to finish a fucking game. This is work for me. Maybe not paid work but work for a grade that influences my future. While you were playing a game. Everything is a fucking game to you, isn't it Mattie?"

My chin retracts a bit more with each accusation flung at me in a heated whisper. "I'm here now. I'm trying to help. And yeah, life should be fun, and if you'll remember, I'm paid very good money to play a fucking game, so excuse me for my outlook. Just because you find it skewed, it works for me."

She shakes off my arm. "Just go. I don't need you. I need someone I can rely on, someone I can trust. You, on the other hand, couldn't even give me the courtesy of a text."

"I apologized. I'm here. What else do you want from me?"

"Not to be late."

My brows draw down because the mascot has turned

to watch us. Not wanting to draw any more negative attention that would affect her project, I say that. "Imma go hang by the table and do what I can. If we stand here too long, it could affect your data. Go do whatever you were going to and come back. We can continue this later."

"Or we can skip it and never talk about it again," she retorts and walks off.

This is exactly why I don't do relationships. I don't want to be accountable to anyone, even for a text. She returns with a bottle of water, and I sense the waves of anger rolling off her. But instead of annoying me further, I find myself wanting to make it up to her. Always before, if I'm late to an event or cancel last minute and the person gets frustrated at me, I apologize and walk away. If they can't get over it, it's their problem and I hang out with them less.

Maybe I feel this way because hanging out with her less is not an option. No, that's not true. Sure, we're in a shared group of friends, but we didn't see each other that frequently until I got involved with this marketing stuff.

So I should step back from helping her with her project. During a lull in foot traffic, I open my mouth to say that and what comes out is, "Please let me buy you dinner to make up for my tardiness. I'll help you summarize the results of today."

I blink.

She blinks.

My relationship phobia belatedly kicks in, but I rationalize my offer as something I'm doing to smooth the way with a pal. I'd do the same with a teammate, no doubt.

She opens her mouth—to refuse, I'm sure.

I throw in, "You can pick the restaurant. Or I'll pick one."

She looks away and calls to a passerby, "Have you met one of our star wingmen for the Tornadoes? This is Mathieu du Près, and you can get tickets to an upcoming game right here."

Merde. She's going to sic fans on me now? A few other shoppers hear her and wander over.

I paste on my most charming smile and lean in before they engage me. I whisper in Nicole's ear, "You better do something similar with the mascot when I'm not here, or the results will be skewed by your aggressive sales approach."

She shivers. Interesting. I doubt it's from my words. I might have a shot at getting back into her good graces and having a nice dinner. My fears of expectations and calendars are nowhere to be found. As for my vow in Vegas, that it would be the last time? This is like a workout regimen. You commit, but if you decommit, you forgive yourself and simply recommit. I'll recommit to honoring her desire not to get hurt after one more bout of awesome sex with the hot pixie.

I have to leave at two o'clock despite my tardiness because we have an afternoon practice. As I go, I do a showy complicated multi-step handshake with the mascot that we'd practiced in the pre-season for social media, and then lean in and hug Nicole. "I'll text you when I have reservations."

Chapter Seventeen

Nicole

Mattie   5:00pm

> I'll pick you up at 6:45

I debate ignoring him. But he's such a spoiled child used to getting his way, he'll probably show up to my place anyway, so I'm going to have to deal with him. I might as well get a free meal out of it. To give him a taste of waiting on me, even though it's petty, I don't respond. I do, however, shower and shave and moisturize my entire body. I'm debating outfits when his next text comes in.

Mattie   6:20pm

> I'm heading your way

You have to give the man points for his optimism, no matter how irritating his always-looking-for-the-party attitude is.

6:35pm   Me

> Fine

Every guy knows what "fine" means in girl speak. Yes, I live my life by a detailed calendar, but this wasn't some casual social invitation. He knows what this means to me. And he fucking *offered* to help. It's not like I roped him into it or something.

Ugh, I'm getting frustrated all over again. First, I need more clothes than a pair of thong underwear, which is the only thing I'm currently sporting. Second, I definitely need wine. Christina's caliber of wine in fact, on his dime. Then maybe I can have a calm conversation with him.

I stand in front of my mirror in my third outfit, trying to find that sexy-without-trying look. I'm not sure why I'm going for sexy. Looking around, I note my personal tornado from rifling through my clothes. We can't come back here, at any rate. I've cock-blocked myself from making a bad decision, which will help reinforce my promise to myself to stop this insanity before I get in deeper. I have to get back to the idea of one-and-done, no emotions. It's too late to avoid that with Mattie despite his deplorable time management skills—he's too fucking nice, hot, and great in bed—but I need to cut it off before I fall back into old-Nicole habits of pining.

I haven't confessed this weird hookup-but-ongoing thing to the girls, so I can't call any of them for apparel advice without a ton of questions, and he didn't say where we're going.

Finally, I channel my inner Maria and grab my best push-up bra and a ribbed coffee-colored t-shirt with a deep vee, and black pencil trousers that I swear make me look taller. Hopefully, this will go dressy or casual.

He picks me up in a rideshare. But unlike most

people in a rideshare, he has them wait and comes up to my apartment. We're dropped off on West Sixth Street, and he tips the driver in cash. The restaurant's parking lot is tiny, so now I get the rideshare choice.

Clark's Oyster Bar. Does he really remember our brief conversation from six weeks ago about me not having tried oysters? Nah, I'm sure he's simply continuing his own quest, and I was handy for this particular research outing.

Whatever. I'm happy to try a popular Austin restaurant when he's paying. But as the host directs us to our seats, several women's heads turn to watch Mattie. A few of the gawkers are here with dates. Rude. And depressing because they are all taller, prettier, and more elegant than I am.

After we order drinks, he asks, "How did the rest of the day go?"

My feelings of inferiority cause me to snap, "Fine. Look, I appreciate dinner, and I'm sure we'll get past today. But your actions made it clear you don't care about my marketing project, and I'm not over my frustration yet. I think we should talk about other things."

"Just because I was late doesn't mean I don't care."

"You didn't even text me to let me know." My voice rises in irritation, although I manage to keep the volume low.

He shrugs. "It didn't occur to me. I didn't track how late I was until I was walking up to the table."

"Where I come from—" I start through gritted teeth but go silent when the server brings our drinks "—being late means you value your time and *game* more than you value mine and my project." My tone may or may not have been caustic on the word "game," but at least, I'm focused on his pretty face now, instead of all the drooling women.

He thinks for a minute, tapping that distractingly delicious lower lip and asks, "Is there something you're bad at?" At my frown, he amends, "Or not good at?"

Attracting men who want a relationship? But I go with, "I can't iron to save my life."

He raises a brow. "Who the fuck irons anymore? But I digress. So if you were to iron a shirt for me…on whatever outdated planet we were living on at the time…and you burned a big iron shape into my shirt, would it be because you didn't care about my clothes?"

"No."

"Well, I suck at time management. I've actually been contemplating getting a part-time assistant because I get in trouble with the PR team for being late to meet-and-greets they set up. The only thing I manage to stay on time for is practice and games because I'd be fined by Coach."

"That means you disrespect a whole lot of people's time."

"Like theoretical-you disrespected my clothing and my time and money purchasing it? No, it was an honest mistake when theoretical-you was doing something nice for me."

"For theoretical-not-late-you."

He chuckles. "Now, you're getting it."

The server returns, and after I order a salad and an entree, Mattie orders all twelve types of oysters on the menu and the catch of the day. The waitress blinks but nods and scribbles it down. "I'll uh, bring the oysters and salad together?"

Mattie says, "Bring the oysters first, please? This

lovely lady hasn't had them before. Oh, and maybe some bread as well as the crackers."

"Of course, sir." She grabs the menus and hurries off.

A few tables away, a tall, lithe blonde stands, showing off her toned stomach in a cropped top paired with low-slung flowy pants. Instead of aiming for the restroom, she circles behind me, stroking her boob-length hair on the way. She drops her hand to her side abruptly when she's alongside our table, attempting to gain Mattie's attention.

Her presence is a good reminder that I'll never be in his league. Yet another reason, along with his inability to manage his time, that I shouldn't allow myself to blur the lines again. Friends. Casual friends are what we need to remain.

To Mattie's credit, his gaze never leaves mine. I replay our conversation before the server came over. Oh, right, he is waiting for me to forgive him because I theoretically ruined a shirt he can easily afford.

Narrowing my eyes, I ask, "Mattie, you're not comparing an article of clothing to a grade toward a degree, are you?"

He frowns and jerks his chin back. "I was trying to explain that it wasn't intentional; it's something I struggle with." His tone turns bitter. "Obviously, I don't know about grades and degrees."

I quickly reply, "Sorry, that was poorly worded. It's not about the degree. Even if it was something for work, I was just saying the scope of the harm is different."

The crease between his brows lingers, then smooths. He wiggles his brows. "I understand. And I am sorry. Pardonne-moi? How can I make it up to you?"

He's far too cute for his own good, but I'm not going

down that easy. "Mattie, this is important to me. I allow myself to rely on very few people, all of whom you know. I accept your apology, and I understand your analogy, but it stung when I found I couldn't rely on you."

"You can."

"Not unless you can commit to being where you promise when you promise, and it doesn't sound like you can."

He visibly shudders at the word "commit."

I roll my eyes. "I'm over it. Really. It reinforced the idea that this needs to remain casual. No commitments necessary. Although, a text would be appreciated in the future."

He clenches his jaw for a second but nods. "Okay. I still want to hear about the day and the project. Hopefully, I've shown you that a lack of skill in an area doesn't equate to a lack of interest. Besides, I didn't get to take a marketing class, so I'm living vicariously through you."

He blushes and looks away. Yep. Definitely embarrassed about his lack of a degree. Which is hard to fathom when he's so successful he can casually choose this as a weeknight dinner spot when it's not even a special occasion.

The server returns with a huge circular tray filled with a bed of crushed ice. The oysters sit on that, still in their shells, with tiny cups of condiments in the center. The interruption gives us both a minute to regroup. He creates a plate for me with each oyster variety before building one for himself. After talking me through the condiments, he slathers on a bit of cocktail sauce and slurps the oyster right out of the shell.

My eyes bulge.

He laughs, correctly guessing my expression as shock at his table manners. "This is how you eat oysters. Honest. Look around."

Sure enough, a couple other tables have been served oysters recently, and people are holding shells to their mouths. The table of tiny waisted women is full again, but they're drinking rather than eating. They're probably debating whose turn it is to take the long way to the restroom next, to pass Mattie.

"Okay, before you eat it, the idea is that you don't chew. That's part of the reason for slurping. You're going for the layers of flavor on your tongue as it slides down your throat." He wiggles his brows again.

I dress mine as he did, hold it up to my lips, and tilt the shell, sucking. I blink at him as I swallow.

He's smiling proudly. "There's my girl. That was some good sucking."

My heart thumps at him calling me his girl before my brain talks me out of my enjoyment. *No, bad heart. You're not allowed in this friendship.*

"So what did you think?" Mattie is asking.

"Um. That's…certainly a flavor bomb." And it was, although I'm not sure whether I like it or not. It's certainly different than anything I've ever eaten.

"What did you taste?"

"There was a strong taste of the sea, as though I'd swallowed a bit of ocean water. A smooth slimy feel, sort of like wet sashimi. Along the way, there's a hint of creaminess and the tang of the cocktail sauce."

"Ha. A great description. But the question is, did you like it?"

"I haven't decided yet. I didn't hate it. It was just a

shock."

He leans in and says, as though it's a secret, "You know these are supposed to be an aphrodisiac, right? They definitely remind me of a certain flavor."

As he's already proven to enjoy that taste, I find myself thinking of that night rather than rolling my eyes at his crassness, and heat rises to my cheeks.

The darned man notices, of course. He's smirking as he watches me.

I finally answer, "Yes, I knew that, and yes, they remind me of that sort of thing as well. *Despite that*"—I grin at him as I emphasize those words, and he chuckles—"I think I liked it. Certainly enough to try some more."

"Excellent. You'll be my partner in finding the best here in Austin then." He sits back and devours most of the oysters, humming in pleasure at some and tilting his head side to side as he proclaims others only so-so. Between slurps, he brings the conversation back to my class. "Talk marketing to me."

I describe how the Tornadoes Marketing Director had told me late afternoons sell more tickets, so I'd deliberately had him come earlier. And interestingly, we sold more tickets than they'd expected both halves of the day, but especially in the time he was there.

"I suspect folks texted their friends at the conference and told them you were there, so they came by and bought tickets even if they missed you."

"I wonder how they formed an expectation, given that this is our inaugural year," he muses.

"That's actually a good question," I say with raised brows. I grab my phone and jot a note in it to ask the Marketing Director that.

The oysters are swapped out for my salad and our meals. When I offer him some from my plates, he accepts. Scooping lettuce and snapper onto his bread plate, he says, "I was surprised you didn't include your family in the people you rely on. If you're up for talking about them, I can be a good listener."

The question is fair, given their call when we were together in Vegas. I'm unsure if I want to spoil a fun evening. This isn't a date, though, it's two friends—or maybe friends with benefits—having dinner.

"My family are cattle ranchers." My voice is flat. I'm relaying facts, keeping my frustration at bay.

Chapter Eighteen

Mathieu

I'd hoped there would be a chance to ask about Nicole's family. Her obvious omission of them as people she can rely on provided that opening. Between her phone conversation and Cam's cryptic remarks, I'm curious. I choose to ignore the fact that I'm never curious about anyone's families, especially those belonging to the women I want to fuck.

I nod silently at her bare bones statement, not wanting to push her.

She continues, "The ranch has been handed down for several generations in my father's family. And luckily, my brothers seem eager to follow in the tradition. I, however, am the black sheep, since I have zero interest in either ranching or marrying a rancher."

"Why?"

Her shoulders relax. "Thank you for asking. Many city boys don't care to understand, having already chosen to live in an urban setting. Ranching life is hard. You're up at the crack of dawn, you work outside in all weather, from searing Texas heat to ice and snow. There are smelly animals and broken equipment all the time. It's very repetitive. In my job, there is analysis and thought needed, not just physical strength. In a temperature-controlled environment, no less."

I bark a laugh but quiet quickly. Dieu merci I'd asked for the seat facing away from the majority of the room to avoid too much recognition. It gives me some freedom to enjoy my meal without interruptions. So far, no one has come by to ask for a photo, although Nicole frowned at one woman when she walked by.

She smiles at my reaction.

"Okay. But why wouldn't your parents support you in finding your own path?" My voice is tentative. I worry about being nosy while trying to understand their relationship.

"It's not that they don't support me," she says, then grimaces. "My mother was a city gal from Oklahoma who fell in love with ranching as much as with my father. She can't understand why I'd prefer a city over that. And frankly, they need every helping hand they can get. They pay my brothers some wages, but it's also understood that they're working toward their future ownership."

"I'd still expect parents to support their daughter in chasing her own dreams, rather than foisting theirs on her." I wince internally at my word choice. "And if they want you back there and pay your brothers so little, they must be profitable, non?"

She presses her lips together, clearly not happy with this conversation. But she doesn't shut it down. "They were, once upon a time. But expenses have gone up, and it takes capital to invest in technology that would make things easier. Unfortunately, market prices haven't increased at the same rate as their costs, so they're stuck unable to advance."

"I don't understand why they'd want you back there then, another mouth to feed, etc."

"Yeah. It's not logical, so don't try to follow it." She

sighs, her frustration creeping up. "They want me back because they want the family working together. But they won't listen to me about taking out a loan to invest in some new equipment that will increase their efficiency and therefore their profit margin. Nor will they diversify, no matter what analysis I put in front of them or what neighbor I point out who has done something similar."

Her voice has risen, her movements becoming more animated. Trying to bring the emotions back down, I say in a mild tone, "Merci, ma chérie. Is there anything I can do to help?"

She cocks her head and smiles. "Most days, I don't know what *I* can do to help, so no, but thank you. Listening is good. And though we're casual, it still is good to talk about it."

She's definitely less angry. Despite what she said at the table in Vegas, she keeps throwing the word "casual" out there. It gives me hope that I can get her to go for something similar to what I had in Florida because I can't get her out of my head. I want more time with her, just maybe not calendared quite so firmly.

However, I know women enough to recognize that if I push too hard tonight, after a disagreement we're barely past, I'm going to lose all future opportunities with her. So half-joking, I throw out, "If you need to take your frustration out physically, I can think of a few ways."

"Aw, Mattie," she drawls, her gaze sliding over to a table of women about her age that she's been glancing at all night. "You're such a good friend. But today was a long day, so I'll pass."

Resigned, I pay the bill and order a rideshare. When I get out at her building to walk her up, she looks surprised.

I growl, "I'm taking you home the same way I picked you up. Just because you refused my ever-so-generous offer doesn't mean I'm going to drop you at the curb and run."

Under her breath, she mutters something about the table of women at Clark's, but I ignore it. Our conversation had kept my full attention on her.

At her door, I tug her in for a hug. When she resists, I protest, "Hey, friends hug."

She relents, and I sigh with pleasure when I can wrap my arms around my pixie. My breath ruffles her hair as I mumble, "G'night, p'tit chou."

"Good night, Mattie. Thank you for a lovely evening." The door closes behind her, leaving me in the hallway savoring the last glimpse of her.

At home, I slouch on the sofa watching sports news. I barely register the hockey scores, though, while I mull Nicole's family situation and why she feels she doesn't do casual well. Even with only a high school diploma, I can guess that she's looking for the love and support she doesn't get from her parents.

The devil in me—or in my pants—keeps telling me I should still make my play for a fuck-buddy gig. My fuck-up helped her get perspective that we wouldn't be good together long term. But damn if we're not fire for the short term. She must see that. And the fact that she let me get away with the dirty reference tells me she does. There's hope.

Chapter Nineteen

Nicole

Three days later, I have an evening with no class and no group meeting. I'm caught up enough on my homework that I text the girls from work.

Me

> GNO?

Christina

> Boys are on a road trip. I'm in. Terroir?

Maria

> Margaritas for a change?

Christina

> What do you mean for a change? You drink margaritas like they're water.

Maria

> <face with tongue sticking out emoji> For a change from you drinking wine like it's water.

Me

> I'm Switzerland. Just tell me where to go.

Christina

> What? No, this was your idea. You pick. Anyway, our project manager can't be Switzerland LOL

Lauren

> If it helps, Terroir is easier for me to get to.

Maria

> I didn't say where the margaritas were!

Lauren

> oops

Me

> Terroir. Sorry, Maria. I'll vote for margs next time.

For a change, I'm the first one there, pulling up my Google doc to see where we are on the wine list. I'll wait for Christina before I order, though, given her persnicketiness about wines.

Maria comes in and hugs me. "What's up that you called a girls' night?"

"Just needed time with my besties and a break from my life."

Christina and Lauren walk in together, and we sort out our wine selection and three dip sampler order.

"What's up?" Christina asks.

"I asked that. No answer yet," Maria says with a side glance at me.

"How's school?" Lauren asks.

"Overwhelming, as it almost always is. I'm not sure I'll make it through. This is only my second semester, and I'm exhausted."

"Are you taking the summer off?"

"I still haven't decided. They actually have two short but intense sessions with limited classes offered. I might only do one of those, though."

"Maybe we can do a girls trip during the other one," Lauren says but then turns to Christina. "Or maybe we'll have a wedding to attend?"

"Doubtful," she said with a big grin. "I told you I've forbidden him to ask this season. We need his contract done and dusted or the press will be ugly."

"Doesn't mean you can't plan the wedding. It's not like you're not going to say yes."

We all laugh. I wonder what Christina's preferences for a wedding are. With her money, she could do anything. A destination wedding—heck, they could rent an island, do the traditional thing somewhere local, or opt for an intimate ceremony and celebration at her and Greg's home. They'd hosted the whole Tornadoes organization, back office and team, for Thanksgiving, so I guess intimate is relative.

But she shakes her head. "Let's see how the playoffs go and how y'all feel closer to the summer. We should do a girls trip of some sort no matter what, even if it's only a four-day weekend. Maria, how's the dance studio?"

"Good. I might have one more instructor coming on. We're talking."

"Anyone I know?"

Maria says, "No. This would be for beginners, she's coming over from the national chain. She competed a couple decades ago."

Christina grimaces. "Gah. You made me realize I competed a decade ago."

"Oops." Maria mirrors her disgruntled expression. "Sorry."

I need advice and changing the subject might be better than Christina dwelling on her time since competitive dance. "You all know I decided to try a new tactic this year rather than looking for the perfect man and coming up short."

"Get your 'ho on," Maria chimes in with a nod.

Lauren laughs. "Hey, I resemble that remark."

I retort, "I used the word 'slut' at Chasers last month and of all people, one of the guys shamed me for using it. Apparently, his sister checks his language and preconceptions. The quote was 'single people have the right to do who we please without being called names.'"

"Ha! I know it wasn't Jack saying that. He embraces his slutty side."

I widen my eyes at Maria in exasperation.

"Oops again, shutting up now." She looks mildly

chagrined.

"Anyway," I say with an exaggerated sigh. "My point is, how do you avoid falling for the guy? I hate that I'm prone to that."

Christina holds her hands in the air. "Don't look at me. I never mastered it, with Cam as Exhibit A."

We all chuckle.

Lauren and Maria exchange looks. Lauren shrugs and turns to me, "I'll take first shot. First, my criteria to take someone for a ride are different than those I might have for a relationship. I think. Actually, scratch that. I'm not interested in dating, so I don't know."

Maria snickers as Lauren frowns and jumps in. "I think what she's trying to say is that I look at the physical more for one-nighters than I would for a boyfriend. It's less about common interests, intelligence, and nurturing than about whether he can get me off twice before he busts a nut."

I breathe a sigh of relief when she lowers her voice for the last part. "But what if he gets you off plenty, and you find out he's a great guy?"

"Ha! Those don't grow on trees, honey," Maria says.

"But what if?"

"I suppose if it ever happened, I'd see where it went. But—and this may go back to the double standard about sluttiness—most guys who get you in bed on the first night don't see you as girlfriend material. They want a lady in the streets and a freak in the sheets." Maria twists her mouth to the side. "It sucks, but it's reality."

"Okay." At first, I'd thought Mattie wanted repeats because I was easy, a known quantity. But he seems interested in spending time with me out of bed, too. So far, not helpful. I push for more information. "What about a casual fling, as in more than one night but keeping it casual."

"Same as one night for me," Maria says, glancing at Lauren. "He might not be the most caring guy, never making me breakfast if he stays over. He may not be the brightest bulb in the chandelier. But if he can rock my world, I'll keep him around for a while until I get annoyed by some other aspect of him."

I was irritated by Mattie's tardiness for the ticket sales event, but it wasn't enough to keep me from dinner that night, and I didn't even get an orgasm. I suspect he'd need to try a lot harder to get me to walk away, which is what I'm afraid of and why I'm asking. I need to figure out how to separate myself without waiting on him. "What if you never get annoyed?"

"Dunno. It's never happened. What's up with the pointed questions? Did you have a one-night stand and already start to fall for him? You know the guy probably has the worst gas ever or something terrible like that. Just assume so, and it'll help you move on."

The others snicker.

I keep my answer vague. "No, no. Nothing like that. I've had a few casual encounters. My questions were hypothetical so I can protect myself."

Christina reads the plea for help in my expression. "How's the marketing project going?"

"Good, I think. I dread putting it all together, but I have most of the data I need. Thanks for hooking me up with the Tornadoes Marketing Department. And Mattie helped."

They all pause in their motions of eating or drinking and stare.

Lauren sneers, "Mattie? As in Mathieu du Près?

What does he know about marketing?"

I glare at her. "What's your problem with him? He's been very supportive."

"Has he ever even taken a marketing class? Guys think they know everything. God forbid a woman who is actually learning a subject actually know how to complete a project."

Oh my God, she is a sniff away from being full-on mean girl. No wonder he's self-conscious about his level of education, but I wouldn't have expected that from my friend.

My tone is stiff when I reply, "Actually, he said he hadn't, but he was interested in learning about it."

"Or in getting into your pants."

I flush. "He doesn't need marketing to do that."

Oops.

"What?" Maria interjects at her usual ensure-everyone-in-the-bar-should-hear volume and slaps my arm. "Girl, you've been holding out on us."

Chris had just sipped her wine but snaps her head around to stare. "You left with him on New Year's Eve. So he was one of your 'encounters.'"

"Yes." I nod.

"And he's been helping you with school?"

"Just the one project. We ran into each other outside the arena when I went to interview the Marketing Director." Everything I'm saying is true, even if it's not quite the complete picture.

Chris, damn her soul, is way too perceptive. "Please tell me he's not the only person you've had encounters with."

I gulp and blink, pinned under her gaze.

"No. No, no, no." Maria slams down her wine glass.

"We're too late. She's caught feelings."

"No, it's more like a series of one-night stands. I've tried to stay away. He keeps popping up."

Maria snorts.

"Oh my gosh, Maria. Keep your mind out of the gutter for a few minutes." Chris smacks her on the arm and turns back to me. "Be careful with him."

Before I can ask why, Lauren adds in a softer tone, "If it's really casual and you aren't already falling for him, shall we assume you're cool with him showing up next week with someone else on his arm?"

"Or cock," Maria murmurs, only to be elbowed by Christina.

"I'm trying. It would help if he wouldn't keep pop—showing up and seeming interested."

Christina is frowning.

"What is it? Why did you warn me to be careful?" I ask.

"From what Cam has said, Mattie is determined to be footloose and fancy free as long as possible. He doesn't like to plan for a disc golf game more than one day ahead."

"In fairness, that might be due to Texas weather being flakier than shit, but I hear you. I don't ask him to plan, I don't expect him to call, text, or take me out. But he does. What does that mean?"

Christina answers, still looking concerned. "Mattie tends to go all in on something new, like a three-year-old with a new toy. But when it's lost its shine and newness, he gets bored and finds something else to hyperfocus on."

Lauren sighs and pats my hand holding the base of my wine glass. "In other words, it doesn't *mean* anything other than you're his flavor of the month, whereas usually it's of the night or week. Maybe you're better than his usual bed partners. Maybe he likes learning about marketing by day and sexing you up by night. Who knows. But what it doesn't mean is that he's changed his tune from being a commitment-phobe to boyfriend material. You'd do well to remember that."

"I'm trying."

Maria adds, "And remember, the best way to get over a guy…"

"…is to get under a different guy. Yeah, yeah, we know," we all respond in unison.

"My work here is done." She raises her glass for another toast.

Chapter Twenty

Mathieu

Me

How's the marketing project going?

Nicole

Fine thanks.

Me

Petit chou, I thought we were friends and you accepted my apology.

Nicole

Sheesh - never mind that my response might have been short b/c I'm at work.

I have to go to the arena to meet the Mktg Dir again.

Me

Oh yeah? What time? Wanna grab a bite?

Nicole

Remember? I have to take those trips as my lunch hour. I still have a full-time job. Unlike you guys with your cushy couple hours of practice then watching movies for the afternoon.

Me

LOL not movies, game tape. It's like you going to a long meeting with a slideshow. Not fun, but stuff ya gotta pay attention to.

Nicole

Yeah, I know. I was kidding. Apparently, my humor doesn't translate well in text. Sorry.

Me

Ok. Not lunch. Dinner. I want to hear what the head of marketing has to say.

Dots appear as though she's typing. Then disappear. Then appear again.

I hold my breath.
Finally, a text pops up.

Nicole

> You gonna find another cool spot like the last dinner place?

Me

> YES. On it.

She's told me twice—New Year's and Vegas—that casual is new and hard for her. I should not be pushing to spend time with her. But she can always say no. Besides, I may want my sexcapades to come with zero commitment, but my pride took a hit when she turned me down after dinner the other night. Also, I still haven't met anyone who appeals more, although if I'm honest with myself, I haven't been looking.

Her admission that she liked my restaurant choice has been added to my bag of tricks. *If not for her, then for my next pursuit.*

The last place was a little loud, but that's because I wanted to be sure to hear every word she said. On my phone, I type in a search for quiet restaurants but need to be careful that the place I choose isn't over the top, so Nicole doesn't shy away, just like she did in the boutique in Las Vegas. I still haven't figured out what to do with that dress I bought for her. I'm dying to see her in it, but for now, it's still hanging in the back of my closet. Tant pis. That's a problem for another day. Today is for restaurants.

I find a place that serves French-inspired cuisine in

midtown on a couple of lists—Hopfields. Perfect. I make a reservation for seven thirty. That should give her enough time to do homework, change, or whatever else she wants without rushing after work.

Texting her the info and that I'll pick her up at seven, I wait with phone in hand. A little voice asks what the fuck I'm doing hanging on a girl's every text. I ignore it. Finally, a thumbs up emoji appears on my message. I exhale and finish suiting up for practice.

After ice time, Coach goes over a few highlights of our next opponent's superstar, pointing out what we need to defend against. Then a few of us grab a smaller conference room and Saint syncs his laptop to the large TV on the wall to watch more game tape. I chuckle at the thought of Mr. Donovan walking in to find all of us watching a movie, as Nicole said.

Later at home, I'm trying to read *Marketing for Dummies*. I bought it online, so no one saw me check out with it. Holy shit, this is boring, so I set an alarm in case I nod off.

My phone playing the intro of "To the Fairies They Draw Near," the tone I use for anything Nicole related, wakes me. The book is on the floor beside the couch, and I glare at it. Seriously, someone smart enough to write that many words about one subject should be able to make it interesting.

Abandoning it, I change out of my t-shirt and shorts into a button-down with purple, green, and white stripes of varying widths and pair it with jeans. Austin is casual enough that nice jeans go almost anywhere.

When I arrive at Nicole's, she's waiting downstairs in a pretty yellow sundress with a lilac sweater clutched in her hand. I bet all of our wardrobes have gotten a lot more purple since the Donovans brought the Tornadoes here.

The dimly lit narrow front room of Hopfields holds only a few tables along a bar. But when the hostess takes us back, there are alcoves on either side of us with only three or four tables in each, which do indeed make it quiet as the lists promised. The lighting will also help me stay incognito.

She takes the seat against the wall, and I smile in gratitude. She remembered I like to face away from the crowd. "This is nice, Mattie. Thank you. You know I was teasing, and I'd be fine with Torchy's Tacos, right?"

"First, yes, but exploring new places is fun for me. And second, I'm not taking sides in the taqueria battle going on between Christina and Cam, so I'm never going to be the one choosing a taco place." Christina swears by Torchy's, and Cam insists that a one-off local spot will always be better than a chain, but he hasn't found one that Christina loves yet.

"All right, fair enough. I had to check where your loyalties lie. Now, before we talk about marketing or anything else, I told you about my family. I want to hear about yours."

A distant alarm rings in my brain. We're getting into date territory here. Ignoring it, I say, "My family is great. My parents have always been super supportive, and my sister is brilliant and funny and keeps me humble."

The waitress returns. I ask about whiskies, and they have a local one I haven't heard of, so I order that. Nicole gets a glass of white wine, and we order our meals.

She looks at me expectantly.

"What?" I ask. "I told you about them."

"Come on, give me more."

I lean forward. "Look, I could rave about them for this entire dinner, probably for an entire day. But do you really want to hear all that?"

She narrows her eyes. "You mean because mine isn't the same? I'm a big girl. I can handle it. Lauren is close with her family and brings me home with her sometimes, and I love it. But I appreciate your concern."

"Okay, then. Here goes. Once they saw how much I loved hockey, my parents researched everything about it and got me into the right leagues, even as a moustique."

"What is that?" she asks.

"I guess the direct translation is a mosquito."

She snorts a laugh. "Why would you call yourself that?"

"It's a youth hockey league term. Moustique is age seven and under. After that, I moved over to Hockey Canada's minors to get into a more competitive division."

"Did your parents push you to continue or to compete?"

"Nope. In fact, it was the other way. They checked in every year before signing me up. 'Do you want to try something else this year? Are you still having fun? You don't have to do this for us.' I told you, they're amazing," I say with a shrug. "Truth is, hockey has always been fun for me. There are some sacrifices, sure. I don't see Maman and Papa anywhere near as often as I'd like, and I'll probably move a lot. But those things are minor. I'm having the time of my life on the ice, and when—if—it stops being fun, I'll find something else that is."

Although I have no idea what that would be, given my lack of skills in anything other than hockey.

"Wow. I wish I loved my job like that."

"Do you like it, at least?"

"I like some aspects of it. And I guess I'd say it's better than bad or I wouldn't be able to go there every day. But there's no love. However"—she draws out the word—"we're here to talk about your family, not my job."

"Okay, okay. Um, what else? My parents had enough money that helping me improve wasn't a hardship. Hockey is a pay-to-play activity; not as bad as skiing, but it's expensive. So I was lucky. I hate to think of the kids out there who love it like I do but can't afford it."

"What about your sister? Was she dragged to all your games?"

"Hey, now. You say dragged, I say enjoyed."

She laughs. "I'll have to ask her."

I pause. Does she realize her words imply that she'll meet my family? I wait for my gut to clench at the idea of considering more than a few days ahead with a woman. Strangely, it doesn't. She could mean as friends, anyway. My conscience pricks me at that thought, but I ignore it.

"She is four years younger than me. So yeah, when she was super young. They were so thrilled when she chose to attend university. They tell me all about how she's doing in every phone conversation, as though doubting I talk to my only sibling. Or maybe hinting that I should have gone." I smile. "They keep encouraging her to find her passion as well. Or passions or interests. It turns out Annabelle enjoys being a—what's the English phrase I've heard? A jack of trades, not a master?"

"Ah, a jack of all trades, master of none. I don't know where it came from, but there's a lot to be said about some knowledge of many things, rather than a deep dive on only one. Ask Christina. She laments her lack of cocktail conversation subjects other than the financial markets and dance."

"Don't forget hockey," I offer.

"I'll remind her to add that to her list."

The food arrives, and since I've ordered approximately twice what she did, I gesture with my fork and say, "Tell me about the marketing thing. And if you want a bite of anything, feel free."

She gives me an update on her conversation with the Tornadoes manager and the project overall, finishing with, "It's due in a few weeks, mid-semester, and I'll be glad to get it off my plate."

"Is it a paper?"

"It's a paper and a presentation."

"Oh! Hey, practice on me. Then I get to hear the highlights without having to read the paper," I tease.

"Sure, okay. It's not done yet, but I'll text you when I have a rough draft."

The server whisks our plates away and asks about dessert.

I look at Nicole. We've had a good evening, with no echoes of our time management issues. Her reference to meeting my sister kept me from trying to offer the idea of a casual, non-exclusive, totally casual but ongoing fling. Also, I hadn't figured out how to suggest it. However, I can't resist trying for another round. I say, "Nightcap at my place? Totally casual, of course."

She presses her lips flat as she considers. My ego takes another blow. Finally, she nods.

I whip my credit card out and decline dessert.

Chapter Twenty-One

Nicole

Goddammit, I shouldn't agree. But Lauren and Maria manage it, and per their criteria, Mattie hasn't fucked up yet, at least too badly. I should be able to as well. Regardless, call me weak-willed, but there is no way I can sit across from this smoking hot nice guy who's asking all the right questions and not want to jump him again. I have no idea why he's acting so interested in my marketing project. It seems to be beyond ego about his involvement. I can only assume it's to get in my pants; either way, it leads to my compliance. I spend the ride berating myself for being a sucker for a few nice words from a hot guy.

This will be the last time.

Back at his apartment, he makes a move toward the kitchen to offer the drink he promised, asking, "What would you like?"

No more conversation. I need to get what I came here for and get out before he says more things my heart wants to hear. "You, naked."

He stops, mouth hanging open for a minute before it curls into a grin. In a fake Texas drawl, he says, "Happy to oblige, darlin'."

When he doesn't move for a moment, I raise my brows.

His shirt comes flying toward me in a motion so fast I barely see it. Damn, hockey players and their reflexes. But then he slows it way down, unbuckling his belt and undoing the top button of his jeans. Hands on his waistband, he asks, "Would you like a drink with the show?"

I laugh and shake my head no, although I'm still mad at myself for being here.

"Well, then. Shall we take this to the bedroom or the couch at least?"

"Couch is closer," I say, turning toward the living room area and tipping one strap of my dress off my shoulder. When I sit, I tug the flared skirt up a little so if he wants access, it's easy. But my gaze remains on him, hoping the striptease will continue.

He saunters around the end table while keeping his hands on his waistband. In profile, I can see his shoulder and back muscles move as he walks. *Yum.*

When he faces me again, the bulge in his jeans is larger than it was in the entryway. He inhales and sucks his stomach in to loosen his jeans, and his ab muscles stand out in relief against his torso.

A flash of wet heat arrows between my legs, and I hope I don't leave a wet spot on his couch. I glance sideways. Eh, it's a warm brown leather. It'll wipe clean.

His jeans slide down his hips, and he toes off his shoes and denim. He stands straight, feet spread, hands on hips, a Superman stance if ever there was one, and damn, all he needs is the cape. That body rivals any superhero's. His cock rides along his left hip under his boxer briefs, a lengthy ridge that makes me salivate.

An idea occurs to me, one that will hopefully cement in my brain the fact that I'm here only as a fuck buddy.

Plus, he's tasted me; I want to taste him. "Come give me a lap dance."

"Oh no, you don't want to see me dance."

"You freakin' twerk on the ice. You can move those hips."

This is so much more lighthearted than sex ever has been for me. *Is that because it's Mattie or because it's casual?* I don't know which I want the answer to be.

"You want hip movements, do you? Those I can do." He steps around the coffee table, nudging it backward with his taut calf, and straddles me on the sofa, careful not to put too much weight on me.

I catch his ass in my hands and squeeze, keeping him from sitting back. Leaning in, I lick across his abs, scraping my teeth along them, though there's no purchase for me to bite.

I nuzzle his cloth-covered cock with my face, rubbing along its length.

He groans. "Who's giving who the lap dance."

I smack his butt lightly with one hand. "I told you I wanted you naked."

"I see we're feeling bossy today. I'm here to serve." He hops up, far more agile than I could be rising off a couch backward, and strips off his underwear. "May I request the same of you?"

I shift and tug my dress up around my waist and lean forward, hands in the air. "Pull."

In the next minute, I'm in my thong and shoes, a recurring trend in my state of dress around him.

He places one knee next to my hip and swings his other over, and I grab his cock in my fist. My other returns to his ass to hold him where I want him as I lick my lips and suck him deep into my mouth.

His hand comes to my nape under my hair, and he murmurs, "Ah, mon chou, your turn to serve, and you do it so well."

After a few strokes, he's thoroughly wet with a mix of my saliva and his precum. I take my hand out of the way of my lips and see how far I can take him. I work him deeper on each drive forward, finding the right angle to get him past the back of my throat.

"Tabarnak." His tone is guttural, so I know it's an expletive. His hand on my neck clenches, although he doesn't pull me into him, leaving me to set the pace and depth. Courteous as always. His ass tightens under my hand.

I want to try something I've read in books, which is why I worked my way to taking him down my throat. Thankfully, I wore waterproof mascara. I trust Mattie, and I need to be clear to myself that this is indeed a passing thing. I'm not a princess or a girlfriend, I'm a fuck buddy, and he should treat me as such. Releasing his cock, I put my hands on his ass and say, "Fuck my face, Mattie."

"What?! Are you sure? I mean, you don't need to do that."

I push him, reminding him what we agreed. "I thought this was casual. If I was a puck bunny whose last name you didn't know and whose phone number wasn't in your phone, would you ask that?"

He narrows his eyes at me. His brain wants to argue, but I give his cock a long lick like a popsicle, putting his focus back where it needs to be. "I—"

"Don't give me 'I can't.' I'm sure you've done this before. You have my permission. Fuck. My. Face. I'll even ask nicely. Please."

"Holy shit, Nicole. Pinch my ass if you need me to stop." Then under his breath, "Hopefully, I'll feel it, and it won't put me over the edge."

I replace my hands on his butt and suck him into my mouth again, swallowing and taking it farther. Then I look up at him and wait.

His hands go to my head, and he pulls me back. I breathe in, and he yanks me forward, but not as far as I had gone. I give a tiny shake of my head, frowning at him.

He sighs, a crooked grin forming. His cock pulses, and he tugs me back. "Okay."

That's all the warning I get before he's holding me still and thrusting deep, retreating to where I can gulp or release a breath as our cadence allows, and thrusting again. After half a dozen, he shoves in and holds it there. "Swallow."

I swallow around him. His eyes roll in pleasure, and he pushes forward a tiny bit farther into my throat. He puts one hand to my throat to feel the bulge of his cock there, a self-satisfied grin spreading across his face.

Needing air, I scrape my nails along his ass, not trying to pinch and stop it all, but wanting a break.

He takes the hint and pulls back. "I don't want to come this way."

I frown again. He is a twenty-six-year-old in prime physical condition who would need only a short recovery period to get it up again. Plus, there are other ways to get me off. It won't take much; I want this, and I'm already halfway to an orgasm from doing it. My nails sink into his butt to indicate my preference.

His lips firm, his eyes go stormy, and he tightens his grip on my head. "Okay, mon chou, since you ask so prettily with those lips around my cock."

I breathe in one last breath, knowing what's coming. He thrusts over and over and over with no time for me to breathe on his withdrawals. I hold on as his cock slides along my tongue, coated in the thick saliva from my throat. Tears leak from my eyes, and drool and precum drip from my chin.

And holy shit, I'm so turned on I could probably rub one out against the sofa cushion right now. His leg fur brushes the hard tips of my breasts on his drives, and flames lick through my body at each contact.

His cock swells, my teeth scrape the sides, and I glance up, worried I've hurt him. His head is thrown back, his teeth are bared, and he's…growling. It's my new favorite sound.

He tips his head forward to stare at me and mutters, "Gobes tout…take it all. I'm going to come down your throat."

After a last two staccato rams into me, he stays deep. His butt muscles flex against my hands and his cock pulses. The semen is so far down my throat, I can't taste it. I swallow against him over and over, and his cock keeps rippling.

A long groan comes from his throat, and his torso bends over me.

After what seems like five minutes, I smooth my hands down the backs of his thighs, begging for air.

He pulls back, but I stop him from withdrawing fully. I gulp a couple of breaths then clean him up, sucking and licking as I release him.

"Merde," he pants. "Best blowjob ever."

I squirm, itchy from arousal. He needs a minute, I need to be patient, but I'm breathing almost as hard as he is.

One minute he's sitting back on my lap, the next he's standing, and the room is twirling around me as I'm tossed over his shoulder. He's still naked and so muscular there's nothing to clutch for stability—my nails scrabble over his back and waist.

I'm airborne again, landing on—I glance around—his bed.

He drags my thong off and places my legs wide. Staring down at me, he whispers, "Such a pretty pixie, with such a pretty pussy." When I squirm again, he raises a brow and asks, "You need something, p'tit chou?"

I nod. "Please."

"Use your words."

At this point, I don't need much. I'm so close, my body is thrumming like a live wire. Waves of heat and arousal undulate through me. I just need that spark, and I'll go up in a conflagration. With a voice rough from the recent friction, I growl, "Touch me. Touch my clit."

"Good girl."

I swear I nearly come without him touching me at those words. My hips twist in desperation.

He sinks down on his belly and threads his arms under my thighs and around, his fingers coming to my pussy lips to hold me. Then his mouth is on me. Too gentle at first, his lips skimming and exploring. His tongue joins the play, tracing the outline of my pussy, making a wide berth around my clit.

"You like giving me head that much, huh?" he asks, licking his lips and smiling up at me.

I nod, as words are beyond me. I can't even be mad at the smirk.

Spreading me with his fingers, he swipes up the

length of me.

My hips come off the bed a little, despite his anchoring hold. I gasp. That lick felt like a cattle prod because I'm so over-sensitized since the blowjob.

Before I can catch my breath or relax my stomach muscles, he latches onto my clit. There's nothing gentle now. His tongue makes micro taps at a furious pace as he keeps suction on it with his lips sealed around it.

"Unh, unh. Holy shit, Mattie, don't stop."

He unwinds an arm, and a finger slides into me and curls.

I'm gone. The world goes white with rapture then dark as my eyes slam shut. My hands go to his hair to clutch him against me, and my hips are stuttering on the bed, tiny thrusts at his mouth and finger. Inside me, ecstasy ignites and spreads searing warmth through me. Outside, my sensitive flesh is contracting and quivering against his hold.

Finally, it's too much. I whine, pushing on his head. "Okay, okay, enough. Please."

He looks up, his lips and chin shiny, and sucks his finger into his mouth. "One is never enough with us."

One bounce and he's somehow above me on all fours. I was correct, his cock is very definitely recovered.

I inhale, exhale, and smile. "Bring it."

He laughs and does.

* * * *

Mattie is dead to the world, asleep on his stomach after our second round. I take a moment to admire his hotness. Back muscles on display with his arms up under his pillow, glutes even at rest making his ass high and biteable, and thighs and calves that should be used as models by sculptors.

I search for my underwear. It's too dark, so I pad out to the couch where my dress, purse and shoes remain. Grabbing my phone, I turn the flashlight on and keep it facing downward. Another pass in the bedroom reveals them half under the bed. Phew.

I return to the living room to dress, and my foot kicks something. Muffling a curse, I bend down.

"Marketing for Dummies?" I whisper. Staring out the window at the darkened city, I consider our conversations. He's been defensive and embarrassed a couple of times about his lack of education.

Does he think he's dumb?

I return the book to where he left it, not wanting to discomfit him further. Donning my clothes, I make my escape, my thoughts swirling the whole way home.

In bed, I close my eyes. It's after midnight, and I have work and class tomorrow. But the longer I lie there, the more agitated I become. He's such a happy-go-lucky guy, always ready with a smile, always up for fun. And he's a top six player for an NHL team, a professional with a skill level only a few out of millions attain.

Here be dragons. This type of thinking leads to my demise and was exactly what I was trying to avoid with the deep throating and sneaking out. My kryptonite is finding a guy's weakness and wanting to bolster his self-image. Investing in him. I want a guy who gets invested in *me.*

Mattie does; that's why he had that book.

Nope, nope, nopedy-nope. Shut up, heart. Head's in charge here. We need to walk away. Sighing at my sleep-deprived brain conversing with itself, I change that. *I* need to walk away, to remain in self-preservation mode.

Otherwise, when Mattie becomes bored, as Christina

says he's prone to do, and moves on, I'll be left shattered yet again. And I'm tired of that. Better to assume he has some terrible habit I have not yet discovered, as Maria so graphically suggested.

I roll over and punch my pillow and read the latest guilty pleasure book on my e-reader until I fall asleep for a few hours.

In the morning, I check my schedule and, thankfully, it's a light meeting day. Working for a West Coast headquartered company can be a blessing. I email my manager and a few local team members who might be looking for me that I'm working from home and then text Maria. She'll be able to give me the tough love I desperately need.

Lauren would be my first choice, but she works business hours like I do. Maria is a barista by morning and dance studio owner and instructor by evening.

I get a thumbs up to my request for a consultation on her break and head to the coffee shop where she works.

"'Sup?" she asks as she slides into the chair across from me, carrying two coffees for us. She does a double take. "You look…"

"Rough? I know."

"I was going to say tired, but okay. What's up? If you're here to gloat about how excellent Mattie is at providing orgasms, I'm out."

I smile, but annoying tears leak out. "Kind of."

"Ugh! I'm such a good friend. I'll stay, I'll stay. You don't have to pull out the waterworks," she jokes, knowing I'd hate for strangers to see me crying.

"So you were right," I start, but I'm not sure where to go from there.

"Always a good lead-in. Tell me more," she says,

leaning in and propping her chin in her hand.

I can't help but laugh at her antics. "I know y'all said his continued attention doesn't mean anything other than I'm new and shiny and bright for the moment, but my heart doesn't understand that message. Maria, he had—" I stop. Mattie blushed talking about not having taken marketing. He would not want me to share about that book. "He keeps texting and inviting me to dinner at super cool places I can't afford. It's probably harmless, but he asks all the right questions and seems interested in more than just my hoo-ha. Then we're in bed again and he's ruining me for other men. Each time, I vow that will be the last time, until he texts again and flirts his way through my defenses. What do I do?"

She sighs and shakes her head. "You know what to do."

My eyes well again. "I hate this. I can't even have casual sex properly. I'm a failure."

"You're not a failure. You're a serial monogamist like Chris. You wanted a break from having to kiss all the frogs to find your prince, and I totally understand that. But I'm not sure you're cut out for one-night stands, even to take the edge off. Maybe investing in a few new vibrators and toys would help. I found a cool—"

I hold up a hand. "Okay, wait. That's a conversation for wine—or margaritas, not coffee."

She shrugs. "When you're ready."

"I should probably block his number. But this whole sharing a friend group gets in the way."

"Really, it's amazingly simple. You say 'no' or you don't respond. Every time you want to reply, just think—"

"It's too early for more fart references, please."

"—that too, but you think that if you don't ghost him now, he'll be the one ghosting you in a week, a month, whatever."

She's got a point. I nod.

"On the surface, y'all kept saying it was casual, right? So consider what he'd do when he was ready to move on from someone casual. He'd either say thanks but no thanks, or he'd go silent."

"It's so…"

"Rude? Yeah, if you're a woman. Guys do it all the time and believe they're being kind by not leading the chick on." She rolls her eyes.

"Hurtful."

She leans in. "That's where you're wrong. It would be hurtful to you. But he's been telling you all along it's a fling, and unlike you, he means it when he says it. It won't bother him in the least. His reaction will be, 'Next, please!'"

Damn, that's cold. But accurate. This fucking sucks. But it sucks way less than it would in a month.

"Okay. I'll try harder."

"You know what Yoda said." Maria deepens her voice. "No! Try not. Do." She returns to her normal tone. "When you want to reply, text me instead, even if it's gibberish. I got you."

Chapter Twenty-Two

Mathieu

Of course, I wake up alone. One of us is obeying the unwritten laws of casual sex, at least, and it's the one who says she struggles with non-relationships. This is three times now, as she had an early flight from Vegas and left that night, too.

She also hasn't responded to my texts a week later. Call me paranoid, but given that my marketing reference book was somewhat visible in the living room, I can't help feeling like she's moving on from the hockey goon.

Cam and Buzz and I are out for a drink, purportedly to discuss Coach's new line mashups. In reality, no one likes to gossip more than a hockey player.

So after we decide which groupings we like from Coach's playbook, we settle in. I'm still concerned about Scottie's drinking, but I have bigger issues at the moment. "How do you feel about dating someone smarter than you?"

Cam snorts. "Thanks for the vote of confidence, du Près."

"Ha. I'm confident in what your girlfriend has done for my net worth. But I was sort of serious. You at least have a degree. I'm the only one in my family who doesn't. And between us, after Vegas, I know more than ever I don't want to end up with a bunny."

"Jessica Rabbit was at it again, huh?" Cam asks, and Buzz rolls his eyes. "Okay, in all seriousness, I appreciate Chris's intelligence and knowledge of finances. She once told me to trust her in her area of expertise, just like if she wanted to learn how to play hockey, she'd trust me in mine. It's about balance. Like she helps me not put up walls with family, and I help her establish limits with hers."

Buzz has been silent so far, so I turn to him and raise my brows.

"I'm with you, man. I don't have a degree, and I'm therefore grateful for Christina's guidance on saving and investing. I also don't have a Plan B other than coaching. At least Cam here has Dancing with the Stars. Although, I like his other Plan B. Let's all marry sugar mamas."

I crack up and Cam frowns at us. "Hey, I pull my own weight."

"Dude, your salary is probably a rounding error for her," Buzz manages through laughter. I'm nearly falling off my chair at Cam's disgruntled expression when Buzz turns and says, "Where is this coming from, Mattie? I thought you were the king of spur-of-the-moment and skirt-of-the-moment? Are you making an application form or something?"

His question catches me off guard, and my face goes hot.

Cam growls. "This better not be about who I think it is."

Buzz glances between the two of us. "Hey, no fair if I'm the only one who doesn't know."

Ignoring him, I say to Cam, "She got a call from her family in Vegas."

"Wait, is this about Nicole?" Buzz asks. He must

have noticed us leaving together. He whistles. "Dude, you can't do casual with Chris's friends."

"First, you can if both parties agree. Second, what the hell is up with her parents? They were giving her a hard time for not doing enough when she's working full time and going to school for a graduate degree." I nearly added, "and sending them money," but I'm not going to share her business, particularly when I don't fully understand it.

Cam shakes his head. "Yeah, none of us are big fans of her family."

"She also has a schedule tighter than a bishop's balls in a brothel. She'd have to schedule me in on her calendar to fuck, much less talk, and you know how I feel about scheduling."

"Ah, there's the Mattie I know and love," Buzz murmurs. "Fucking is the priority over talking."

I ignore him and continue, "Meanwhile, she's taking these classes whose descriptions I can't figure out. That's another reason to keep it casual. There's no way she's going to want some dumb jock around, even if I was into commitment."

"Okay, first, Buzz has a point. You asked about 'dating,' but you say you don't want strings." Cam sits back, twisting his drink on the table. "If you don't want them, then act like it. Take the opportunity to bust a nut when she's available—*if* you're sure you're both on the same page about that, which I doubt—or move on if it doesn't come frequently enough."

I frown.

"You don't seem to like that answer. Which to me says you don't like things as casual as you think." He stares at me. "And now you look scared. Make up your mind."

Buzz snickers.

"As for the dating someone smarter, who is to judge intelligence? Everyone has their strengths and weaknesses. If those fit and you have shared interests, why not see where it goes?"

Buzz has gone silent, listening to Cam's words of wisdom, despite Cam being the youngest of the three of us. He nods, then shakes his head. Confusing much? "I agree, but I also agree with you, Mattie. It's intimidating as hell when you see them as more intellectual."

Cam and I raise our brows. Cam asks, "Who are you talking about, Drew?"

He blinks twice. Waving a hand, he says, "Just in general. You know, from my past."

He's a sucky liar, but I can't worry about Buzz's dating woes. I have my own to stress over. I thought I wanted what I had with the bunny in Miami, a non-exclusive arrangement for good sex when our schedules aligned, with an understanding it would end whenever one of us was ready to move on. In that case, I'd been the one ready.

Maybe I'm not ready, or maybe it's harder when the other person is done before you are. Or maybe, like Cam said, I want more. Problem is, I don't know how to do "more," especially if it includes a calendar and scheduling.

* * * *

A week later, I still haven't gotten a reply from Nicole. After a few more texts, I stopped trying. Going on what I'd do if someone stalked me via text, I won't win her attention by pestering her.

Cam is right. If someone didn't respond to two texts

153

in a row from me, I'd write them off as too much work and find the next lucky woman.

But I'm not done with Nicole yet. She intrigues me. And I don't like that she doesn't have family to support her career and studies.

I just got home from a team-mandated appearance. I love visiting the pediatric units of the hospitals here, but today I selfishly wished that it was a PR appearance because Nicole might be there.

My phone rings, and I sprint to the kitchen island where I left it. It's not Nicole, but it's one of my other favorite people. I grab it.

"Salut, Maman. Ça va bien?"

"Ah, so you do still remember your family and your French. I thought Texas might have converted you to full-on American English, bébé."

"Maman, don't be like that. You know how my schedule is during the season, and that was when I was in the same time zone as you. Besides, I wouldn't want to interrupt your important job."

"So call in the evening," she retorts.

"How are you? I do miss you guys. Any chance you can come down for a game or three?"

"Not right now, sweetie. Actually—" A long pause ensues. "—I'm calling because I have some news. I debated doing this, but since we usually come down for some warm weather at this time of year, I thought you should know why we can't this year."

That was a whole lot of words that sparked off alarms but didn't tell me anything. "What is it? Are you okay? Is Papa? Annabelle?"

"I'm sure it will all be fine. But…"

"You're killing me. Please, say it. I can be on a plane

tonight."

"Mon dieu, this is why I wasn't sure I wanted to tell you. Don't do that. But my most recent mammogram showed a lump."

I suck in a breath and put her on speakerphone to pull up my game calendar and flight information.

She's still talking. "It's near enough to my lymph nodes to give them concern. They're going to do a biopsy in ten days."

"*Ten days*!" I roar. "What about tomorrow?"

"Ten days is not unreasonable."

"Come on. Isn't it better to catch—" I stumble there. I can't say the C word. I don't want to put that out in the universe "—whatever it is sooner rather than later? I'll fly you to wherever the best experts are and pay for the tests in the U.S. Please, Maman." My voice is thick with tears I'm choking back.

"It will be fine. Ton père is okay with it. Please try not to worry. I don't want this to affect your job."

Even when she's worried about her health and at her own job with the government, she is respectful of my work as though it's important, rather than treating me like the overpaid *player* I am.

"I want to be there for the scan. What can I do to help?"

"Non." Uh-oh, that's her mama bear voice. "I forbid you from coming home. You are paid to do a job, and it's not one you can call out from. Even if you were fourth line, you're part of a team, an organization that depends on you."

"Mamaaan…" I whine.

"Non. I don't want to hear another word about it. I don't know how long it will take them to analyze the biopsy. But ton père et moi, we are assuming it's nothing to worry about until we're proven wrong, and I expect you to do the same. I will call you after the biopsy."

"Tell me exactly when it is."

"Only if you promise not to fly here for it."

I look at my calendar. Ten days from now, the team is in Toronto for a game. I'm pretty sure Coach will let me take a short detour to Ottawa on the way back to Austin if I give him the circumstances. I need to hug my mother. But I won't be flying there for it, so I can answer honestly. "I promise."

She gives the date, and sure enough, it's the day of the game. So I won't be there for the test, but I can at least go home and reassure myself that she's still whole and healthy-looking, and let her know I'll do anything I can to help her no matter what the diagnosis.

"Thank you. Papa is truly okay? And you?"

"We really are. There is nothing we can do until we know what it is, so it's business as usual here. Once you have time to assimilate, it will be for you as well."

"It would help if I knew what 'assimilate' means," I grumble.

She laughs. "Oh, you. Stop playing the woe is me card when you make more than both of us put together. We're very proud of you. That's another reason we want you to stay there. Watching you play is one of the highlights of our week. Once we're past this, we'll talk about a trip later in the season."

But we don't know what she'll be going through then. What if she's too sick to travel? What if the team makes the playoffs and I can't go home until June? I never thought I'd not want to make the playoffs.

"Mathieu, I can hear you spiraling. Stop it. Please.

Go do something, don't sit in your apartment and brood."

I'm choked up again. But she's taking her usual, stoic approach, and I don't want her worried about me. I swallow the tears back and lie, "All right. Someone just texted me, so I'll see what they're up to. I'll call you in a day or two. Je t'adore."

"Je t'adore, bébé. Please try not to worry."

And she's gone. The silence of a phone has never felt so deafening, and Ottawa has never felt so far away. She's right. I can't stay here, or I'll lose my mind or renege on my promise and get on a plane.

Chapter Twenty-Three

Nicole

Mattie

> Hey, do you have a few
> minutes? I really need
> someone to talk to.

Me

> Sure, what's up?

My doorbell rings just then. I look down at my sleep shorts and braless top under a tank and shrug. Whoever it is should have called first if they wanted something more formal.

When I check the peephole, I'm surprised to see Mattie. Wow, he really does need to talk. Old-Nicole kicks in, ready to bend over backward. But when I consider where to place the boundary, I realize I don't want one. He's a friend in need who came to me. Therefore, I will help to the best of my ability. Everything else doesn't matter.

Realizing my phone is still in my hand for his answer, I toss it on the hall table and swing the door wide.

He looks rough. His eyes are tight and a little red, and he keeps running his hand through his hair.

"Hi. You okay?" I ask.

He shakes his head.

"Sorry." I step back to give him room to enter. "Can I get you a drink?"

He nods, then shakes his head, then nods again.

"Well, that clears things up." I head to the kitchen, getting the very small bottle of the nicest Canadian whisky the liquor store had. It's not Wiser's or whatever he charmed Renee into stocking at Chasers, but the guy assured me it's not swill either.

I pour us each a glass and bring it over to him on the couch.

He's hunched forward, elbows on knees, head hanging down, and he doesn't move to take the drink. It clunks on the table, and I sit beside him.

He turns and pounces. His arms are tight around me, clutching me to him. His head is still lowered, his forehead almost on my shoulder despite our height difference.

My arms wind around him and squeeze. "Hey now. It's going to be all right. Whatever it is, we'll get through it."

My conscience is in self-preservation mode. *No, no, no. There is no "we." Boundaries. He's not just a friend and you know it. You know what happens when you go all in to help someone. This is why you sat on your hands to not respond to texts for two weeks.*

"Ma maman. Elle a trouvé une bosse dans un sein," he mumbles against my neck. His arms tighten further, and he sniffs.

Is he crying? Holy hell, I wish I took French rather

than Spanish—not that I remember any of that either—in school.

I got the "my mother" part so I ask, "Is she okay?"

"Nous ne savons pas. Pour dix jours!" His hands scrabble against my back as though he wants to absorb me into him.

I rub his shoulders, all I can reach of him when he has me in such a tight hold. "You're okay. I'm here."

I shouldn't be, but I will be. This sounds bad.

"Now, take a deep breath."

He does.

"Another. Okay, now, can you maybe tell me in English so I can see if I can help?"

He grunts, a small part of him responding to me trying to lighten things up. Sitting up, he wipes his eyes with his wrist, then wipes it on his shorts. Such a guy. He explains the situation again in English—that his mother found a lump.

"Oh my god, Mattie. I'm so sorry. How are she and your dad doing?"

"That's the thing." He flings out a hand. "They are fine with the small wait. I want to fly them down here and get the biopsy done tomorrow so we know what we're facing. But they won't let me pay for it. They say they're not worried and going through OHIP, er, our provincial healthcare system, is fine."

"I understand. I'd probably want the same thing. Although, there'd probably be a longer wait than that here, too, no matter how you paid for it."

He frowns at me.

"Okay, okay. Not the right time to debate the merits of socialized medicine. Sorry. What can I do?"

He sighs. "I don't know. They won't even let *me*

help."

"Hey, I wasn't talking about helping them, although I'm happy to if you think of something. I'm concerned with helping you." Whatever our status or situationship, I want him to know I'm a safe space he can come to when he needs to talk, cry, or scream into the void.

"Merde, I don't know. I feel selfish thinking about that. My mother is facing a huge health issue, and I'm crying on your shoulder. A grown man afraid of losing his mother," he bites out with a dark bark of a laugh.

"There is nothing wrong with worrying about those you love. I'd be upset as well. Besides, they're our parents. We're used to being on the taking end of support, so this sort of thing throws us off."

"Doesn't make it right."

"Come here." I hold out my arms. "Hugs help."

"Yeah. That's why I came here instead of to Cam and Jack's house," he jokes with a half-laugh.

I snort. Then he's in my arms again, and I'm in his, and all is right with my world. It took everything in me to not reply to his texts, and this single hug has undone all of my efforts. On top of all the things I'd found to lov- ah, *like* about him, now he's here being vulnerable? Whatever half-assed wall I'd started to build around my heart is in dust at his feet.

His mother will get through this, I'm almost certain. There are eight hundred things it could be, and if it is worst-case scenario, Mattie has the means to get her the best care in the world, whether it be in Canada, Europe, or the U.S. I push those confident vibes toward him, rubbing his back.

After several minutes, he heaves a breath and says against my neck, "I'm so scared. I'm not ready to lose her, even if she's more than a thousand miles away."

"I know," I say gently. "But you're getting ahead of yourself. If your parents feel it's safe to wait the ten days, then you must try to be patient as well."

He pulls back. "How? How do I go play a stinkin' *game,* which has always been fun, when there is life and death at stake."

"I don't know how your parents are doing it, but for now, you have to say it isn't life and death. It's a medical condition that you assume will be addressed once they identify it. Using distancing language might help you remain calm."

He weighs my words, nods, then shrugs. "I'll try."

I reach for our drinks, handing him his. He sips and looks at it. "This isn't bad."

"I stocked it for you," I admit. Stupid, stupid girl buying liquor for someone who was supposed to be a one-night stand and with whom I don't know where I stand, but there it is.

"Thank you. Look," he says, then winces, "you've moved on, and I showed up here unannounced. I know we said casual, but we also said friends, so thank you for listening. I should go…but can I please stay? I can hang on the couch. I probably won't sleep much anyway. I just don't want to be alone right now."

I'm quiet for a minute while I war with my conscience.

I'd do the same for Christina.

You've never been fucked to multiple orgasms by Christina.

He's worried about his mom; he was crying.

He starts to look nervous. To hell with it.

"Sure. Have you eaten?" I ask, standing and sipping

the last of my whisky. It's after ten o'clock, so I'd eaten before he arrived, but his mom could have called hours ago.

He nods. "I grabbed something on my walkabout. I actually walked here from my place."

My eyes widen. There're several miles of city streets between us, with some sketchy spots near the highways.

"Will you need a ride tomorrow morning?"

"No, I'll grab a rideshare. Thank you, Nicole." He reaches for my hand and squeezes it.

I tug him upright and pull him toward my bedroom. In for a penny, in for a pound. If I had just heard similar news about my mom, I'd want to be held. "Come on. You can have half the bed, but I need sleep. I have a long day tomorrow. What time to do you need to get up?"

"Uh, six?" At my cringe, he says, "I promised the guys I'd meet them at the gym for an early workout, and I know I'll need that. Physical activity helps keep my head on straight."

I eye him.

"Oh, I, uh, didn't mean sex."

I arch a brow.

"I'm digging the hole deeper, aren't I? Sorry, mon petit chou, I'm not in the right mind for that, even with my hot pixie."

"I understand. I was teasing you."

His smile is wan but present. He strips down to his boxer briefs while I use the bathroom and find a toothbrush for him.

He takes his turn and then slides into bed next to me. I scootch over, and he raises an arm for me to rest on that soft—well, less hard—spot just below his shoulder.

"Thank you." His voice is quiet in the dark.

"Any time." *No, you stupid girl.* "Try to sleep."

He actually does. When his breathing evens out, I slip out from under his hold and prop myself on a bent arm to watch him. This is the soft underbelly of Mattie. Mr. Happy-Go-Lucky, Fear-of-Commitment, and Calendar-Averse has a hidden jelly donut center. Although to be fair, his support of my project, his reaction to my parents' attitude, and his calling me on slut-shaming all had been very clear signs, too.

This is why I was falling. But seeing him cry over his mom? I'm lost. He hides a kind and gentle soul under that rough and tough winger exterior. Now, I understand it more, and I'm as worried as he is about how he'll play for these next days until they know the results of his mother's biopsy.

A selfish part of me preens that he came to me with this problem, rather than a teammate. Maybe there is more here than a casual fling after all.

* * * *

The next morning Mattie is up and out early, thanking me again for my hospitality.

After he leaves, I head to the bathroom. Might as well start my day, too. I nearly scream at the bedhead in the mirror. My hair is a strange, lopsided combination of matted and fly-away. Mental note—make the bathroom my first stop whenever I have a guest.

All my glamorous thoughts of a relationship seem stupid this morning. Mattie has been clear about his phobia regarding scheduling, obligations, and anything else resembling a relationship. Add to that the fact that I'm nowhere near as beautiful as most of the women he has access to, this bedhead, and what I'm sure is morning breath, and I was clearly delirious.

I cram all those dreams down, knowing I'll continue to put myself in harm's way by texting him later, and get on with my day.

That afternoon as I'm trying to wrap one last Gantt chart up for work so I can get to class, I get a text.

Mattie

> Leaving on a jet plane. But I know when I'll be back again. Thank you for last night.

Me

> Bet that's a new text from you to a woman—especially when you didn't even get off. <laughing emoji>

Mattie

> Ha! I mean it, though.

Me

> Just trying to keep things upbeat for you. How are you?

Mattie

> Eh. We'll see. We're on a three-game road trip in the northwest. I wish we had home games. It would help to have friendly faces in the stands. Hint hint.

Me

Hint hint? You want me to come to more home games? You know my studies don't allow that.

Mattie

Was thinking more like flying you out this weekend to one of the games. I need my good luck pixie right now.

I'm tempted to send an eyeroll emoji right now, since I suspect he's tugging my heartstrings deliberately. But after last night, I can envision him being serious about this, even as self-centered as it is.

Me

You may not remember this, anti-calendar boy, but my marketing project presentation is due next week. I have to create the PowerPoint this weekend.

Mattie

First class has plenty of room to work, and I'd have practice and pregame stuff on Saturday…<hands together pleading emoji>

Me

> This is shit timing, but I have to remind you—this kind of thing messes with my head.

Mattie

> You're right. I'm sorry. I know how important school is for you.

Ugh! Now he's being all nice and stuff. If he was selfish about it and pushed, I'd have had no problem saying no. Maria's voice echoes in my ear. *You should have no problem saying no anyway. It's the right thing to do to protect yourself.*

But it's his mother, and he's super close to his family. Heck, I'd be a mess about that kind of thing even with my family.

I kick myself as I type.

Me

> Let me see how far I can get on the deck in the next day or so.

Silence. The plane must have taken off. Good. I need to focus on my own world. I head to class, and after that I stay in the school library and pound out an outline from the paper that I've already drafted. They both need to be handed in together. I realized halfway through the paper that I should have worked on the presentation first, since that would have acted like an outline for the highlights of my findings. But oh well. Maybe this will go fast, and I can go hang in Seattle like a baller or a WAG or whatever those jetsetters call themselves.

Bunnies. Maria's voice is loud.

Okay, I probably shouldn't think of it like that. I'm going to support a friend during a difficult time. Yeah, that's it.

I stay in the student center until midnight, trying to fill in the PowerPoint from the slide headings that were my outline. When I finally get home, I crash.

The next morning, I'm surprised not to see any more texts from Mattie. It's Thursday and their first game of this trip, so I text Christina to see if she wants to come over and watch it. I'll study during the intermissions, but it would be nice to have company.

She does, even bringing dinner. I keep the conversation light, and she lets me study during the breaks, like I warned her I'd need to.

The team wins, although Mattie seems to have less ice time than normal. The commentators in the post-game wrap-up also comment on it, so I know it wasn't my imagination. Luckily, when he did play, he played hard; there was no noticeable effect from his mom's news. He'd told me that they watch all his games, even if they have to record the West Coast ones, so fear of disappointing them probably kept him focused.

The analysis segment finishes up at midnight again, and Christina heads out. Knowing Mattie is two hours behind me, I text him.

Me

> Congrats on the win! You played great.

Silence again. WTF? He offers to fly me to a game, pleads with me even, then ghosts me? This freaking guy runs hot and cold like nobody's business. When I think of the circumstances, I calm down, though. Maybe he's struggling, and it was all he could do to play.

My conscience weighs in. *Or maybe you're making excuses for him, like you did when boyfriends ghosted you.*

Dammit, my New Year's resolution was to avoid this very thing.

I shrug and go to bed. I'm more than halfway through the presentation, but I'll see if he responds to my text before bombarding him with my progress, in case he's changed his mind.

There's nothing the next morning, so as I eat at my desk, I debate. I should let the weekend trip idea drop. I know I should.

But what if he's sunk into a depression and really needs someone there for him?

No, he's got the whole team.

But he didn't tell them about it. He told me. And maybe Coach. Giving up because my brain will circle this until I text, I grab my phone.

Me

> I've made good progress on the deck!

Mattie

> What does a porch have to do
> with your marketing project?

Me

> Oh, sorry. They call it a slide
> deck, a deck of slides like a
> deck of cards, as an alternative
> to PowerPoint (slides) or
> presentation…Probably a
> language barrier

Mattie

> Or an education barrier. :/

Me

> No. At most it's a type of job
> barrier. Your marketing team
> would know it, but why would
> y'all need that term as players?
> :)

Mattie

> Congratulations. Well done.

Me

> So…do you still want me to
> come for the Saturday game?

Silence.

Wow, this sucks almost as much as trying not to

respond to his texts after our hookups. He's changed his mind. Maybe found a local bunny to keep his thoughts and dick occupied. He could at least respond, but on top of all of his other anti-relationship issues, the guy is giving me the silent treatment.

The more I think about his lack of an answer and the late hours I've pulled the last few days after giving him my support when he showed up unannounced, the madder I get.

Chapter Twenty-Four

Mathieu

Coach saw that I was distracted during practice and asked me what was going on. It's rare for me not to be laser-focused on the ice. He gave me light duty in last night's game but made me swear I'd have my head on straight for today's.

Nicole's text yesterday threw me for a loop. I'd already vowed not to push her to come. And I made an ass out of myself not knowing what a PowerPoint deck was. I took a quick poll. Cam knew what it was, and he has a college degree. Buzz didn't and he doesn't. Scottie knew, but that's because he's nearly a decade younger than me, and they were using PowerPoint in freakin' high school. Great, so it's an age *and* an education thing.

My first instinct was to buy the ticket and get her here, but the more I stewed over the gap in our vocabulary, much less our lives, I couldn't.

Merde. I wanted her here, and it sounded like she rushed things to make that happen. But maman, who I've texted with every day since her call, and Nicole keep telling me to be patient and wait to see what the doctors say.

I need to grow a pair and let Nicole focus on her studies because I've already messed with them once by being late. Her grades can't slip because I'm weak and need moral support when we'll only have a couple hours of face-to-face time for all the travel time she'd need to put in.

But if I text her, I won't be able to say that because when it comes to her, I have zero self-control. I'll buy the ticket and tell her to come. So I held back yesterday, figuring I'd text her this morning.

Instead, Coach called a film review meeting, a light practice, then bam, we're warming up on the ice before the game.

Angry at myself, at the doctors in Ottawa for their lack of instantaneous availability, and irrationally at Nicole for not being here, I pour it all into my game.

I might have been in a fog for Thursday's game, but tonight, I'm back, baby, with a vengeance. Seattle isn't going to know what hit them.

First period, I make an ass out of myself when I'm so focused on the puck that I hit the boards and wipe out with zero contact from another player. But even prone on the ice, I flick the puck to a teammate with my stick. Then I'm up and racing after it again. Buzz gives me shit, but it helps dial me in another degree.

We're back and forth, neither team is able to get one past the other's goalie. I swear I spend half my play time grappling for the puck below the goal line. Cam is going to have a crick in his neck from guarding the net as he watches for it to come around.

I'm on an adrenaline high during intermission, bouncing my leg while Coach gives us a pep talk and makes a few observations about the other team.

Second period, we press them harder, racing to intercept the puck, to keep it in Seattle's zone. One of us is always in the slot, blocking the goalie's view and hoping for a pass or a rebound to sneak a shot by him.

Jaden Eskola has started to come into his own. The young kid came from the AHL and was overwhelmed with the size, speed, and skill needed to play at this next level. Coach has brought him up and sent him down once already, and now he's back, lingering on the fourth line. He's French, with an Afro-French mother and a white father who played European hockey for a few years before an injury took him to the coaching side of the game. He's spent time in the weight room and with the skating coach; more importantly, his first language is French, which makes him an excellent addition to Boulanger's and Bergstrom's line.

They shout commands in French back and forth, barking them so Seattle doesn't clue in. Then Buzz, Saint, and I are back over the boards and it's on. I sprint for the puck when it flies up the boards from an around-the-net swipe by Seattle. A Seattle player and I get to it at the same time, and I don't hesitate to slam into him and the boards, digging my stick at the puck to fling it toward the white and purple uniform in my peripheral vision.

Buzz sails it to Saint in the slot with a wrist shot, and it flies into the net over the goalie's left knee as he slides to close the gap a second too late.

Saint pumps his fist, skating by the bench to high five the guys, as we change out again.

In the third period, they're on us like white on rice, an American-ism I learned from of all people, Emil Bergstrom, who seems fascinated with them. I get shoved when I'm nowhere near the puck and the refs aren't looking, smashed into the boards in every corner of the rink, and nearly tripped with players' sticks multiple times. I hop, skip, and jump over them, as light on my skates as I am in sneakers. But the physical play takes its toll, and Coach puts the other lines in a bit more. Gauthier, Dunard, and Petrovsky play tight, and Petrovsky gets an amazing breakaway and manages another goal. Meanwhile, Cam is holding them to zero.

The minutes count down. Seattle is down two and pulls their goalie to try to close the gap. They get one past Cam, and he bangs his stick on the ice three times, frowning, before he clears his expression and refocuses. The buzzer finally sounds with no more goals, and we've won.

I'm exultant at the win and my performance, but the joy is shadowed with a tinge of disappointment that Nicole wasn't here to see it. It's a completely selfish thought, so I stuff it away and head to celebrate with the team at the hotel for a bit before we crash for an early flight to our third and final stop on this tour.

* * * *

Needless to say, I do not get a congratulations text from Nicole after that game. And being the giant man-child that I've already proven myself to be with her, I let her question about the weekend slide into the ether unanswered.

I hate that she bent over backward for me, and I love that she bent over backward for me, showing what a good friend and kind person she is. I, on the other hand, am all about doing what feels good. I'll never be a friend like that, and especially not a boyfriend who shows up on time, remembers birthdays, and drops everything to support my girl because she came to me crying. On top of that, I don't relish her having to explain half of what she says to me because I'm stupid. I'm a selfish bastard and the idea of any of that does not feel good, so I need to back off and make sure she doesn't give more than I deserve.

We lose the next game, leaving us with a two-out-of-three record for this trip, which feels good despite the loss.

There's an optional team breakfast before we board the jet to head home. I'm chilling with Buzz and Petrovsky over coffee when a text chimes on my phone.

*You've been added to the group text **Birthday Phone-A-Friend***

Cam

> Can y'all help please? What do I get Dancer for her birthday? Yes, I should know this, but I'm struggling.

I glance around for him. Apparently, Cam has adopted his billionaire-to-be attitude and declined to eat with the masses. He must be upstairs exchanging kissy faces with the girlfriend he'll see in a few hours. How can he not know the perfect gift?

Me

> I kinda figured it would be a ring…?

Cam

> No. She insisted we wait until
> after my next contract is
> signed, and my agent agreed
> with her. So after the season.

Me

> Lingerie? Diamonds? Lingerie
> with diamonds?

Nicole

> <rolling eyes emoji> Lingerie is
> a gift for himself. Maybe try
> something that SHE wants.

Oh, shit. She's in this group? Who else is? I check the top of the thread. There are only three circles. Dammit, Cam was the one who warned me not to mess with Nicole's feelings. Why would he do this?

Calm down, dummy. It's just a group thread. I take a deep breath and read the screen.

Cam

> Yeah, but that's my question
> <smiling face>

Nicole

> ...I see your point. We all get
> girly things for each other, but
> that wouldn't be romantic
> enough.

Cam

How about a trip? But it would have to be after the post-season, and I don't know how she feels about delayed gratification.

Me

Then you're not doing something right <ROTFL emoji>

Cam

For birthday gifts! Sheesh!

Me

She's got that kick-ass dancer's bod – no offense intended – how about one of those boudoir photo shoots? That'd be for both of you <smiling devil emoji>

Cam

Nicole?

Okay, she must be busy. See what she thinks about that, the trip, and any other ideas you come up with?

Me

> Me? She's the project manager.

Cam

> Exactly. She'll manage you.
> <winking face>

My inner voice spoke too soon. It's not just a group thread anymore. The pair of us has been given an assignment.

We land at three o'clock in Austin because of the two-hour leap forward in time zones. I go straight from the airport to the gym to work the kinks out of four plane rides in as many days.

After a light workout, I dig through my suitcase to grab casual clothes, having no desire to rewear my travel suit.

There's an internal debate before I turn my car toward Nicole's. Despite my avoidance of all things calendar-related, I know Nicole's schedule as well as my own. Better, actually, since mine changes by day and week, and hers remains the same. She has class tonight, but it's a short one.

We need to talk—*shudder*—and then maybe we can get this birthday help done quickly. Better to clear the slate and step back into the friends-without-benefits zone. That way, I don't continue to embarrass myself with my ignorance, and she doesn't get hurt.

I pick up Thai takeout, but since I suck at details almost as much as schedules, I don't know what she likes, so I get eight different dishes with various spice levels and proteins. And so many spring rolls because I love them.

Her car is in her assigned covered spot when I pull in.

At my knock, movement sounds come from inside. Footsteps near, then pause. This is where I pass or fail. She's looking through the peephole.

My voice loud enough to carry through the door, I say, "I brought Thai food for birthday planning."

She swings the door open. "How about an apology?"

I gulp. I guess we're going to face this head on.

"That's the appetizer?" I venture.

"It better be." She turns away, leaving me to come or go as I please and plops back on the sofa where her laptop and papers sit. No invitation. Her message is clear. "And I don't have time for birthday planning tonight. Her birthday is in three weeks. I'll remind you since you suck at calendars. My project is due this week."

I wince. Pixie is furious. I'd expected tears, but knowing Nicole, she's angry out of self-protection. Merde. Either way, I fucked up, and I have to pay the price.

I set the bag of food on the kitchen counter and grab plates and utensils out. "Water? Something else?"

"I have water already."

Not even a thank you, from the politest person I know. *Best get to it, dumbass.* "First, I want to lead with a giant thank you. For the night I showed up here again, but also for busting your butt to try to come babysit me when I was needy."

She opens her mouth to speak, but I raise a hand. "S'il te plaît, err, please, let me finish. That request was selfish. I—of course—had forgotten your project was due this week when I asked. It wasn't right for me to put my *game*, or job, if you want to call it that, over yours. I appreciate your effort and offer. But I never want you to think I don't respect your work and your studies. The ticket sales day taught me that. I'll do my best never to put you in that spot again. And as you see, I got through it okay in the end. I just needed to man up."

Her face had softened when I told her I respected her obligations, but now she frowns and snorts. "Who told you that? The Cro-Magnons you play with?"

I frown and ask, "The who?"

"Your teammates."

"No. I didn't talk about it with anyone, except to tell Coach about Maman's pending test."

"Well, I don't agree with your thinking."

I hear, *"Well, you're stupid."*

She continues, "Everyone needs someone in their corner. Most of the time, you have your family. But in this instance, you needed someone else. You were right to come to me, and there was no harm in asking. I also had the liberty to decline...or to make my own decision."

I shrug. "I made it through."

"But it was probably needlessly tough for you when I could have helped. Even if it was just by text if you'd actually responded."

"Our travel schedule was nuts," I say, hunching a defensive shoulder. She's right, but I've already apologized, and now she's harping.

"I don't think you get it. I don't want you to apologize for needing help or asking for it. Everyone does sometimes. You helped me with my marketing project; this was far more important."

"So, what then?" I'm clueless.

"You invited me then blew me off when I tried to

make that happen. You ghosted me and made my decision for me. That's what I need you to stop doing."

Now's probably not the time to mention that she's ghosted me in the recent past, so I nod. "You're right. I'm sorry for those things, too."

She stares at me for a long moment. Judging my sincerity, maybe. Or ensuring I followed what she said, given my ongoing challenges with her vocabulary.

I raise a plate. "Are you full from the appetizer, or do you want some dinner?"

She cracks a smile finally and comes over to grab the plate.

I hold it out of reach, saying, "I won't feel forgiven until I get a hug."

"More like, your apology is not complete without a hug," she mutters, allowing me to enfold her.

Now, I'm home.

We're back to being friends. There's no need to *talk* about stepping back, as long as I do it, right? No more fucking or fucking up. Chicken that I am, I stay silent and enjoy the dinner with a side of platonic friendship.

Chapter Twenty-Five

Nicole

I've mostly forgiven Mattie. I'm not positive he won't do it again, and I'm trying to stop myself from jumping back into bed with him.

It was surprisingly easy to avoid that on Tuesday night when he brought in Thai food, maybe since he didn't even try. My ego took a small hit over that, but it's for the best, or so I keep telling myself.

During my lunch hour Wednesday, he got on a video call with me to be my practice audience for a read-through of my PowerPoint. A couple of his questions helped me clarify a bullet point here and there.

Now, it's Thursday and I'm done! I presented the project and handed in the paper, and I'm ready to celebrate. It's time for a girl's night out with margaritas.

Maria has class later on, so we meet at 5:30. I take orders via text and get there a few minutes early to preorder for the group.

They all arrive right before the drinks are delivered, and I raise my glass. "To being done with my big marketing project and halfway through this semester!"

"Cheers!"

We clink and drink.

Christina gets a call from her brother. Cam knows better than to call her when she's out with us, but Greg doesn't have her schedule, and they work together closely enough he might need something.

When she steps outside to take it, we all lean in. "So, birthday ideas?"

Maria leads off with her usual hilarity. "I guess sex toys are superfluous now, huh?"

"Ha!" A laugh bursts out of me.

Lauren is on task. "Spa certificate? We did that two years ago, but if we give the gift card and schedule it as a group like we talked about in Vegas, that could be fun."

Maria tilts her head, saying, "I was considering sexier dance clothes for her. She was always conservative, but now, she's got that hot permanent partner, I bet she'd love them. But if y'all decide on the spa thing, I could go that way instead."

"What do y'all think of a boudoir photo shoot?" I say slowly. "I mean, not from us. Don't tell Christina this, but Cam asked for help. As we all know, she's not the easiest person to buy for."

"Why'd he ask you and not us? I'm insulted," Lauren says, frowning.

"I have no idea. He asked Mattie and me on a group thread. Why he'd think a guy who's never hung with a woman long enough to know her birthday, much less shop for it, would have worthwhile input, I don't know. As for me, I assume it's because I'm a planner." I shrug.

Maria narrows her eyes at my need to elaborate on Mattie's less than stellar qualities, then fist bumps me in support.

"Damn. When I think more about it, I understand his dilemma," Lauren mused. "This is the first impression for birthday gifts. She's freakin' richer than rich, and she won't let him be public. He can't even fly her somewhere sexy for an experiential gift because of his schedule. See, this is why people shouldn't date. Just keep it casual. So much less pressure."

"Hey, some of us like some pressure with our sex," Maria jokes, and we snort. She answers my question with, "You know, the boudoir photo shoot is similar to my idea of sexier dance clothes. Showing her that he sees her as super sexy and wants her to see herself that way. Maybe we go with that theme."

"And what, we get her lingerie?" Lauren asks. "That would be weird."

"I sure as fuck could not afford the shoes she likes," I add. "I don't know about the lingerie."

Maria tilts her head. "Those could work if she opens them after Cam gives her the boudoir package, but if you don't like that, maybe there are other things that could set the scene. A candle and a soft blanket, a gift card to iTunes since she's always downloading new music, a satin pillowcase, I dunno."

"Romantic gifts for romance with someone else. I could Google that," I muse. "You don't think the photo shoot is too much 'for him?'"

Maria argues, "It's for both of them. Sure, he'll want to hang it in their bedroom or studio, but she'll get something out of it as well. And it's not a trip where they might be seen together, which would have to wait until after the season, which would be my other idea."

"Let's all think about it, and see if we come up with anything else, but thanks. This helps," I say as Christina winds her way back to our table.

At home, I grab my phone and check on Mattie. The birthday plan is on my mind, but I also want to check on his mental state. His mom's procedure must be soon. We may be past our fling, but I still want to support him as a friend.

Me

> How are you holding up?

Mattie

> Nutting up and dealing. Heading to Toronto on a road trip so I got permission to detour to my family after the game and at least hug her the day after her appointment.

Me

> Awesome. I bet that will make you both feel better. Want to have a call about Cam's birthday ask?

Mattie

> OMG it's only a birthday. I have a game tonight, road trip tomorrow, and my mother's health to worry about.

Well, okay then. That puts things in perspective. Mattie's not the multi-tasker I am, but his texts read more brusque than normal. I get that he's worried about his mother, but why did he show up to discuss the birthday the other night, if he's going to shut it down now?

I put my phone away. I tried. And just as I had the

right to push that conversation before my project due date, he has the right for something this important.

But it also hurts, even knowing his circumstances, that he didn't ask if I finished the paper or how my presentation went.

Chapter Twenty-Six

Mathieu

There have been too many times when I didn't understand a word or phrase Nicole used, and I really hate feeling stupid.

I keep telling myself that hanging with her is hard on my ego, which offsets the fact that it makes something else hard.

I'm so on edge about my mother's health as well as the pros and cons of Nicole that I'm rude in text. I mean, Cam asked us to help, and I went over there to discuss it, so why would I shut it down now? Okay, I went over with discussing that as an excuse to get past my stupidity on the last road trip. Yet here I am being a dumbass again.

I have to figure out what I want. I can't say I want to be friends and then keep acting like an asshole. But nor do I desire to feel stupid, since that's what prompts my assholery. *That one I got from Buzz, referencing a past teammate.*

All that must wait, however. I need to hold Maman. Hear that the lump in her breast is something easily fixable. Only then can I think beyond that and hockey.

Toronto is always tough to beat on their home ice. Normally, we'd do a sweep of Toronto, Ottawa, and Montreal in the same trip, but our team's addition to the league probably made the schedule more complicated. We've already played Ottawa, and my family attended.

Knowing I'll see my parents tomorrow and they'll comment on my performance makes me play harder. I want to make them proud, even if it won't be with a university degree.

We try the setup that got me a couple of my tallies in my hat trick games, but Toronto's done their homework. So instead, I get the puck to Saint and Buzz and even Jack or Scottie. Jack's goal count is high for a D-man already this year, a testament to his speed and power.

Tonight, I take the puck down the ice with him trailing me, and as practiced, drop the puck back to him. He sets up the circle, passing back and forth to keep the Titans' attention fractured. Buzz slides through the slot and out the other side, drawing the D-man, and there's a second with a clear path between Jack and the goalie. One wicked slap shot and the goal lamp lights. I swear the goalie's ear should be hot even in his helmet from the speed of the puck as it whizzed past him.

We give up one but notch another hard-won goal of our own. Then it's the end of regulation with the score tied, Cam is banging his stick to shake the second miss off a little harder than usual.

We come out swinging in OT. But my poke check goes wrong, and I'm in the sin bin for tripping. We're on a two-minute penalty kill. The outcome is almost inevitable. Toronto in their own house come back strong and finish it with one more past Cam.

Merde. This, too, was my fault. My teammates would never say that, but I feel it. And my best supporters are either focused on Maman's procedure today or, in the case of Nicole, not talking to me.

I apologize in the locker room, but the guys back me and dismiss it like they always do. Then I shower, change and crash so I can get to the first train to Ottawa. It's a four-hour trip, so I'll only have the afternoon and evening with them and then a six-hour flight home, missing one practice.

The procedure was this afternoon, and Maman had said she was taking the afternoon off work. The minute the rideshare pulls up in front of our Orléans house, Maman is at the door. She yells to Papa then flies down the steps and walkway to throw herself into my arms as soon as I have my suitcase out of the car. "Mon bébé! Je suis très heureuse, mais ça va bien? Pourquoi es-tu ici?"

I think more in English after several years in the States, so I answer that way. "That's a silly question. I needed to hug you."

"Hmm, I think you needed a hug from me more, oui?" she says with a wink.

My father is at the door grinning at us. He gestures and calls, "Viens à l'intérieur."

We go inside as directed, and Maman bustles around the kitchen making tea and putting cookies out.

I talk with my mouth full. "I'm not supposed to be eating these during the season."

"I am quite sure you can work off one cookie."

"It's good to be home. I mean, I wish I could sneak off like this without this reason, but I needed to see and touch you two."

They nod. Maman pats my forearm on the table. I look at each of them. My mother is her usual self, unbothered by any adversity. My father looks tired, though, like he hasn't been sleeping well.

"How did the biopsy go? What did the lab say about

when your doctor will have results?”

“Eh, my boob hurts.”

I blink at my mother. I'd prefer not to talk about her breasts if possible. Then again, they might end up being the focus of many conversations if the news is bad.

She smirks at me. “You asked. They said they'll try to get the results to my doctor next week.”

“*Try?*”

My father's lips flatten.

Maman says, “We mentioned that it had been ten days, and they offered to try for early in the week, but Mathieu, it always takes time to get the pathology.”

I want to cry. I might lose my mind if I have to wait another week, but they are so calm. What right do I have to complain? Instead, I suck in a deep breath. “Okay. No promises I won't show up again to get another hug, though.”

They smile, but Papa chastises me. “You have work. As it is, you must be missing at least one practice, non?” At my nod, he continues. “Your job is not one you can simply call out of to take a holiday. You are an important member of the team.”

“It's a game, Papa. I'm not helping run the country or saving the environment like you two.” He's an engineer with a company focused on solar power.

“Hey. You give thousands, maybe millions, of people a way to unite in a shared interest, to take their mind off the drudgery of their day. And you're one of less than twenty-five. Your mother and I are small cogs in very big wheels.”

“Hockey feels like a less important wheel, especially right now.”

“What would you do if you were here? Sit and wait

and probably annoy the heck out of us. We're trying to get on with our lives. Whatever the test results say, we'll deal with it. And then we'll still move forward and expect you to do the same."

"Mamaan," I whine.

"Don't 'Maman' me," she replies, shaking her head. "Go. Do what you're paid so handsomely to do. And if you have spare time, find a nice girl to bring home for me to meet."

My flush gives me away.

Her eyes widen. "Mathieu? Mon dieu, Henri, he's met someone."

"No. I haven't. She doesn't have time for a relationship, and nor do I. But she's a friend. She was there for me when I got your call." *Whether she wanted to be or not, given that I showed up on her doorstep, but whatever.*

"Friendship is a good start. It lays an important groundwork for a marriage."

"Marriage! Maman, we're not even dating. Please stop."

"Maybe not, but you want to. Mothers know these things."

"Do mothers also know what's for dinner? Because I'm starving. Can I take you to one of your favorite spots since I'm here?"

Papa rolls his eyes, and Maman says, "I think you mean one of your favorite spots, but fine. I'll call ahead and ask for a table in the back, so you're not mobbed."

"Merci beaucoup, Maman," I lean in and kiss her before running upstairs to change clothes in my childhood room.

* * * *

For the second time in three months—unheard of during the season normally—I'm touching down at AUS on a commercial flight. This time, I arrive right as practice is starting for the guys, so I hop a rideshare.

Despite the lack of knowledge and the continued wait time, I'm rejuvenated from my visit with my parents.

I pull up my phone to text Nicole about it and see our last text exchange. Merde. My response was a little harsh.

I scroll up and realize I never asked her about her project. Aannddd this is why I am not boyfriend material. I'm a selfish, self-absorbed—I'm not really sure of the difference—asshole. Okay, let's try to fix some of this.

Me

> Um, remember my calendar issues? They raised their ugly head again, didn't they? <troll emoji>

Nicole

> ??

Me

> How was your presentation?

Nicole

> New phone, who dis?

Me

Ha. I'm sorry. I was preoccupied. But that's not an excuse, I still should have asked and supported you.

Nicole

It's ok. I knew you were preoccupied and for a legit reason. It went ok. It's done, which is the most important thing. Any word from your mom?

Me

I went to see them after the last game, just landed in Austin. But no word on the test results until next week.

Three dots appear, hover, then disappear. Finally, a text pops up.

Nicole

Keep me posted when you hear from them?

Me

Will do.

I should be grateful that her bar for friend behavior is lower than that of boyfriend behavior. Instead, I'm disappointed.

I should leave it all alone and let her move on. Hell, I should move on. But my thumb hovers over my screen.

Me

> If I find another cool restaurant, can I buy you dinner to talk about the birthday gift thing?

Nicole

> Depends on the restaurant. Most of the good ones won't have reservations available for tonight, Mr. Anti-Calendar.

Me

> Like where?

Nicole

> Uchiko

Me

> Hold, please.

This feels like a test…or maybe a challenge. I don't know why she's testing me, but I can handle this. I'm going to do something I try to avoid—use my celebrity status to see if they'll fit us in. But I'm not doing that from the rideshare and risking backlash on the team. So as soon as I'm in my apartment, I place the call. I apologize for the last-minute notice, stating that we just got back from a road trip and my friend has something she wants to celebrate and picked their place, and ask if they could squeeze us in tonight perhaps, under the name Mathieu du Près.

I have an 8:30 slot in no time. I convey my extreme gratitude and happily agree to sign something for the manager taking my call when I arrive. Hell, for this, I'll see if I have any merch in my place I can bring.

Me

> 8:30. I'll pick you up just after 8pm in a rideshare so we can sample sake.

Nicole

> You're full of shit.

Me

> <screenshot of reservation that just showed up in text from the restaurant>

Nicole

> OMG. I'll do all the birthday work on my own for this.
> Thank you!

Chapter Twenty-Seven

Nicole

Fuck. Here we go again. On Saturday, a traditional date night, no less. This is going to mess with my head. The more time we spend together, the more I like him. However, his actions make it clear that when I'm out of sight, I'm out of his mind.

I swore to myself I'd stay away from him. We need to move on and find someone more suitable for us. Or in his case, a string of someones. If I can only get this birthday gift sorted out, for Christina's sake, then I can block him or something to give myself a bit more time to get past his charm, abs, and random thoughtfulness.

We'd barely texted, and I came super close to offering to get him at the airport. I'm so stupid. I shouldn't consider offering to drop everything to wait on him when he had forgotten about my presentation. Yes, it's his mother, and it's scary. But who knows what the next stressor will be that will absorb him so completely he forgets about me or what's going on in my life?

I dress for Uchiko, not for Mattie. So while I look nice, my silky blouse is crewneck, and my black dress pants are simply that—pants. I may or may not be wearing lacy underwear underneath because I want to feel sexy, not because I have any plans for him to see them.

Who do you think you're fooling? You're wearing them just in case.

I shut down the devil on my shoulder and go wait for him outside my building, silencing another call from my mother. I'm not ready to listen to her pleas for me to move home right now.

Sure enough, at Uchiko, the manager ushers us to a table. Not a corner one this time, and Mattie has a signed baseball cap with him that he gives to the manager. Ah, Mattie used his charm and prestige to get his way. Yet another warning flag about getting involved with him. Why should he take no for an answer when he can wheedle his way to a yes using his clout? Which leads me back to my original concern from before New Year's. Why should he settle for the ugly duckling when he can have any swan in the lake.

He still seats me facing the other diners while he faces the bar in the hope of fewer interruptions. Which is fine. This will give me reason number three hundred and eighty-seven of why not to date a hockey player. I can only imagine the comments on social media if someone snaps us together. If my self-confidence was low before, I suspect I'd become a shut-in after reading those.

The server comes over, and Mattie gushes, "Thank you so much for having us. We were a last-minute reservation, and I see how busy you are. Is it always like this?"

The server—a guy, no less—kowtows and simpers. "Yes, sir. But we're always happy to support our local athletes."

"What's your name?"

"Sam, sir."

"Samsir? That's a unique name." Mattie winks at

him, and I swear the guy is going to be a puddle on the floor. I don't know if he's into men. It's Mattie's way. "Mind if I call you Sam?"

"Ha, of course."

"I'm Mattie, and this is Nicole. This is our first time here. What do you recommend?"

Sam does his spiel, and Mattie asks questions and orders, checking in with me about how exotic I'll go with my sushi.

When I answer, "I'll try anything once," he sucks in a breath and raises a brow at me before continuing with the order.

In minutes, we have orders of edamame and roasted Brussels sprouts between us, and our own sake flights.

Mattie leans in and opens his mouth to say something, then slides his glance to the right. I follow his gaze. The guy at the table next to us, who is seated on my side, is staring at him. When Mattie meets his eyes with a professional smile, the guy tilts toward him. "I knew it. You're Mathieu du Près."

At Mattie's nod, the guy sticks out a hand to shake, "I love you guys. You're having a great season. And two hat tricks, buddy! Hey, any chance I can get a quick pic with you, please?"

Mattie looks at their table. They're almost done eating. "Can we do it when you leave, outside, so I don't get mobbed please? I love our fans, but I also want to enjoy dinner with my friend."

He tilts his head toward me and winks at the guy like there's more than friendship between us.

"Oh, yeah, of course, man. Thank you so much!"

Mattie leans way over to me, gesturing for me to come close, and whispers, "Probably should have kept the hat, huh?"

I roll my eyes at him. "If you're going to play the celebrity card to get a last-minute table, which is totally cheating by the way, then you have to be willing to pay the price."

He frowns. "How is this cheating?"

"I gave you a challenge from a normal person's perspective, and you took the easy way."

"Bah. You call it cheating, I call it using all the tools at my disposal. After all, you gave *me* the challenge, not a normal person."

"You can say that again," I mutter under my breath. He's definitely not normal. And his charm is turned to eleven tonight. My panties may go up in a plume of smoke; he's making me so damned hot.

He clanks a sake cup against mine. "Which sake do you like best? We can get a bottle."

"Slow your roll, du Près, I've only tried one. So…" I need to get this exchange out of flirtation and into co-conspirator mode. "Christina's birthday."

"Oh yeah. I have to tell you, I suck at these."

"Yes, that was obvious from your texts, but I appreciate the self-awareness."

He laughs.

"Have you ever gotten a girlfriend a birthday gift?"

One eye closes as he rifles through memories. The unsurprising answer comes out, "Nope."

"I'm going to explain, in case you ever come across this situation. Counter to your thought in text, it's not just a birthday. It's the first birthday of forever birthdays for them, another first impression, wanting to prove himself marriage material, not that he needs to."

"If he doesn't need to, then why is he so nervous? It

was so much easier when we could kill something and bring it to a woman to cook as a grand gesture."

I stare in shock for a minute before throwing my head back and cackling. "Oh my god, you are the textbook definition of a Neanderthal."

"Ha ha. You know I was joking." There's a little thought bubble over his head with "mostly," but I won't call him on it.

"He wants to because he loves her. It's as simple as that. You don't have to understand it all, but I'm trying to give you the framework, so you don't text him something like 'OMG it's just a birthday.'"

"As if."

"I never know with you. Frankly, you're a bit of a Jekyll and Hyde, at least with me." He frowns at that, but I keep going. "I can keep trying to find gift ideas, but I'd like you to weigh in on if they're romantic or not."

"I'll do my best. Why can't I come up with ideas?"

"You were cut off after lingerie."

"Hey, I didn't say vacuum!" He teases with a chuckle.

"She's extra difficult to buy for because she can buy herself anything she wants," I mull out loud. "She's protective of the environment, she's creating a nonprofit dance program for young girls who couldn't afford it…"

The couple next to us gets up to leave, and Mattie doesn't miss a beat. Excusing himself, he keeps his head down and follows them outside. He's back before I finish my next bite.

"My jokes aside, I like the trip idea. Or tickets if there's a cool show in town. Isn't it theater season now? Maybe there's something with dance in it. All of us—" He glances at me and amends his statement. "Most of us can buy what we want. But finding an experience we weren't aware of to share with a friend is cool and makes more memories than just the birthday. The problem is timing with our games."

"Oh, I like the show idea." I'm already on my phone scrolling one of the theaters here in town. "There is a Cirque show coming through in May. Would that work?"

"Hopefully not."

I frown.

"May is playoff season. In fact, playoffs—or late April to mid-June to you non-hockey people—are harder to schedule. We don't know who we'll play, which will inform where we'll play, and each round dates are set based on the outcome of the preceding round. Plus, all the guys are saving every ounce of energy for the ice. It's a brutal timetable after eighty-two regular season games. I don't even hook…"

He trails off and blushes while I stare at him with pressed lips.

"Um, sorry? I was thinking through planning a birthday celebration. I might have overshared a little there."

"You think?" It shouldn't matter. Rewording that thought, I say, "It doesn't matter. You can do what or who you like, when you like. Or not."

"That's not what I meant, Nicole." He's backpedaling now. My big question is why.

Chapter Twenty-Eight

Mathieu

I spy two seats opening up at the darkest end of the bar where I will attract the least attention. I don't like Nicole giving me that much freedom, although I haven't analyzed quite why. So I'm not ready for the night to end.

Gesturing, I ask, "Could we stay for a bit, but free the table for any late reservations?"

She waffles. "That's probably not a good idea."

"Come on, 'tit chou. I need a minute to get my foot out of my mouth to be able to walk again."

She sniffs a sort-of laugh and nods.

I catch Sam's eye and motion with my chin, so he knows we're not deserting him. He can deliver our check to the bar. I order a club soda. Nicole debates, then orders a white wine.

Taking a deep breath, I say, "Hey. I really was speaking of the past or the theoretical. Not this season. Regardless, it was an insensitive comment, and I'm sorry."

Nicole raises her brows at me over the wine glass tipped to her lips.

"Don't give me that. Just because I don't do relationships doesn't mean I'm a dick. I am upfront about everything and wouldn't be deliberately hurtful."

She narrows her eyes and nods. "Okay. And thank you. I'll look into shows more and check dates against your season if I can find one close enough to her birthday."

"Thank you. Now, enough about other people. How is school going? When will you get our grade on our project?"

"Oh, it's ours now, huh? Because you helped on a couple of aspects? I didn't see you next to me writing that paper."

My smile fades. "Trust me, you wouldn't have wanted that."

She frowns. "Stop that. I would have loved more of your input, but I would never ask that of you given your work schedule."

"I wouldn't know enough to help. Let me know when you get your grade, though. I'm rooting for you. What do you want to do once you have your degree?"

"I'll have to work for my company for two years after I graduate, or I'll owe them their portion of my tuition back. After that, I don't know. My real hope is that those three letters will legitimize my advice to my family."

She's loyal; I'll give her that. But her loyalty seems like a one-way street. "Do you think it will?"

"I'm worried. That, more than anything, is what keeps me up at night."

I lean an elbow on the bar, trying to appear casual and turn toward her more. "Really? Are they proud of you for getting the advanced degree?"

Her lips flatten. "Considering they didn't come to my undergrad commencement ceremony, I doubt it."

"Do they ever come to visit you?"

She shakes her head. "It would be too hard to leave

the ranch. They say they can't afford any more help, and everyone's plates are already full."

I inch closer, keeping my voice gentle. "I worry you're setting yourself up to be hurt again. What do you want to do for you? If you could pick any job given your skillset and the MBA, what would you choose, money aside? Would it be consulting to the ranch?"

"Ha. No." She stares at the shelf of bottles behind the bar until I think she's not going to answer. "Something using my organizational skills for sure. I don't know. Maybe an all-woman consulting firm helping women-run businesses."

"That's cool. I'm sure Lauren would be proud, too."

She giggles and elbows me, then sobers. "Honestly, I am not sure of the possibilities. I've never thought about it. I'm too busy putting one foot in front of the other, just in a different way than my parents. But you make a good point. I don't want to be them, trudging toward retirement in a job simply for the money."

I smile, proud of her for thinking beyond her family.

She turns to me, eyes wide. "I want to be you."

"What?" I say with a huffed laugh. "A dumb jock?"

"Stop that. I hope to follow my passion and do something I love, and be good enough that I'm compensated well for it. You're such a success story. Why do you always put yourself down?"

My mouth drops open, and I nearly fall off my barstool. I look away for a second to get my bearings. No one has ever admired me before, other than my parents, who are biased. Sure, fans admire my game, teammates admire plays. But her looking at me as a person and seeing success blows me away.

I lean in and cup her face. Right before I lay my lips

across hers, I say, "Good girl, that might be the nicest thing anyone has ever said to me. Thank you."

Her eyes go molten at my lead-in.

I wasn't saying it to take advantage. Her kindness simply overwhelmed me.

She tastes like chardonnay and heaven, and my lips linger on hers.

When she moans quietly, I give in to my desire and am more deliberate. Pulling back a fraction, I ask, "Is there anything I can do to make you feel as good as I do right now?"

Her eyes flash open, locking on mine, and her sudden exhale gusts over me. "I can think of a few things, but we can't do them here."

Having doubted I'd get anywhere with that offer, I need a second before I straighten and throw cash on the bar for our drinks. Sam had brought our dinner bill earlier, so all that's left to do is call the rideshare, which Nicole is already doing.

Then we're out on the sidewalk, in the car, and finally, hustling into my apartment.

I find the one button behind her neck to loosen her silky top and slide it over her head while she's still closing the door.

Pressing her forward into it, my hands roam her shoulders and arms. I tuck her hair behind one ear and ask, "Now, about those ideas…?"

"I can't think when you do that."

"When I do what?" I press my hips into her ass. "This?" I unclasp the lacy bra she's still wearing and smooth my hands beneath it, pulling her away from the door an inch to cup her breasts and thumb her nipples. "This?"

"Any of it," she gasps. "All of it works."

"Excellent." I undo her pants and shove them down. Our heights are too different for me to take her this way, so I lift her into a cradle hold and have her kick her shoes off, letting the pants follow. Taking her to the couch, I bend her over the back and tell her to brace herself on the seat cushions.

My shirt is tossed over my head, and my dark jeans are unfastened in no time after fishing a condom out of my wallet. I caress her folds, circling her clit once before dipping in to spread her wetness and make sure she is ready for me. A second later the condom is on. I bend my knees and thrust up into her, not too hard, but one long thrust that makes us both groan out loud.

"'Tit chou, tu m'as manqué. It's been too long since I've been inside you. T'es si belle."

"Mattie, that's nice and all, and I hope you'll explain what you said to me later, but for now, *move*. Please."

I choke out a laugh. "You're cute when you're demanding, good girl."

She shoves her hips backward.

I inhale sharply and do as she says, to our mutual rewards.

As I find my release, listening to her cries of pleasure, I stare down at her. I'm so not done with this girl, and this thing between us feels less and less casual every time.

Chapter Twenty-Nine

Nicole

Once again, I snuck out of Mattie's place in the dark of night, fulfilling my part as his repeat one-night stand. The ride home and the next day are spent berating myself for letting a romance book phrase be my undoing. Well, that and the infinitely sexy mouth it came out of before I was finished off with an epic kiss. But damn, I've probably had more orgasms in these first few months of the year than I did in the past two years, despite our hookups being casual, unplanned, and on-and-off. He's impossible to say no to, especially when I like the man behind the crazy bedroom skills.

I avoided texting him and watched the game from home last night because Zoe and Christina get priority on Cam's seats now. They'll attend his game tomorrow as well, but next week, I'll get Zoe's seat because she has a term paper due.

I need to rebuild the walls around my heart and stop letting my past ways interfere with my new approach to life. If only my body was designed to have walled off feelings and a wide-open pussy, but alas, it's not to be. Kitty will have to go without. However, I'm dying to know if there has been any news regarding his mom, and I got my project and grade back. He told me he wanted to know when that came in.

Me

> Hi. Sorry about the loss last night. You took a couple rough hits. How are you doing?

Mattie

> Eh, the pads and the ice bath after the game solved most of it.

Me

> Ouch. That sounds worse than the hits.

Mattie

> Ha! It's up there.

Me

> Any word on your mom?

Mattie

> :/ No. But thanks for asking.

Me

> Keep me posted. So…wanna know my grade?

The phone rings, "Mattie" showing on the screen. It's after ten pm even though he needs to sleep to be ready for tomorrow's game, but hey, he's calling me, not the other way around.

"Hi—"

"How'd we do?" He's so eager, it's sweet, but it also messes with my head and makes me think he's interested in more than sex.

I don't tease it out. "We got an A."

"Woohoo!" he shouts, and I hold the phone away from my ear. "I knew my good girl could do it!"

I gulp, wanting to be his good girl, his bad girl, anything. And hating that I want that.

"Petit chou? You still there?"

"Yes. I did my celebratory dance when I got the email, I was letting you get your groove on," I manage. Another nickname that makes me wish things I shouldn't. Somehow the words sound normal despite my throat being tight against the image of him repeating that phrase as he holds me, pets me, does delicious, nasty things to me.

"Speaking of celebrations, we should do that over dinner at a new spot."

"Only if I pay. The professor's comments made it clear that your contributions made a difference in evaluating the conversion rate."

"Christina is the only non-family member who has ever paid for one of my meals. I'm not comfortable with that."

"Neanderthal."

"With the knuckle scars to prove it, bébé. But what's a conversion rate?"

"Oh, sorry, I thought I'd explained that along the way. It's the rate at which your marketing efforts convert to income-producing behavior, like buying a ticket. Sometimes, there are multiple steps. For instance, social media…" I trail off. "You probably aren't interested in this."

"You sure you don't mean you probably wouldn't understand this either? Sorry you have to explain to the dumb jock."

"Wait a minute. You've said that before. That is not how I see you."

"How could you not? It's what I am. That's why you have to keep explaining words to me."

"First of all, English is your second language. I don't have a second language. You'd have to explain every single word of French to me, not just specialized vocabulary for a field you don't work in."

He starts to say something, but I continue.

"Second, you're my friend, and your contributions helped me, according to someone with a PhD, not just me. I don't like it when you put yourself down. Intelligence and education are not the same. Lauren and Christina might know the term conversion rate because they're in business, but they might not, because it's a marketing-specific term. Maria might, because she's in business for herself, so she wears all hats including marketing. But if none of them do, I don't consider myself smarter than them or think less of them in any way. Same goes for you. I'm sure I know about a thousandth of what you know about hockey rules, strategies, history, you name it. Because that's your area of expertise."

When I stop to take a breath, he says lightly, "Wow. Tell me how you really feel."

I snort a laugh. "I'm serious, Mattie."

"I, too, am serious when I say thank you. Those are all very nice thoughts. I don't agree because you're smarter than me. But I appreciate your enthusiasm, good girl."

If he were here in person, I'd be half naked by now with all his sweet talk and name calling. Since we're on the phone, I manage to dig deep and find the strength to preserve my sanity, if not my heart, saying, "Ugh, Mattie, I need you to stop calling me that. I've told you any number of times, I can't keep falling into bed with you and still believe it's casual. You do *not* want me to become a stage-five clinger."

"What's that term? It's not marketing-related."

"I don't know where it came from. It's basically a severe case of clinging as though we're inseparable in a relationship."

"How the fuck am I supposed to keep up when you use terms *you* don't even understand?" he says with a laugh.

I sigh. The most wistful sigh in the universe. Then get real. "I'd say, hang with me and I'll explain them, but that's my whole point. I am afraid of ending up hurt; you've said all along you don't do commitment or calendars, which are two of my favorite things."

"Okay. I'll try to respect that. It's hard when you're such a smokin' pixie, but I'll try."

"Grr. Try harder."

He laughs. "I have to get some sleep. Goodnight, p'tit chou."

"'Night, Mattie."

Chapter Thirty

Mathieu

We touch down in Denver for the start of a quick two-game road trip. From here, we'll bounce to St. Paul then home.

As the bus heads for the hotel, my phone rings, *Maman* flashing across the screen.

I answer in a hushed tone, but before I finish greeting her, Maman says, "Ce n'est qu'un kyste."

"What-what does that mean?" I hold my breath. I have no idea if a cyst means it's cancer or not. But she said "only" so it has to be good?

"It's benign. They can drain it or remove it if it becomes larger or painful."

"Maman," I breathe, tears of relief springing to my eyes. "Dieu merci."

"Oui." I can hear the smile in her voice. Papa is muttering in the background. "Papa says I should have checked where you are, sorry, mon bébé."

I sniff and pinch the bridge of my nose in an effort not to bawl in front of my teammates. After a watery laugh, I keep my voice low and say in French, "Only on the bus surrounded by twenty plus macho hockey players."

"Oh non."

"It's okay, Maman. You know I wanted to hear this

the minute you got the news."

"Yes, we tried to reach you earlier, but the call wouldn't connect."

"I was on the plane. We just got to Denver, and we're pulling into the hotel now."

"Ah bon alors. Go check in. Play well tomorrow. Je t'adore."

"Je vous adore. Dis salut à Papa pour moi."

I blink and scrub my face. Never mind tomorrow's practice and game. I'm ready to take on Denver single-handedly right now. "Conquer the world" has new meaning for me.

In my room, I stare at my phone's text screen. My thread with Nicole from her getting her project grade is still on the screen. She made it clear that we need to be done with hookups but that she still wanted to hear about my mom's biopsy.

Taking a breath, I open the thread.

Me

> Maman called me. Cyst is benign. I'm riding high.

Nicole

> Yay! I'm so glad. Do they need to do anything with it?

Me

> Not right now. They'll keep an eye on it.

Nicole

> Even better. I'm so happy for you and your family.

Me

> Thanks.

I shut it down before I get into trouble with texts.

Me

> At the hotel. I learned a new term from Emil: hitting the hay

Nicole

> Ah yes that's a good one for living in Texas. 'Night

Me

> Sweet dreams, mon petit chou.

So sue me. I couldn't resist. I sleep better after that exchange, though.

* * * *

Saint and Cam knew about my mom in addition to Coach. As two of the more mature, perceptive guys on the team, they could tell something was up. I tell them all the good news, and they nod. Saint's comment is, "I expect you'll be back to your usual self in the games."

I'm not, though; I'm better. Like the Tasmanian devil

in the American cartoons, I'm everywhere on the ice for our two road games. Fighting to get the puck away from our opponents, winging passes to him and Drew. Hell, I'm even down at our end, helping Jack and Scottie and the other defensive pairs. Both games fly by in a blur of assists, then we're heading home with two wins under our belts.

Tonight, we're back on home ice, playing the Las Vegas Desert Kings. We're within a few weeks of the end of the season, and if we win, we almost certainly will make the playoffs. Despite being an older squad, they're a tough team.

Jack played for them before coming here, which means we have the inside track on some of their weaknesses, but they also know how to play against him. This is our second game against them, and we are neck and neck for securing the playoff berth, so a win would be a mind fuck over them.

Because they know Jack's speed, they play an aggressive forecheck strategy, ensuring they have a chance of regaining any puck sent into their territory. That means we spend the first period chasing that black disc up and down the ice with no one managing to score. I'm frustrated. Even with their heavy forecheck, we should have been able to beat them with our speed and get behind the forwards. But their goalie is on point tonight, stopping everything that flies his way.

I'm panting by the intermission, happy with the eighteen-minute break to rest and regroup. Coach points out that we're not getting enough rebounds, we're not setting up in the slot enough. I want to say, "because we're basically doing a bag skate out there," but I don't. We all nod. We'll try harder if that's what it takes.

Saint points out what a fast game it is, and Coach decides he'll put a few of the more agile players together on a line and give them more time. Petrovsky and Bergstrom brighten, always looking for more playing time, even in a high-speed chase situation like this.

We're back out there. The game is a blur, whether I'm on the ice or riding the bench. The Kings score. Cam taps the ice three times and shakes it off, hunkering down and looking fiercer than ever. Within minutes, we head back into their zone and I'm near the boards, looking for Saint to pass me the puck from the other side of the ice. No one is in the slot again, but Drew is next to the goalie, just outside the crease. Saint rips off a slapshot. The goalie sees it's going wide and doesn't go for it, but Drew raises his stick and in midair, not even a one-timer, deflects the shot off the blade into the net at a new angle, too close for Vegas's goalie to react.

Drew raises his fist, and we gather around to give him backslaps. We're tied.

Third period, and time to make this game ours. We're on home ice, the fans are loud for us, and we dig deep to keep the speed up. Bergstrom and Boulanger are out on the ice together again with their shorthand French commands to signal plays and passes.

Coach puts them out when there are fewer European and Canadian Desert Kings playing, and sure enough, Bergstrom gets closer to the slot than his usual spot near the boards. The goalie's attention is divided, and when Emil calls that he wants the puck, that's all Boulanger needs. He wings it in past the goalie's mask, barely clearing the post. We're up, with four and a half minutes left.

Jack is running his mouth when I head back out, and

I grumble at him as I skate by. He's going to start a fight and doesn't seem to care. We're pressing their defense to keep the puck down at their end of the ice, when one of the Desert Kings starts trash talking in my ear. They're looking for a power play, so I ignore him.

But then he says, "Pussy, why don't you go home to Mama, or won't she have you?"

Everything with my maman's situation comes rushing back in. Shoving him, I drop gloves.

He's startled. I'm usually the last one to fight.

I grab his sweater, shove him against the boards, and swing a fist. He shoves me back, and my blades are so sharp I lose my balance and go down. He's on me, catching my jaw with his now-also-gloveless fist. The refs pull us off and point me to the sin bin. Dammit.

Jack skates alongside me. "What happened? Do I need to deal with him?"

"Nah. Sorry, man. Just hold the line. Don't let 'em get past you."

"Not a problem," he says with his usual confidence. I'd say cockiness, but he's damned good at what he does.

And we pull through those last couple minutes, no thanks to me, to get the W.

* * * *

I lean against the bar, holding my glass of Wiser's to the bruise along my jaw.

Renee stands across from me, wiping down the bar. "You know that stuff works better when you drink it."

"Why can't I do both?" I ask with a grin.

"Seriously, do you need an ice pack?" She keeps a few behind the bar for those injuries that linger beyond our post-game cool down and showers.

"Nah, I'm good thanks."

As Renee strolls down to check on other customers, a bunny sidles up to me. "Oh, Mattie. That looks painful."

I lean back when she reaches for it. Touching it is not going to help it feel better.

"I could kiss it and make it better," she offers with what is probably supposed to be a cute pout.

"Ah, thanks, but…" I trail off. Normally, I'd flirt back, telling her that kissing a different part of me would make me feel way better. But I'm not into it tonight.

"I think it needs to be left alone for the moment." I throw back my drink, wasting a delicious whisky, and now, I'm annoyed at her and myself.

Heading toward a cluster of players who are not entertaining bunnies for the moment, I shake my head at my thoughts. Since when am I annoyed by bunnies? They used to be my reward for winning a game, my consolation for losing, and straight-up fun. Even when I wasn't looking to get my dick wet, flirting has always been fun. Tonight, it feels like work.

I look around. Cam told me that Christina and Zoe used his seats for this game, which means Nicole won't be here. I shouldn't care. Sexy pixie or not, she has said she can't deal with me dipping my wick in her well any longer without catching feelings, and I need to respect that.

This whole caring about someone else's feelings is annoying. I've always been respectful of the women I fuck, and I have always been clear about what it was and what it was not. If we were up for seconds, we'd gone into it eyes wide open, like the arrangement I had in Miami. So until I determine what I can manage and what I want from my pixie, I need to leave her be.

I pause mid-step. It's a good thing I'm used to balancing on skates because if I fell over, I'd never hear the end of it. Always before I've been annoyed by a woman's clinginess. This time I'm annoyed by *mine*.

But I'm not relationship material, especially for a smart girl like Nicole. Which means I should move on. Now. Ready or not, it would be best to get back in the saddle again.

Narrowing my gaze, I scan the room again. There are a few very attractive, scantily clad women hanging off Jack. I could help him with that. Pasting my most charming smile, I pull forth my French accent and redirect my steps.

"Bonsoir, mes amis. Can I get anyone a drink?" Mon dieu, American women are suckers for accents. I can almost see their panties melt.

"Oh yes, please."

"Hi, Mathieu, I'm…"

I don't even hear her name. Definitely don't need it for my plans.

"You played so well tonight," Bunny One says.

"Oh, were you at the game?" I ask, catching Jack's smirk.

"No, we were waiting here for y'all," she says, stroking her blonde hair. Her hold is reminiscent of how she'd hold a cock, and the last curl hangs on her left tit.

All of which *should* work for me, dammit. Instead, a sigh echoes in my head as I woodenly take drink orders and go fill them. When I return, Bunny Two takes her drink and leans in. Between the game and the silent conversation I'm having with myself, my reaction time is slow, and she gets me right on the lips.

I manage a weak tip up of one side of my mouth.

Come on, get it together. You're not getting Nicole anymore. This will have to do. It's what you deserve.

I try to engage, asking them questions and joking with Jack about his antics during the game. But when Bunny Two's hand lingers on me, it feels wrong. When she scratches her long fake nails along my forearm, I shiver.

She takes it as pleasure when it's closer to fear. Leaning in, she asks, "Want to go back to my place?"

Yes. Say yes.

"Aw, thanks, chérie. But it was a long game. Maybe next time." I give my standard wink, nod to Jack, and put my barely touched bottle of Topo Chico on the bar to head home.

Even if I wanted a relationship with Nicole, I'd end up hurting her, given my complete inability to manage my time. And I want more than anything not to hurt her. But it seems I don't want anyone else right now either.

I'm twenty-six. I should be living large, as Jack likes to say. Life has always come easy for me other than school. Hockey remains fun no matter how hard the coaches push us, no matter how disappointing it is when we get knocked out each year without the Cup. Finding the next fun activity, woman, or party was the goal. Now, I'm dissatisfied by all of it except hockey. And Nicole is anything but easy. So now what?

More exhausted than ever by my circling thoughts, I crash into my cold bed and hope to sleep off this funk.

Chapter Thirty-One

Nicole

I race to finish updating the project plan for my team before pulling warm clothes on despite it being in the 80's, so I can get out of here and meet Christina at the Tornadoes game. There should be a warning about how cold hockey arenas need to be to maintain the ice. A detail I would never have known if not for Mattie—hockey players love a hard ice whereas figure skaters like a softer ice. As I'm saving the file, my cell phone rings. "Mom" lights up on the screen again.

I sigh. My father's leg muscle pull has still not healed fully, even though it's been over a month. My mother has been calling me every week to try to convince me to move home. She tells me how hard it is for my father to do his share, her own aches and pains, and that there aren't enough hands.

I've avoided the last two calls, but this will escalate, and I need to focus on work and school, so once again I'll have to shut it down.

"Hi, Mom." I gather my things and start the walk to my car.

"Hi, honey. I was thinking. You must have vacation time at that job of yours. How about you use some and come home and see how you feel after a couple of weeks? It would lighten our load while your dad's still not a hundred percent."

"Because I have school, Mom." *And that's not how I want to spend my vacation.* I'm still hoping to be able to go with the girls for a summer getaway, although I probably won't share that with my mother. Just as she won't know that I'm attending the hockey game tonight. If I have time for that, then I'm living a life of luxury at their expense.

"I'm worried about your father reinjuring himself. Then where will we be?"

"I suspect you'd need to hire some temporary hands. In fact, as I said in our last two calls, it would be better to do that now and avoid reinjury."

"Your brothers are looking so tired, too. Did I tell you one of them seems interested in a rancher's daughter in the next town? Apparently, they went to high school together for a couple years."

"That's great, Mom. Maybe she'll be another set of helping hands soon, if they decide to get married."

"Hmm, yes. At least I'll have a supportive daughter-in-law."

I grit my teeth. "Really? That's the thanks I get when I send you every spare dollar I have? When I offer suggestions on how to make the ranch more profitable? I contribute a lot even from here. Why should I bother if it's not appreciated?"

She sucks in a shocked breath. My self-makeover and Mattie's reaction to their lack of support or interest in my life outside the ranch is giving me new perspective—and attitude, not only with men apparently.

"I meant someone to support the workload on the ranch," Mom mumbles.

I'm not convinced.

"I'm going to say this one more time. After that, I hope our calls will be to see how I'm doing and how school and work are going, as well as updating me on what's going on in your world. I will not be coming home to help on the ranch in the foreseeable future. I do understand and respect that it's hard work, and if or when it's too much, you should hire more help."

"I guess I know where you stand, then, don't I. I'll tell your father he'd better get back out there since he can't rely on you."

"Fine. Bye." I hang up on another gasp from her.

I drive over to Christina's, managing not to pound the steering wheel in residual frustration. As always, we'll take her car for her primo parking.

Christina answers my knock with an excited smile, but it falls away when she sees my expression. "Oh no. Come here."

I accept the hug gratefully and sniff back tears.

"Your parents?"

I nod against her.

"I'm sorry, Nic. I love you. And you are right to carve your own path here."

I take a deep breath and take a small step back. "Thank you. I needed to hear that so much. They keep pushing and pushing. I actually came on a bit strong today about them not appreciating the help I do offer. Instead of hearing me when I called her on bad behavior, my mom doubled down and got bitchy."

"-er," Christina tacks on.

"Yeah, that." I grin. "Anyway, let's go watch hockey and escape real life."

"Sounds like a plan."

* * * *

At the game, we settle into our seats. After Christina drools over Cam's warmups, we snag food and sodas before the game starts.

I try to get lost in the plays, but my mother's guilt trip niggles at me.

Cam and Christina make goo-goo eyes at each other as he comes and goes at the intermissions. My gaze follows Mattie surreptitiously. I didn't tell him I was coming tonight, and while Christina and I had planned to go to Chaser's after the game if we won, I'm rethinking that after our week of silence following his text about his mom. I need to stay away from him. His hotness and charm are like a magnet for my clothes. On top of which, I still like the rest of him too much.

Maybe I go and watch him with the bunnies and force myself to get over him.

Or maybe you're making excuses to go.

Ugh. At my huff of irritation, Christina glances at me and asks, "Why the sigh? We're winning. Are you still in your head about the ranch? Don't let them kill your night."

If only it was that easy.

Midway through the third period, Buzz gets the puck on the breakaway, and he's so damned fast no one can catch him. He's one-on-one with their goalie, and the goalie blinks. Buzz sails a shot over the guy's heavily padded shoulder into the net, and the goal lamp lights. It's 3-1 with less than four minutes remaining. An NHL team would never play out the clock, but Coach is playing the checking lines more to keep the defensive pressure on with the lead.

We head to the friends and family lounge because of course Christina can't wait until Chasers to congratulate her man.

A few of the guys start trickling out of the locker room. Jack's voice echoes down the concrete hall as he nears, "To Chasers! Let's gooo!"

I'm smiling as he enters because his shenanigans are already putting me in a better mood. Mattie steps in right behind him, sporting a deep eggplant colored suit. Holy hell, that nod to his team colors and willingness to be bold in his apparel is as hot as him in jeans and a clingy polo. Not as hot as him in nothing at all, but—

Dammit, stop thinking about him naked.

I'm basically grinning like a loon because my brain ran away when confronted with him. He looks surprised, then winks like the player he is. His long legs bring him straight to me. "P'tit chou."

"Don't pateet shoe me. Still not a cabbage."

"It's a common term of endearment. Not every translation can be word for word. What would a French person say if 'hitting the hay' were translated piece by piece. They'd think Texans were crazy."

"We might be."

"Come on, little cabbage. Let's go get a snack. I'm starving."

I roll my eyes. Of course he is. His gesture to Chris that I'm riding with him gets a raised eyebrow and a nod, and then we're in the car.

"Well, you know how my day was. How was yours?" he asks, glancing over at a red light.

Damn. The game and joking with him had done a great job taking my mind off my mother's call, but with that question, all my frustration and guilt come rushing back.

"Oh no. What happened?" he asks. My expression

must have given me away.

"My mother called. My dad's leg isn't healing as quickly as they'd hoped, and they want me to take vacation time to help."

We park and head into the bar where he pleads for a rush order of his favorite pizza. Turning back to me, he leans an elbow on the bar. Frowning, he says, "But they know you're in school. You can't take vacation from that."

"See? Even the most calendar-challenged person in my life can figure that out, but they don't care." My throat tightens. "God, Mattie. I lost it a little today. I might have shocked my mom."

He reaches over and squeezes my hand. "I'm glad you stood up for yourself. Wait until they hear that you're going to be a rock star consultant after school and they'll have to pay top dollar for your help."

"Ha. I never said I was going to do that. I said that's what I would do if I had my choice. But if my family needs my help…" I trail off, unsure now how I'd handle that. I can no longer see myself going home afterward to fight every day to be heard regarding improvements and to have drudgery fill my days in the form of ranch tasks. If I'm honest, I haven't been sure I'd be able to force myself to do it from the minute I left home.

"If your family needs your help, you give it in the best way you can—consulting on business practices with all that knowledge you're stuffing in that cute pixie head of yours," Mattie says in a matter-of-fact tone.

"You know it's not that easy."

"It *is* that easy, Nicole. If you offer a life preserver to someone drowning and they decline it, it's not your fault they drown."

"That's a terrible analogy. I could jump in and help them. I'd want to do everything I could."

"What if you couldn't swim?"

"But that's where your analogy goes wrong. I can swim—er, work the ranch. I just really really don't want to."

"Normalement, I'd say you know better. But honestly, Nicole? In this case, I don't think you could work there. You'd lose your soul, your will to live, and be right back here or in another city with only ranch work on your resume, and your relationship with your family even worse off because you'd resent them for usurping your twenties."

How dare he? "You have no business saying any of that," I grit out. "You haven't met my family. They love me. We'd find a way to make it work."

"Would you though? Because it sounds like they love your willingness to help them either with your hands or your money, but not your brain. That's not love, chérie. That's selfish and toxic."

There might be steam coming out of my ears, I'm so furious. "Says the guy who will only hang with people if they're doing something fun because he doesn't want any downers or commitments."

With that, I walk away. I'm glad that my anger keeps me from crying at the hurtful picture he painted. I tug Christina's sleeve as she's talking to Cam and gesture.

Cam looks at me and says, "Hey, hang on. Do I need to beat up Mattie? Did he upset you?"

I shake my head.

He tries to wrap me in his huge arms, but I throw up my hands. "No, please," I gasp. "If you do that I'll cry. I have to go."

Christina and he exchange a glance, and he tilts his head up. She grabs my arm and walks with me.

"You don't need to come. I'm sorry."

"It's okay. I know where to find him later," she says with a half smile meant to conjure one from me.

I sniff.

Once we are in her car, she asks, "What happened?"

I recount the whole conversation. "Gah! He was so out of line."

"Exactly what are you mad about?" Christina asks. "About how wrong he is? That he dared to say it?"

Something in her tone makes me turn to look at her as she pulls through her family estate's gate.

"All of it."

"Okay." She nods as we walk the path around the pool to her cottage. We settle at her kitchen counter. "Let's break it down. Do you feel he wasn't in a position to say anything about your family without having met them?"

"Some. He's heard snippets of phone conversations and what I've told him and extrapolated from there. So he has a lopsided picture."

"But if he's heard most of that from you, and you generally defend your family, then his position wouldn't differ from yours because of his limited source."

"Then he's making stuff up. I don't know."

"Or as someone who cares about you, he's observing the effect on you despite what you're saying with words."

"But—"

"Look," she holds up a hand. "I agree that unsolicited opinions, especially negative ones, about one's family are not polite and should be tempered or reserved for extreme situations."

"Right. It's the idea I can say what I want about them; they're my family, but I'll defend them to the death to outsiders."

"I'm going to ask you to consider whether he's really an outsider, given how much y'all have been hanging out. It's nice that he noticed you were upset. Maybe he felt the situation was extreme enough to defend you when you wouldn't, seeing as they've been pushier since your dad's injury." She quirks her brows before continuing, "What was he wrong about?"

I stare at her for a minute before answering, "He made me sound like I'm weak. That I'd buckle and go back to the ranch and bury myself there even though I hate it."

Christina nods, her mouth scrunched. In the softest voice possible, she says, "Until today, until this very last conversation with your mother, isn't that what you've been telling all of us?"

I frown. "Are you saying you agree with him?"

She reaches for my hand and holds my gaze. "I'm seeing things from both sides here. I guess I'm saying that I can understand where he might have gotten that idea. Literally from things you've said to all of us."

"He tells me all the time that I'm smart. Why wouldn't he trust me to be smart enough to do what's right?"

"Whether it's because you're such a kind person or because your family has put this guilt on you, we all worry that you'll do what you think is 'right' rather than what is 'right for you.' This is your life, not theirs. You didn't ask to be born on a ranch, and you didn't ask them for college tuition. They chose the ranch over the city.

You're not telling them they have to move back to the city to be your family. Why should it work the other way?"

Whoa. This took a turn. Instead of referencing Mattie, it's become "we"—she's including herself and others. I feel ganged up on, like this is an intervention, when I haven't done anything wrong. "Who is we?"

"What?" she asks, then waves a hand. "Oh, the girls, Cam."

"You all feel this way? But no one has ever said anything to me." I'm crying in earnest now. It's one thing to be the ugly duckling of the group, the eternal wingman who will talk to the hot guy's friend, and the project manager everyone looks to for organizing group activities. But they're talking about me behind my back, criticizing me and my family.

"Hold on a minute. It's not like we were discussing this without you. They feel this way from comments or looks when we've all been together. But aside from a few suggestions we've given you, we've sat back and tried to be supportive because you kept signing a new lease, taking a new job, things that kept you here, where you've told us you want to be. If you came back after Christmas and told me you suddenly saw it all in a new light and fell in love with ranching, we'd support you going home. But this has always been a bone of contention between you and your parents. You're twenty-five. At some point, you have to make your own decision and not let them dictate your life."

I understand what she's saying, but I can't handle it all right now. Now, I understand how Mattie feels. They all think I'm stupid for giving my family this much control over me. "I gotta go."

"Nic, no, please wait. I'm sorry if I upset you." Christina reaches for me, but I grab my purse and run back around the big house to where I left my car in the drive—mere hours ago, but it feels like my whole world has been flipped.

Cam is parking his car as I reach mine. I've beeped the car open, but I can't find the damned door handle through my tears.

He pulls me in for the hug I rejected before and holds me for a long moment while I wet a spot on his dress shirt and sob. Leading me around the car to the passenger side, he opens the door. "I'll drive you home and rideshare back here. Give me your keys."

"What? No. I just need a minute."

"Take ten. I'm not letting you drive like this." He's an immovable object holding the passenger door.

The ride home is silent, as is the walk to my apartment, where he unlocks the door before handing me my keys and hugging me again.

"Thanks." The word comes out muffled against his still-damp shirt. "Tell Chris you give good hugs."

"One would hope she already thinks that," his voice rumbles in my ear.

"Mmph," is the only laugh I can muster. Normally, I'd tell her myself, but I'm not sure when I'll be ready to talk to her again. Or anyone.

Chapter Thirty-Two

Mathieu

Trying to shrug off Nicole's reaction—I was defending her for fuck's sake—I hang with Jack and Scottie. With them, I need to stand and nod, and the conversation will flow around me either between those two jaw waggers or with bunnies they pull in.

Women come and go, Jack objectifying them in both directions while Scottie nods. At least he's drinking less these days; maybe that is why he's quiet tonight.

When Scottie takes orders for the bar and trots off to refresh drinks, Jack elbows me. "What's up? You're gonna scare the women off with that mug."

I attempt to relax my jaw and forehead. "Nothing. Sorry."

"Doesn't look like nothing. But it better not be Nicole."

I lose my shit. I turn on him, although I keep my voice low so I don't overshare with the people around us. "Why the fuck not? Cuz I'm not good enough for her? Cuz the graduate student deserves better than the hockey goon? She's the one who said she wanted to keep it casual. And oh by the way, she seems to have less of a clue about what she wants to be when she grows up than I do."

"Whoa," Jack's brows are at his hairline, and he

brings his hands up.

I glare at him.

"Does Mattie need a wittle pat on the back?" he says in a baby tone, then returns to his regular voice. "There is no reason to mess with the friend pool. Look around you, asshole, you have your pick. Hotter than Nicole, too."

I growl at him. "Shut your fucking mouth."

His hands are still up facing me. Now, he circles his wrists and brings both middle fingers up, laughing like the hyena he is. Apparently, that comment was a test, and I failed. Or passed. My brain is so muddled, and Jack is such a pain in the ass, I can't tell.

"Fuck you more. I'm outta here." I stomp off.

Lying in bed, I pull up my text thread with Nicole. My last text hangs there, wishing her sweet dreams. She doesn't say things like that to me. It's because she told me she's trying not to catch feelings. But damn, it would be nice to have someone offering happy dreams, being in my corner when I'm in my feelings.

I don't know how to deal with this family situation because my own is so different. My parents would never guilt-trip me like that, about anything. Even if I were playing OHL or ECHL hockey, barely scraping by and having to have part-time jobs or seasonal gigs to pay the rent on some shitty apartment, they'd say they were proud I was following my passion. Although, spoiled brat that I am, I'm not sure it would be my passion under those circumstances. I don't like to work that hard for things.

Until Nicole. Damn, that girl makes me work. And I like the challenge most of the time. But this thing with her parents bugs me. Family shouldn't be like that.

It's...dysfonctionnelle. I don't know the word in English—I've never needed to learn it.

Jack was poking the bear, but he's right. I need to hook up with someone else and keep moving forward. But will that upset the delicate balance of my friendship with Nicole?

Eh, I've probably already done that. So why am I lying here alone instead of getting my groove on? And nope, gonna have to tell Emil that one sounds weird.

Or maybe Cam was right. If I don't mind the work Nicole makes me do, then perhaps it's time to do my best at a relationship. She said she'd teach me her words.

Gah. I roll over and punch the pillow and hope for sleep.

* * * *

Despite not having practice until the afternoon, I'm up early the next morning, only having slept for an hour here and there. I sip espresso and stare at my text screen again.

Me

> Hey. Sorry I upset you with my terrible analogy.

Delete, delete, delete. I'm avoiding the real issue.

Me

> Hey. Sorry I upset you. Of course you should do what you think is best.

Silence. No three dots, nothing. Once again, ghosted. Nicole is the only woman to do so. Sure, women have occasionally not answered my booty calls, but I didn't care. This sucks.

I check my phone before I leave it in my locker for practice. After, I stare at it as I ride the bike in the gym for forty-five minutes.

When a text chimes as we're wrapping up, I jolt and nearly fall off the bike. Scrambling, I open it.

Jack

> Figured I'd give you something to stare at so you don't burn a hole in your phone <rolling laughing emoji>

My head snaps up. I'm ready to go to the mats. Enough is enough. Unfortunately, I catch the back of him ducking out of the gym toward the locker room. My phone chimes again.

TEAM
Jack

> Anyone up for wings?

How he eats the junk he does and remains as fast as he is remains a mystery. But wings with a bunch of annoying team members sounds like a great distraction right now.

Me

I'm in.

Jack

Sucker for punishment, huh?
Phones aren't allowed at the
table, Mattie.

Me

<middle finger emoji>

What can I say? Hockey players, especially Jack, have a warped way of showing we care. If only someone could explain that to Nicole.

Before I walk into the wings place, I text her again.

Me

Hope school is going well. Let me know if you're coming to another game soon. Or if you want me to find another cool restaurant for us.

I hit send and cringe. Was that too much? Do I sound desperate and needy? Or maybe I don't care if I'm willing to give a relationship a shot. It's starting to feel like I figured that out too late, though.

At dinner, Gauthier is complaining about how much work his new girlfriend is. Saint is with us, and Gauthier looks at him. "Is it worth it?"

Saint replies, "If she's your person, you'll know without asking others."

I swear we're going to have to rename him Yoda. He always finds a complicated way not to answer a question.

Cam's answer is almost as bad. "It's like the NHL. Nothing worth having is easy."

Except hockey *is* easy for me. Sure, we don't win every time, but I love all those hours practicing and playing. I revel in keeping my body in the best shape to beat our opponents, in strategizing with my line and reading the guys we're up against.

Women, on the other hand, are challenging. Or rather, caring about people is. My mother's health scare, Annabelle's future, and my dad's age all worry me, particularly because they are so often too stubborn to accept help. If my dad would at least let other people do household repairs when they happen, ideally on my dime, I'd worry less, but that hasn't happened yet.

Now, I worry about Nicole, too. Whether she'll be satisfied with her grades, get enough sleep, eat between work and school, and of course, whether her family will add to all her stress. The fact that I included her with my family as people I care deeply about reinforces how badly I've fucked this whole thing up.

Jack chimes in. "I don't know why you'd want to work that hard when you can have any girl you want."

Cam rolls his eyes at his roommate. This is a debate we've all heard before. "Some of us want more than a warm body."

"I have you losers for 'companionship.'"

"Don't you want kids?" Gauthier asks.

"Not in the foreseeable future. I'll think about that when I'm done playing hockey."

That's how I've always felt, too. In fact, I'd said as much when my parents asked me when I was going to settle down and give them grandchildren. Even now, I can't picture it, but I find myself wondering if Nicole wants children, given her family.

It's weird to see Saint's and Cam's points when I'd always been on Jack's side of the conversation.

After the plates are cleared and guys are finishing their beers, I'm talking to Gauthier about a play I screwed up in our last game. There's movement on my other side, then a tap on my arm. Cam has pulled up a chair next to me at the end of the table.

He jumps in with, "What the fuck, man?"

"Excuse you?" I reply with a frown.

"You don't get to pass judgment on other people's families just cuz yours is perfect."

"I wasn't… Well, okay, maybe I was a little, but fuck, she's still thinking about going home after her MBA, when she hates the place. If she was doing that because she felt like it was the right thing without a guilt trip, I could maybe stay quiet. But her family's influence is hanging over her."

"Don't you think I know that? Don't you think her girlfriends see that, too? Fuck, Christina tried to talk it over with her after your fuck up, and she got upset with Christina, and now, she's gone radio silent with all of them."

"What did Christina say to her that hurt her?"

"Oh no. You don't get to blame Dancer for this mess that you started. It doesn't matter. That will be resolved between them. And I have no doubt it will be. They've known her a long time, and she knows they have her back, just not always in the way she thinks they will."

That makes me wonder if Christina's thoughts were maybe along a similar line to mine. I was trying to have Nicole's back.

"Either fix this or stay away, Mattie. But if you fix it, you better be clear on what you want from her. You can't keep doing this on again off again thing. It messes with Nicole's head. She's not Maria or Lauren, who change men as easily as you've always changed women."

"I've already apologized."

He snorts a laugh. "By text? Cuz I know you haven't talked to her. If she's not returning Chris's calls, she's definitely not returning yours. All I know is, I better not have to drive her home again because she's crying so hard she can't drive."

My eyes widen. Merde. How do I fix this? Because challenge or no, staying away is not an option.

* * * *

So much for wings and hockey jokesters being a distraction.

I drive home still dazed from my conversation with Cam and my determination to mend the tear in my friendship with Nicole, rather than walk away.

Other women haven't held any appeal in months. I memorized Nicole's class schedule without trying. And I miss her even on the road when I wouldn't be enjoying that hot pixie body.

I gulp. I hate the word, have always hated the word, and can't believe it, but I want to try a *relationship*. I tilt my head, letting that idea roll around in there. I mean, it has a lot of space to do so.

It doesn't put a pit in my stomach or make my lip curl or send a shudder through me, which are my normal reactions—sometimes all at once. Instead, it kind of sounds as though it's the right label, the right step.

But how do I convince her to take a risk on me. She's been worried all along about being hurt; she's not going to want to move forward with someone who's admitted he's a bad bet.

I wander my place, staring at the couch where I got the best head ever. The *Marketing for Dummies* book that put me to sleep every time I attempted to get past the first chapter. My bed where my good girl was naughtier than I ever dreamed.

I flip on the closet light and step inside to toss my clothes in the hamper, and my movement rustles a dry-cleaning bag. I turn. In the back corner at the end of the rod, nestled against the wall, hot pink flashes.

The dress Nicole drooled over that I bought in Vegas on a whim. Our on-off casual fling and her warnings had me on alert for giving her the wrong impression, and I'd put it away and forgotten about it. But now…now it could be the perfect tool to show thoughtfulness, even if timeliness is missing. To get her to take a leap of faith.

I need my sister's help. I'm not smart enough to solve this alone.

It's late, so I wait until morning to text her. When she says she's not in class for another hour, I call.

"Bonjour, ma soeur."

"Oh non. Je suis Anna when you're calling to chat. I'm your sister when you need something," she says with a sigh.

"You wound me," I respond, fighting a laugh.

"What's up? I should have known since we texted a few days ago to catch up. You must need a woman's perspective."

"Actually, before I say anything more, I have to

ask—"

"Of course I won't say anything to Maman et Papa. I know better. *Especially* if it's about a woman. Mon dieu, they'd be booking a church for you, never mind flights."

"Oui. Anna, I think—" I'm still wrapping my head around the idea, so I need a breath before I say it out loud. "I might be interested in dating someone exclusively."

"Aw. Look at my big brother, all grown up."

"Maybe. Hopefully. But how do I go about it? I kind of fucked up."

She sighs. "Of course you did. You're a man. Tell Anna and I'll see if I can help."

I give her the highlights of the past few months, along with the argument.

"You need a grand gesture. An apology, but with more. But you said 'might.' You need to be sure you want this before you go all in."

"Duh. Even the dumb jock knows that much. I was easing my way into saying it out loud."

"Stop that. We hate it when you call yourself dumb."

"Facts are facts."

"And your opinion stinks like the asshole you are. Stop it." I can pretty much hear her eye roll, so I subside. She continues, "I can't design a grand gesture for you. I don't know her well enough. And it has to be genuine, from your heart, not from me or a book or anywhere else."

"You won't help me? Come on," I whine. "S'il te plaît."

"I'll go one step further. This is what I will say— you're smart enough to figure this out on your own Mattie, especially if you want to be with her enough. Stop thinking of yourself as dumb. See yourself like I do—a wonderful man who cares as much as he's carefree. You'll do great."

Fuck. I might have to call her Yoda as well.

There's no way I'm asking the guys. Most of them would be too busy laughing at the fallen player, and Cam would lecture me again about hurting Nicole. I guess I'm doing this on my own, a sure recipe for disaster.

Chapter Thirty-Three

Nicole

After Christina jumped on the pick-on-Nicole's-family bandwagon, I needed time to regroup. The past two days have been accomplished on autopilot. Sleep, eat, work, school, repeat.

I've shut down thinking about anything outside of that and set the focus feature on my phone, so I don't get notifications except during lunch when I'm surrounded by coworkers and not able to do more than read or delete.

On the third day, the receptionist calls my desk to tell me I received flowers. I walk out to get them, my heart beating double time in my chest. Mattie wouldn't send me flowers, would he? That would send a message he wouldn't want. But a seed of excitement has been planted and is flowering in the short time it takes me to get to the front desk.

I open the card and read, "I'm sorry. I love you. I support you. ~Christina." My shoulders drop, although I manage to school my expression.

The receptionist notices anyway. "Too many flowers, not enough apology?" she guesses.

"Nah. It's a really nice apology." *Just not from the person I wanted.* "Thank you." I heft the vase and carry it back to my cubicle.

Of course they're from her, she's so thoughtful and

along with me, the most traditional of us. I have no business being disappointed the gesture wasn't from Mattie. We're over, lame text apology or not. We weren't going to be anything more than a hookup anyway. Turning my thoughts to my friends, all of whom have reached out, I bring up a group text.

Nope. I'm not ready to deal with all of them right now. I thumb that down and send a thank you to Christina only, asking for one more day to think about it all.

Christina

> But I'm forgiven? <hands pleading emoji>

Me

> Yes. I know you have my best interests at heart.

The next evening, I go to her brother's house to watch the game and catch up. The Tornadoes are on a short two-game road trip, and until the playoffs, it's always hit or miss whether we'll get them on regular cable channels. She and Greg have some hockey subscription so they can stream any game they want.

I get there early, and we order pizza, which is my favorite cheat food. She's made a delicious salad with chickpeas and all sorts of veggies on it, so we get a small sausage and mushroom with the understanding that we'll eat as much salad as pizza and have leftovers.

Chris pours us generous glasses of wine, some Argentinian Malbec, and sits next to me on the couch.

She jumps in. "I'm sorry."

"You said that. And I forgave you."

"I thought it worth saying again in person. But thank you. I've agonized for a while over whether to say anything. Your new outlook this year emboldened me. But I want to support you in making your own choices, not direct you like your parents."

I wince, and she catches it. Sighing at herself, she says, "Poor choice of words. I'll try to do better. Anyway, if I was going to say anything it should have been couched more gently and shouldn't have been dumped on you after Mattie's verbal diarrhea on the subject."

"I concur. But it did force me to look at things, hearing similar feedback from two different sources."

"Oh?" She keeps her tone neutral but is fishing.

"That's why I asked for the extra day. I wanted to see if I could sort through the mess."

"And?"

I shake my head side to side. "And I wish I could say it's clear. I'm still unable to figure out where I'm comfortable drawing the line between what's right for my family, what's right for me because I love my family, and the guilt."

She nods, considering all this. "I think— Wait. Do you want to hear my thoughts?"

I chuckle and nod. "Yes. You really are forgiven. I would love help from someone who's known me for longer than a few months."

She lets that slide and says with a shrug, "I was going to say that it's a good start that you see a need for a line at all."

"Ha! You're probably right. And isn't that

depressing."

"Here's the thing. I agree with Mattie—sorry—that you should decide what's right for you. As an adult, that is the definition of what's right. Your parents got to decide that. I—all the girls—will support you no matter what path you choose. On the flip side, you're twenty-five. An adult yes, but young enough that your choice doesn't have to be carved in stone. Try one direction and if you don't like it, try a different one. I hope—" She takes a deep breath. "—that you'll only try one that you think there is a chance of happiness with."

"That was a whole lot of words that didn't help me get to a decision," I say with a grin, so she knows I'm kidding.

"Yeah, well, I would love to make the decision for you, but I can't."

"Obvs. Damn."

"Maybe use your parents as an example? What did they do when they had a similar decision, if they did. Or what would they do in your place? They seem pretty focused on their own world. Start from that place and see where it leads you."

I nod. "Okay, thanks. I'll try that. At the very least, it'll be a new angle, rather than circling the same thoughts over and over."

"So…" she hedges, giving me the side eye, "…about Mattie."

"Nope. Not talking about him. That's a whole other ball of yarn to untangle."

I get an eye roll for that. "Okay, Grandma. Hockey?"

"Hockey."

* * * *

The next day, I get up early. I can either talk to my

oldest brother after his workday or before, and I'm relying on wine in the evenings to smooth out my thoughts before bed. Given the length of his workday on the ranch, I should do this in the morning.

I dial.

"Hey, city slicker. How are things in the corporate world?"

"Hi Corey. They're going okay, thanks."

"Let me guess why you're calling. Mom's been annoying you with requests for your presence, either temporary or permanent, giving you a guilt trip about Dad's leg."

"Hey, they're not the only reason I call you."

"Um, I beg to differ. You and I usually text about how we're doing or hockey or whatever."

He has a point. Dammit. "I'm sorry?"

"Nah. Texting works for me, or I'd have told you. But I agree, this subject warrants a discussion."

Oh no. He's going to ask me to come home as well.

"How is Dad, really?"

"Eh. He's in his fifties. Even light duty on a ranch does not allow a leg muscle to heal the way it should at that age. I'm trying to hire someone, but he won't stay down."

I'm afraid to reply. My dad's bad behavior is what's causing his recovery to be slow.

Corey continues, "River and I have asked them to allow us to take over management and have them step back. We suggested they pick and choose what work they do and maybe take a vacation. But they're so damned stubborn, and neither wants to leave the ranch."

I groan in frustration. Their universe is so small. I'm glad it works for their happiness, but it makes their world view rather myopic.

He snorts at my reaction and says, "Yeah, I'll see you a moan and raise you a pounding headache trying to bring them into this century. Do you have any idea how long I tried to convince them to take your recommendation on solar windmills?"

I catch my breath. "You did? How did you know about it?"

"I happened to see the paperwork on Dad's desk. Because of course he prints everything out to read it. I didn't tell you because I wasn't successful."

"It would have helped me to know that I wasn't completely unheard," I say. "I feel like the odd one out most of the time."

"What? Why haven't we talked about this before? I always assumed you felt relieved you'd gotten away to forge your own trail. You made it obvious you didn't love ranch work."

That's a good question. "We haven't talked about it because even on holidays, the ranch requires you to be focused there, and I knew Mom and Dad were going to give you a hard time if we sat around talking. And like you said, they were the decision-makers, so I was too busy trying to convince them of things to save them time and money. I'm sorry for not including you more."

"And I'm sorry for not doing more to show you that River and I are on your side. We'd love to hear more ideas when they come to you. Or maybe as that fancy degree teaches them. How's that going, by the way?"

"It's hard work, but I'm passing everything, at least."

He grunts. "Pretty sure that means A's and B's like it did back here."

I smile. Yeah, but that's not what's important in this

conversation. "Did you see any of my other suggestions?"

"There were others? Oh my god, you're going to make me spend time at my desk, aren't you?"

"Yep. I'll email them to you. Hey, you said you were gunning for a leadership role. That's what happens," I retort with a laugh.

"Yeah, yeah, but then I'd be able to hire someone to replace me as a ranch hand. Anyway, please send them over. I'll look at them as I can, and I may have some questions. I probably heard this phrase from you, sis, but I want to work smarter, not harder. I'll take all the help I can get, even if it's all the way from Austin."

"You say that like it's the other side of the world. You and River should come check out how the other half live one weekend. I'd love to have you. And now's the time to get away before you're running the whole shebang."

"I'll think about it. I do miss you. But I also understand why you don't come back all that often. In the meantime, ignore Mom when she pushes. Better yet, let her know we talked and tell her I said you're not needed. Maybe this whole 'who runs what' will boil up sooner rather than later."

"Really? Thanks, Corey. That means a lot."

"Hey, what are big brothers for? Just because I like working out here with my hands doesn't mean I'm not willing to use my brain."

If only Mattie recognized that in himself.

But I'm not thinking about him right now. I'm focusing on me and my future, and that just became a whole lot clearer thanks to my brother's support.

Chapter Thirty-Four

Mathieu

I still have no idea what I'm doing. I've thought of and discarded and re-contemplated dozens of scenarios. I've reread every text exchange we had. Ugh, I really need to avoid messing up in the future if she is willing to give this relationship a try because grand gestures are *hard*.

I'm about to Google "grand gesture" again, despite the pages and pages of smutty books it spat out at me last time, when my phone dings.

Cam

> Coffee?

Me

> Any place, any time.

He offers to come to my neighborhood, since he'd have to drive halfway to me just to get out of the swanky area where the Donovan estate is located.

After we grab our choice of caffeinated but low-fat drink, we sit in a corner, angled away from the other patrons for anonymity.

I ask, "What's up, man?"

"I wanted to say thank you. Nicole approved your boudoir photo shoot idea and added your second alternative of a show, with a short list of a couple specific events she thought Christina would like. I'm going with the show, just debating whether I do it as a group thing and make it dinner and a show as a birthday party, or the two of us."

I nod, unsure why it's such a big decision. Oh, wait. "Nicole said something about this setting the stage for future birthdays, another first impression. You can always do something splashy later but maybe keep it romantic and between the two of you. And anyway, you don't want to start with an idea you can't top."

He's staring at me, mouth open.

"What?"

"You said that without a drop of sarcasm or snark. Are you okay?"

"Har har. So sue me for listening to a smart person."

"It's more than that. You're finally starting to understand the give and take of relationships," he says with a chuckle.

I look away and don't answer.

"Man, I'm going to keep that boudoir photo shoot idea in my back pocket though. Dancer remembers her competition weight, and I swear she has no idea what a smoke show she is with the curves she has now."

That's it! Thanks to Cam, my grand gesture plan is fully formed. I stand and gulp down the thankfully lukewarm remnants of my coffee. "Sorry, man, I gotta go."

"Uh, was it something I said?" he asks, staring up at me.

"Sort of. I'll explain later. Sorry," I repeat before bolting out of there.

I run around between practices that day and the next until I have my multi-step plan in place. It's designed to wear my pixie down, so she'll accept my apology; I hope it works before the end of the week because my parents are flying down for a game. I want to introduce them, so she has a little time to get comfortable with them before the summer. That way, when I go home for a visit, she'll be more comfortable joining me.

Tabarnak. Who am I? This feels like an out-of-body experience and yet so right. Jack teases Cam all the time about being whipped. Hell, I did, too. But I get it now. Nicole's not demanding these things. I *want* to do them.

Well, she's not expecting anything and doesn't want anything from me right now, but I hope this plan will change that.

I text Annabelle my plan.

She responds, "Good luck."

WTF, Anna. You couldn't give me a hint as to whether that will work or not? But it's not worth arguing with her.

My family will love Nicole. I have no doubt Maman worried I'd knock up some bunny and have to marry her—or worse, not marry her and continue with my fuck boy ways. Even if they guessed at who I'd marry, it wouldn't be someone as smart as Nicole, with an education and a job similar to theirs.

I can't think about that, though, or I'll spiral and give up. Nicole has no reason to settle for a dumb jock— sorry, Anna. She can do so much better. But I want her, so I'm going full offense. No dekes, no passes, I'm heading straight for the goal. Her goaltender has nothing on me.

Okay, that's starting to get sexual. Never mind.

Chapter Thirty-Five

Nicole

I hate Mondays. Most of my weekends are spent juggling errands, housecleaning—occasionally—laundry, and homework. Hockey games are a nice addition, particularly when I can watch them at home so I can study during the intermissions. But I'm never rested and ready for the week like everyone else probably is.

Suck it up, buttercup. It's better than ranch work, which doesn't give weekends or Sundays off. Fuck, even my usual Monday morning pep talk is sounding tired.

After lunch, I get summoned to the front again by the receptionist, who is giggling. There's a box this time, wrapped in pink, with a small card in an envelope. I open it.

#1

That's it. No signature, nothing. I open the box. There's a six pack of grapefruit seltzer and a martini glass wrapped in bubble wrap. I frown. This screams "Mattie," but why would he send me a random gift? And not sign the card. Don't players want credit for gracing a girl with their affections?

The receptionist is staring. "Still not enough apology?"

I smirk. I can't resist. "No, I think this is an apology from a second source."

Her eyebrows shoot up to her hairline. "Damn, people everywhere pissing you off, huh?"

"Pretty much. But hey, silver lining—presents." I shrug and grab the box and the card to lug to my desk. I'm going to have to deal with her interest again if I'm not mistaken, given the fact that he numbered this gift.

Sure enough, the next day, the receptionist calls again about a half hour before lunch. "Delivery. Smells delicious. If you need help, my lunch can sit in the fridge for a day."

There's a cauliflower crust pizza from Chasers waiting for me. I look at my watch. I'm surprised their pizza oven was up to temp by this time unless Mattie called in a favor. Renee does have a soft spot for him, like so many of us do. Scrawled on the inside of the box is a big number two in Sharpie.

If the grapefruit seltzer represented our first hookup on New Year's Eve, this refers to his demand for the second round after the mid-January game. Assuming I'm right, Vegas was the third time we fell into bed together under the guise of a one-night stand.

Sure enough, the next day brings a number three note with a bottle of hand lotion. It's the brand he smoothed into my back in the hotel room in lieu of après-sun cream.

This has been a fantastic game, but I still don't understand what he wants. Okay, he probably wants me to thank him. He's had things too easy with women though, and I'm no longer interested in being his bed warmer, even if I've mostly forgiven him for what he said about my family. So I'm hesitant to open up communications again, despite this fun.

Our fourth date—

No, Nic, not a date.

Our fourth hookup was at his place when I experienced the best oral sex of my life, both giving and getting. I'm almost scared to think of what he's going to send to mark that.

The next day, I can barely concentrate on my meetings, writing things down rather than trying to update them directly in the project plan in case I screw it up. As the hours tick by, I'm more and more antsy, getting up to get water every half hour because I can't sit still.

It's four o'clock when my line rings from reception. I'm half out of the cubicle when I remember I should answer the phone first.

I'm out front, and there's a box a bit bigger than a shirt box with a gift bow. I open the card and am surprised at the number of words.

I considered throat lozenges with very fond memories, but I thought you'd enjoy this more instead. I'd love to take you somewhere in it. #4.

I snort. Our memories of that next night align.

Being the girl I am, I heft the box and shake it gently. It's pretty light, and the only sound is a rustle. Apparel? Maybe a backless top since he likes them on me so much.

I untie the bow and ease open the box. Drawing back the tissue paper covering the item, I gasp when magenta and purple flowers are revealed.

No! He didn't! Holy hell. How did he find that after this long? How did he know what size? And fuck, I remember the four digit price tag. Maybe it's not the same dress but a knockoff. But when I open the box further and spread the tissue fully open, it's the exact dress I fell in love with in Vegas. The designer label mocks me from inside the back seam.

Tears well. It's not the money. It's the fact that he saw how much I liked it and understood I couldn't or wouldn't get it for myself. These—all the gifts, not just this one—are not the actions of a fuck boy. He's said all along he doesn't do relationships, so I'm more confused than ever as I stare at this gorgeous piece of wearable art. Fuck, I wish he was open to relationships. He cares so much and so openly. Calendars I can manage. Protecting my heart if he loses interest, I cannot.

Staring at the gorgeousness in my hands, I realize my heart is no longer mine to safeguard. All my hard work has been for nothing. No, not nothing. Everything, if these gifts mean what I think they do. Either way, I've fallen in love with this tender, supportive, self-deprecating man.

The receptionist has been watching every move, but when I tear up, she stands. "Hon, you okay? Do I need to send this back where it came somehow?"

"No!" I clasp the half-open box to me clumsily. "Oh my God. I can't— He didn't— Oh my god."

She sits slowly. "Ah. Those are happy tears. Phew."

"Maybe more confused tears, but can you do me a favor and tell my boss I had to leave an hour early please? I need to deal with this. I'm going to grab my purse and sneak out if that's okay?"

"Absolutely. I'll tell him you were in a meeting last I saw you," she says with a wink.

"Thanks." I tuck the box flaps closed and pat it.

"Don't let this out of your sight. I'll be right back."

I snag my purse and phone, retrieve the box, and get to my car. I debate calling him from here. But I can't remember if he has a game tonight or not. Me! The calendar expert.

Even if he doesn't, no one calls unsolicited anymore. I settle for texting, then I'll drive home with my phone on DND, so I won't be tempted to look for replies until I'm no longer navigating the roads.

Me

> OMG.
>
> Mattie.
>
> What did you do? How?

> Thank you for all the gifts.
> They're all very cute. Today's,
> though...<mind blown emoji>

I drive home on autopilot, debating whether to call Christina. She'll encourage me to give him a chance, which I'm already prepared to do. Lauren and Maria, I'm not so sure about, though. Really, the only person who can solve this with me is Mattie.

I pull into my parking spot and can't wait to get upstairs to turn my phone off DND. And there it is.

Mattie

> You're welcome. I'm glad you liked them. Can we talk? I have a reservation (the other half of #4) if you want to do it over dinner, but I can come to you or you can come here if you'd prefer.

I'm dying to see what restaurant he found and would love to put this dress on again, even if it's a bit much for dinner out in such a casual town. But if our conversation takes a wrong direction, my beautiful dress might be forever ruined for me. Besides, I don't like to cry in public. Not taking the time to change, I pull up a rideshare app before texting back.

Me

> I'll come to your place.

* * * *

Mattie greets me with a glass of wine. He's in a dress shirt and flat-front trousers again, I suppose in case I took him up on the reservation.

"Am I going to need alcohol for this conversation?"

"Hopefully not, but I know your work and school schedule, possibly better than I know my own. I figured you might like a glass," he says as he walks away, and holy shit the rear view is as distracting as the front. I probably shouldn't drink wine until after we talk, so I maintain some semblance of focus.

There's a lowball glass with whisky sitting on the coffee table, the ice block in it still solid. He sits next to it on the table with his knees bracketing mine, so he can face me on the couch.

After a moment to enjoy the feeling of being surrounded by Mattie, I start. "Thank you again for the gifts. I don't know how you found that dress again or knew my size, but ohmigod, Mattie. I probably should say it's too much, too expensive a gift, but I can't bring myself to care. I'm keeping it."

He chuckles. "Good. I couldn't return it now anyway. I bought it as soon as you walked away from the shop while we were still in Vegas."

I blink. "You did? Back then? And kept it? Why wait and give it to me now?"

"Yeah. I still can't tell you exactly why, other than the look in your eyes when you stared at it in the window. I wanted you to have something you craved that much."

"Remind me to look at a Lambo that way."

"Ha. I didn't know how to give it to you without sending mixed signals. We kept talking about keeping things casual, and I know that gift isn't casual."

"Why now?" I repeat.

He reaches for my hand, then retracts it as though worried I don't want his touch. How wrong he is.

"Because it sends exactly the message I want to send now."

I frown. "Forgive me for being dense, but I'm going to need you to spell it out for me."

He wipes his hands on his pants without breaking our gaze. "I want you to figure out how to share your calendar with me so I can see it on my phone. To set reminders for me to actually look at it. I want my number on your back at games. Most of all, I want you. Your sense of humor, your hot pixie body, your huge brain. All of it. I'm not your type. You could do better. And you'll have to explain words and other things to me a lot, but please. I want to try."

I stare at him, at a loss for words. My nose pricks with threatened tears. He said everything I want to hear, except an apology for being so harsh about my family. Fuck, I want him so bad. Last year, I would have left it there, letting the rest go, but I need to be strong for once, rather than the ragdoll I've always been with men.

Grabbing my wine glass, I gulp some. "Before I consider that, we need to talk about the last conversation we had."

He hangs his head. "Yeah. About that."

I ask, "What would our relationship look like if I decided to move home after school?"

His gaze shoots to me, and he blinks twice.

"I see Mr. I Don't Plan didn't think about that."

He flushes. "You're right. I didn't. Because I hope you won't. But I want to be with you, regardless. I want time to show you how good it could be. If you decide to be a rancher, we'll figure it out. Maybe we summer out there. Maybe you give me a few extra years of hockey and we retire there." He shrugs. "I'm willing to see it and try it."

"Says the ultimate city boy. You wouldn't last a day," I scoff with a giggle.

"Hey, people change. Case in point, I never thought about a relationship until I met the right person. I'm here, saying I'm willing to try. What about you?"

"That conversation can't happen again." I won't let him off that easily. "You don't get to tell me what the right path is for me, careerwise or familywise. You need to respect my career as I respect yours. And you can't disrespect my family like that."

He leans in and, braver now, takes my free hand in both of his. "I know. I'm sorry I hurt you. I was already falling for you, which was overwhelming and confusing, I was on a high from the game, and I was hungry. I stand by my opinion and my feelings of protectiveness for you, but it came out horribly wrong, and I apologize. And I do recognize that the decision has to be yours."

I nod. "Thank you."

He straightens. "Now what?"

It's my turn. He's been honest with me, and I need to do the same. Taking a deep breath, I lay out my fears. "I'm super afraid of being hurt. You're...you. Larger than life, hotter than hell, funny, flirty, caring. You could have anyone. I worry you'll get bored with me."

He reaches behind him for a gift bag I hadn't noticed on the corner of the low table. "Gift number five addresses that. You still don't see yourself as I see you, mon petit chou. You are the hottest pixie around, and if I could keep you in backless tops for the rest of our lives, I would. Sadly, the rink is too cold for that."

I snort a laugh.

"I meant what I said. Je veux tout. I want the whole package. But the physical is indeed part of that, and you are smokin' hot, as well as gorgeous. This is to help you see that."

I toss the wad of tissue paper aside and look in the bag. Lingerie—a lace underwear set in lavender. My lips twist. Seems like a gift for him, to try to make a silk purse out of a sow's ear.

"Keep digging." Damn, he sounds nervous.

An emerald-green negligee with only a few straps across a very lowcut back. I put that aside with the bra and panties and the tissue paper. A nightshirt like the ones I like to sleep in—cotton, with a cartoon sheep on it and the phrase "Good night, sheep tight." I snort and put it on the pile.

The next item, seemingly the last, is a Tornadoes jersey. Not game weight, it will still sit at hip length on me and has clearly been tailored to nip in at my waist. I flip it. Sure enough, there is his name and number. The idea of wearing his name in public or in private warms my insides—my heart as much as my sex. I hope this means what I want it to mean, even if he's not ready to say it.

"There's one more thing in there," he murmurs.

There's an envelope at the bottom. Drawing it out, I open it, and the assortment of apparel makes sense. It's a gift card to a boudoir photo shoot.

"I promise, you don't have to show me a thing if you don't want." His words are rushed. "This is all for you, so you can see how sexy you are. Christina helped me with sizes, but of course, if you don't like them or they're the wrong color, they can be returned."

My hand holding the card drops to my lap. How does this man believe he's the least bit stupid? He came up with an entire week's worth of gifts tailored to me, he remembered details of all our times together even though it was supposed to be casual, and now, he wants to bolster my self-confidence.

"Mattie, I—" But I'm too choked up to continue. Instead, I gesture with grabby hands for him to come hug me.

When I'm in his arms, practically on his lap, I

manage, "This, all this, all week, are the most thoughtful gifts anyone has given me."

"Really?" he asks from above where my face is buried in his neck.

I can't tell if he's eager for the praise or appalled, but it doesn't matter. "Really. Just don't tell the girls that, please."

His body shakes under me in silent laughter. He pulls back so he can look me in the eyes. "Pixie, does this mean you'll give me a chance?"

"You promise to talk to me if my calendaring gets too much for you? And to try to be on time to things? And to give me space regarding my family?"

"I do."

The gravity of those two words is not lost on me. I raise my head from his shoulder and swipe at my tears to stare at him.

From his solemn expression, his word choice appears to be deliberate.

"Then I do, too," I say with a nod.

His mouth hits mine almost before I finish the last word.

Chapter Thirty-Six

Mathieu

Dieu merci. Elle a dit oui. She said yes.

Now, I want to show her how much I worship her. These days without her have been miserable. I never want to experience that again.

Nicole's eyelids flutter open when I draw back from my attack on her lips. She takes a second to focus, looking as dazed as I am from the emotion behind that kiss.

She's wearing a silky strappy tank top over fitted capris, so I cup her butt and warn her to hold on as I lift her.

Her legs wrap around me where I wish I could wear them forever, and I carry her to the bedroom. Tossing her onto the bed, I shove up her top and lick her nipple before gently running my five o'clock shadow over it.

She arches and grabs my hair, clutching me to her.

I suck while my hands scrabble for a button or zipper on her waistband. There's none, and I draw back, confused.

She snickers and tugs on the waist, showing me they're elastic, then without waiting for me, she shoves them down to her hips.

"Ah." I drag them the rest of the way off. In only lacy panties and her top shoved up around her armpits, she's so hot my bed might ignite. "Take the top off so I don't rip anything, s'il te plaît?"

She flings it aside, and I stand between her knees at the edge of the bed and take her in.

"Fair's fair. You're wearing way too much clothing," she says, staring right back.

I strip in record time, then place one knee on the bed and lean in to kiss her again. I need all of her tonight, not just her body.

"You are"—after a long, lingering lip lock, I punctuate my words with kisses down her neck—"gorgeous, hot as fuck, and cute all at the same time. How do you do that?"

She giggles, but the sound cuts off when I suck her nipple into my mouth and lave it with my tongue.

Her hands roam my shoulders and back. It's my best feature, and her delight in me turns me on more. Sliding back, I nip at her belly before kneeling on the floor. My breath washes over her pussy as I say, "This is mine now. Exclusive, unfettered access."

She moans and opens her legs wider.

"Good girl."

Her thigh muscles clench in reaction to her favorite phrase. I soothe them with my hands before closing the gap to lick her, exploring her nooks and crannies with my tongue and nose.

She squirms and breathes, "Mattie, please."

"What do you need, good girl?"

"You."

"You've got me, for as long as you'll have me."

"I want you in me. Now. Please."

I shake my head, enjoying the brush of her soft inner thighs against my cheeks. "Sorry, no can do. Not done worshipping."

She grabs my hair. She doesn't tug or push. It's as though she needs to hold it for stability.

I return to my exploration, sucking her nub into my mouth and flicking it fast with my tongue.

"Oh!" Now, she's holding me to her.

Maybe I can give her so many orgasms she won't leave me for someone smarter.

As though I conjured it, she shudders, her clit quivering between my lips and her pussy soaking my face. Prying her clenched fingers out of my hair carefully, I rise over her and bring us to ecstasy again before collapsing next to her.

* * * *

Nicole snuggles into my side. A beat later, her head pops up. "Oh, I need to tell you something else about my family."

I narrow my gaze. "Is this a test?"

"No, I mean it."

"Merde, I nearly forgot. I need to talk to you about my family, too," I say, shaking my head at my calendar-challenged brain. My stomach rumbles under her hand. "How about I order us some food and we talk over dinner?"

"Yes, please."

With takeout from a Mediterranean salad place I frequent often, we sit at the kitchen bar. I drag my barstool around to the end of it, so we can talk without getting cricks in our necks. "Okay, you first."

Nicole nods eagerly. "You'll like my news."

When she relays the call with her brother, I pause in hoovering food into me. "Damn, Nicole. That's awesome. Did you send him your other ideas?" At her nod, I continue. "Would hockey tickets help get them to come visit you?"

"Maybe. But I'd rather they make that decision without a bribe." She straightens on her stool. "I should be enough."

"Aw, Pixie." I reach out and grab her hand that doesn't have a fork in it. "You're right. And you are. I didn't mean to imply you're not. Tell me how I can support you."

Look at me, trying hard to be a good boyfriend when I haven't earned that title yet.

She smiles. "Thank you. I will. And we'd love hockey tickets if and when they do come if it's during the season. So, tell me about your family."

I swallow hard. I hope she's not going to freak out at the short lead time. Reminding myself that this is a girl who wants a relationship and all the things that come with it, I say, "My family is flying in for tomorrow's game, and I got you a ticket for the box with them. I'd like you to meet them."

Her eyes widen. "Tomorrow?"

I nod. "Yeah, they follow all my games and know tomorrow is important. If we win, we not only are in the playoffs for sure, we will end up first or second in our division. So they picked this one. They'll love you. I've already told them a bit about you. How smart you are. How you don't let me get away with tardiness."

"Oh man. That's scary. I'm not sure whether I'm relieved I don't have more time to freak out or stressed because I have to figure out what to wear, do, say."

"Let's go with relieved. I like that one. And"—I smirk—"may I suggest something backless?"

She hits me with her napkin. "No! That rink is cold,

among other things!"

"Okay, okay. How about that?" I lean my head to where the tiny DU PRES jersey is thrown over the back of the couch.

Holding my breath, I wait for her answer. She's only forgiven me, and now, I'm pressuring her to meet my parents. If it doesn't happen now, I'll live. But damn, I crave seeing my name across her shoulders.

She glances over and bites her lip, sliding me a sideways look. "The lilac lingerie? Yeah, I could wear that."

Too busy managing my disappointment, I don't follow that she's teasing me.

She laughs and adds, "It'll go perfectly under that jersey."

My breath gusts out in a whoosh, then catches again. Because if the pixie's going to layer those items, I won't get my cup on, much less be able to play in it. Holy hell, that image is hot.

"Send me a picture? S'il te plaît? But *after* the game."

Leaning in, she kisses me on the corner of my mouth. "I'll wear your jersey and meet your parents. Maybe they can give me tips on how to keep you in line."

I groan. This might not have been my best idea.

Chapter Thirty-Seven

Nicole

I wake feeling invigorated. I stood my ground, and Mattie not only apologized but wants to try a relatio— Holy shit, I'm meeting his parents tonight.

My eyes fly open, and I throw my legs over the side of the bed in one motion. Whoa, wait, this isn't my room.

Looking over my shoulder, the other side of *Mattie's* bed is empty. Oh my. I spent the night. In fact, I distinctly remember him spooning me and whispering, "Stay."

Checking the clock, I calculate. I don't have any meetings for the first hour of my day, so I have time to run back to my place and get changed.

There is a note under my phone on the bedside table, telling me he went to the gym and practice and my ticket will come to my phone after that.

I wander out to the living room and see the jersey still hanging on the couch. Grabbing it, I head to the bathroom, throw it on, and take a picture over my shoulder. Flipping it so the name reads right, I send it to the group thread.

Me

Look who turned from a hookup into a boyfriend—his choice, no less.

Maria

Phew. Cuz you were failing at the casual thing, girl.

Christina

Don't listen to them. Monogamy is lovely, as he has now discovered. Congrats!

Lauren

Congrats

Maria

Good luck <rolling laughing emoji> Oh, I mean congrats.

Me

Thank you - even you, Maria.
But he's moving fast - I meet his parents and sister tonight.
They're flying in for the game.

Lauren

Well, at least you don't need to worry about what to wear. Although, I'd recommend pants with that look.

Maria

> <rolling laughing emoji> No,
> really, then—GOOD LUCK!

I close that thread and pull up Christina's name. She gave Mattie instructions on lingerie labels and sizes and that is some seriously sweet underwear.

Me

> Thank you.

Christina

> Happy to help. Glad it worked
> out. Come down and find me
> in Cam's seats if you need an
> escape.

As I hit the sleep button on my phone, it buzzes.

Mattie

> Assuming you have work
> today, but just in case, my
> parents have a key to my
> place and will arrive there
> around noon.

Me

> Ah, thanks. I do have work, but
> I'll be sure to make the bed and
> tidy up.

Mattie

> You don't need to do that. Ma
> maman will probably
> rearrange half my apartment
> no matter how tidy it is. It's
> her thing.

I start to ask if they're staying here and if he needs me to do anything—make up a bed, put out towels, grocery shop. Then I remember, I don't need to do that shit like I did with past boyfriends. He likes me without that. Hell, he liked me enough early on to buy that crazy expensive dress. I'm still not over that.

I review what Mattie has told me about his parents and sister. It's all been positive, but there must be some reason he's still insecure about his lack of education.

Yesterday was all about me, his apology to me and showing his commitment to trying this thing. But it won't work unless we both see ourselves and each other as equal partners.

Maybe his family can shed some light on this issue. The question is how or when I could raise the subject with them. On the other hand, we have to talk about something during the intermission, and better the subject be him than me since I still don't know what I want to be when I've grown up.

* * * *

I arrive early to the box, hoping to beat his family and get my bearings. Okay, and salivate over Mattie stretching at the start of warm-ups.

But when I walk in, there are three du Près jerseys in

various sizes by the bar keeping an eye on the ice as they chat.

Sucking in a breath for courage, I stroll over with fake confidence. *They speak English, don't they?* My steps falter. Shit, I should have asked Mattie that. But no, he would have told me if they didn't, and I'm quite sure Anna does.

They turn as I approach, smiling when they see his number on the front of my shirt.

"Mr. and Mrs. du Près?" I ask.

"You must be Nicole," his mother practically coos. Her French accent makes me "Neecol," which I love.

"It's so nice to meet you." I offer my hand, but Mrs. du Près tugs me in for a hug.

"C'est magnifique to meet you. Mattie has told us very little about you. You must sit next to me during the game."

Mr. du Près gently disengages his wife's arms from me and gets his own hug in, keeping it brief. He leans in and pseudo-whispers, "Don't worry, she'll be completely focused on the game in no time. Just escape for the intermissions."

I snort a laugh, my shoulders dropping an inch.

Turning to Annabelle, I don't bother with a hand out, I lean in for a hug. Turning to face them all, I smile and say, "Mattie talks about you so highly, I was kind of expecting you all to have angel wings."

"Ha!" His mother laughs.

Anna shrugs. "I left mine at home. Didn't want to show him up."

Her dad elbows her. "You can't show him up when he's playing first line for an NHL team, even if you deserved wings, which you do not."

Huh. So they are proud of him. That makes me more confused as to why he's so down on himself.

We chat during the break before the game, with them asking me about work and school, and me asking them the same—work for his parents and school for his sister.

Once the puck drops, we're all in the stadium seating at the front of the box, leaning forward to watch every blade swish and every stick slap.

During a timeout after Cam makes a glove catch near the end of the first period, I get up to use the private restroom. When I come out, Annabelle is lingering near the bar with a fresh drink in her hands, something clear and fizzy with a lime in it. She's watching the game on one of the hanging TVs, but when I emerge, she gestures me over.

"Hey, I wanted to warn you. Mattie has never wanted us to meet a woman before. He talked a bit about you when he was home for that one afternoon, apparently, but claimed you were just friends according to my dad. But Maman was sure there was more to it." She shrugs. "Mother's intuition, I guess. Plus, Mattie is way less sly than he thinks he is."

I snicker. "True."

"Anyway, Maman may come on strong. She says she's past ready for grandchildren, but the world is different than when they married and neither Mattie nor I are ready to entertain that yet. Just let it roll over you if you can. We'll be gone in another day, and you'll be safe for a while. Mattie can take the heat in phone calls."

"Thank you. I appreciate the heads up. What about your future—not kids, of course, but what do you plan to do after university?"

"Ah, the question they hound me about. Mattie's

older so he gets more of the settling down stuff. I get the career pressure.”

“Oh? I got the impression they were thrilled at you attending uni, and happy with whatever you chose for your future.”

“Where’d you hear that? All I hear is ‘Mattie knew what he wanted to do from age seven on. Mattie is already hugely successful in his career.’ Will you be able to say that in four years? Etc. Etc. It’s like he can do no wrong.” She rolls her eyes, but she’s smiling.

I stare, solemn.

“What?” she asks.

“Ah…I don’t want to speak out of turn, and you should talk to Mattie about this, but he tells me that they talk about how proud they are of you and how excited they are for your future *after university*, to him. In fact, he seems to have a bit of a complex about it.”

“Huh. Is that where his silly ‘dumb jock’ comments come from? Damn, they annoy all of us.”

“Yeah, me too. I don’t know if that’s where it started, but they do seem to be linked. Maybe you two need to get on the same page, and maybe ask your parents to rethink their method of encouragement?” I gasp, realizing I’ve criticized their parents within an hour of meeting all of them. “I’m sorry. I don’t know what I’m talking about, obviously. I’ve only just met you all.”

Annabelle smiles. “Actually, I agree. And I love that you’re protective of him.”

I flush, not sure what to say. Before I can figure it out, the elder du Près join us for intermission. Checking the score on the jumbotron, I breathe a sigh of relief that it’s still the same. I didn’t miss anything. That would have been a bad first impression as Mattie’s girlfriend.

"What are you two discussing?" Mrs. du Près asks.

"My lack of clarity on what I want to be when I grow up," I jump in, throwing myself under the bus to protect Anna.

Anna's eyes go round.

Mrs. du Près responds, "Ah, a common problem around here, non? But you have time. And until Mattie secures a multi-year contract, you don't know where you'll be next year anyway."

Mr. du Près tsks at his wife. "Sweetheart, stop pushing. They've only been dating for a short while."

I add, "I will be here next year. I can't change programs halfway through an MBA, at least to a similarly competitive school. But after that, assuming Mattie and I are together, I'm open."

Annabelle mouths, *"Now you've done it."*

"You'll be together. My son would never have insisted we meet you and flown us down to do so if he wasn't in love with you and planning your future together." She ignores my gasp. "Which means I'll be hoping for grandbabies. Peut-être he can get traded to an Eastern Canadian team to be closer to us."

Annabelle rolls her eyes and grimaces at me from behind her mother's shoulder.

My smile is serene. I suspected he felt as I did and simply didn't recognize it, but having his mother confirm it reassures me. I'll worry about the future later, especially after I talk to my brothers again. Right now, I'm just glad I may have helped Mattie feel more confident.

Chapter Thirty-Eight

Mathieu

We score in the second period, then Cam misses one at the start of the third. The whole team doubles down and skates our asses off, scoring again with two minutes left. We're tense as they pull their goalie. But they can't get it done; we want it too damned bad.

I'm on the bench as the final seconds count down, and when the buzzer sounds with a 2-1 win for us, we all pile over onto the ice to group hug. We've secured our playoff berth in our first year!

The whole team has more energy than we know what to do with when we should be exhausted after a tough game and a long season.

In the dressing room, Champagne bottles are already popping, and the guys are spraying each other down. Saylet could barely get Saint to talk to the media for a few questions.

As someone shakes a bottle and aims at him just inside the door, Greg steps in behind him.

His however-many-thousand-dollar suit is immediately doused. We quiet for a second, and someone behind me mutters, "Oops."

He laughs, unable to stop grinning, practically vibrating with excitement.

The room gets louder again, but he holds up a finger,

asking for a moment of our time.

"For the past three years, I've dreamed of the Stanley Cup, coveted the feel of it under my fingers, my lips. I told myself it wouldn't happen this year; a team hasn't won the Cup in their first year in the League since 1918. And it still may not. I get that. But I am here to tell you that I picked every last one of you based on that dream. And every single player here tonight has far exceeded my expectations. I could not be prouder. Congratulations! Drinks are on me tonight! Uh…if it's okay with Coach Steele?" he looks sheepishly over.

Coach shakes his head. "Yeah, fine. But I'll be watching you—Landry, that means you especially. And don't overdo it. But take tomorrow off, and I'll see you Sunday morning at the flight."

Jack yells out his standard response. "Let's fucking goooo!"

Greg gestures, and more Champagne is brought in. He plucks at his suit and calls, "I'll meet you at Chasers. I'll be the stinky wino."

I change in record time, manage to dodge most of the fizz, and get to the family lounge to find my family and girlfriend. Sighing with happiness, I see them all together chatting away. Thankfully, Maman did not manage to run off Nicole.

Christina checks in with Nicole and shakes my family's hands, then turns to me and hugs me. "Congratulations, Mattie! You all played great out there."

"Thanks, Chris. You coming to Chaser's? Apparently, your brother is buying." I raise my brows, knowing I'm outing him to his financier, but that she'll be all in, especially now that she's with Cam.

"Excellent. Then I am absolutely coming. I wonder what Renee's wine menu looks like," she muses with a wink.

* * * *

We only stay for one drink. Turns out my family booked hotel rooms once they heard I was inviting Nicole to the game. I'd say it was considerate, but Maman's hope for grandbabies makes itself known in far too many ways. I roll my eyes at her antics but slide my gaze to Nicole.

The next morning, Nicole and I have to swing by her place to grab fresh clothes for her before heading to my parents' hotel for breakfast with them.

After we've ordered, Annabelle jumps in. "Mattie, I've never told you this, but Maman et Papa used you as encouragement for me to find a career and pursue it. They mention how proud they are that you identified your passion early, pursued it relentlessly, and now are already at the highest level."

I blink and put my coffee spoon down. Where is this coming from?

My gaze slides to Nicole as Anna talks, and she looks equally taken aback at first, but her expression smooths to…satisfaction? Maman and Papa look as surprised as I feel, so the girls must have gotten up to something last night.

I'll play along. "You didn't. Did you know that they can't say enough to me about how proud they are that you're in university and are finishing higher education?"

Maman is looking decidedly guilty right now. We turn to her. "Am I not supposed to be proud of my children?"

Anna speaks up. "Of course, you are. Mais, Maman,

perhaps it would make more sense for you to tell us how proud you are of us directly. This feels like a bit of playing us against one another."

"Oh no! I would never!" Maman looks truly upset at the idea.

Papa, however, is nodding. "I have mentioned that you take it a bit far, ma chérie. Oui, your intentions are good, but maybe we try another tact from here on out."

Maman looks at each of us, her mouth in a regretful grimace. "I worry with Mathieu so far away that he doesn't see your accomplishments, Anna."

"We text at least a couple of times every week, Maman," I say, not waiting for Anna. "But it was hard to keep hearing about her doing so well in school when I will never be smart enough to attend university."

"Non! Ce n'est pas vrai, mon bébé. You are plenty smart, just in different ways, as we always tell you. And after you needed that tutor for math in high school, we knew you weren't suited for college. You were destined for bigger things, in a field you excel in."

I gape.

She frowns and tilts her head.

Finally, I find my voice. "You knew about that tutor?"

"Mais, oui. Of course. The school notified us."

"Why didn't you say anything? I tried to hide it from you because I was so ashamed, realizing I wouldn't make it through university when I knew that's what you wanted." I reach sideways under the table and clutch Nicole's hand. All these years, feeling like I had let them down, knowing I'd lied to them and acted like I never wanted to attend uni. They'd known the whole time; indeed, they'd been fine with it.

"We assumed you didn't want to talk about it. You acted like it didn't matter, that you were happy to talk to the scouts for the AHL. As were we. You had found your calling. Look at you now. We couldn't be prouder."

Nicole squeezes my hand in happiness. It's all I can do not to tear up.

Anna is watching silently, clearly pleased with herself for putting all this in motion. I narrow my eyes at her, and she sticks out her tongue, and everything is right in the world again.

Maman's next words come slowly. "Wait, is this why you so often call yourself a dumb jock? Because you thought we were disappointed in you?"

Papa pats her arm on the table as he observes us.

She rallies. "We tell you all the time how proud we are of you."

I shrug one shoulder. "Yeah, but you spend more time talking about Anna and her studies."

"Because—" she cuts herself off, shaking her head. "It doesn't matter. Mon dieu, je suis désolée. I am so sorry, mon bébé. Please, say something sooner next time. But either way, never, ever call yourself stupide encore, s'il te plaît."

She comes around the table and leans in to hug me. "Merci, Maman."

Papa nods, Nicole sniffles, and Anna smirks and takes a sip of her mimosa.

For the rest of the meal, I keep glancing at Nicole, overwhelmed by what my pixie did for me to show me that others see me as she does—a success, someone who is worthy of her. The realization opens my eyes to endless possibilities. I'm not just ready to try a relationship. I'm ready for forever with this smart, thoughtful woman.

* * * *

Cam took my advice and kept the show tickets for the two of them. But Greg had other ideas for his sister's birthday and invited the Tornadoes' organization as well as her friend circle.

Cam grumbled to me about it, but I saw Greg's issue. If he invited some of the team she's closest to through Cam, it looks unfair. I suspect Greg also saw it as an excuse to celebrate our playoff berth. We're still fighting for home ice advantage and will be for a couple of weeks, but we've all been hyped this week. Coach had to threaten us with a bag skate to get rid of some excess energy.

So here we are, back at the Donovan mansion. March in Austin means temperatures could be in the fifties or eighties but mostly are somewhere in between. So while we're poolside, we're not cannonballing into the water like we were at Thanksgiving, and there aren't kids. This one is employees only.

Even better, they forbade gifts. We're here to party. Nicole and the girls will give her their gifts at a girls' night out, and Cam gave her his gift in private. I'm off the hook. Which is excellent because I may have used all my creative energy on my grand gesture to Nicole. A little time to replenish the well before another event—or fuckup—is appreciated.

Jack pulls me aside after we stuffed our faces from the build-your-own-taco bar—Christina's request.

"Mattie, Mattie, Mattie," he says, shaking his head sadly. "Please tell me this is not what I think it is. Tell me I'm not down a wingman."

I snort. "Sorry. Can't tell you that."

"Dude, what are you thinking? Nicole's a lovely girl, don't get me wrong, but you're *twenty-six*. The world is your oyster."

"Don't 'dude' me. Twenty-six isn't that young. I mean, it's more than a third of the way through my career as a player. I've been playing full time for eight years, which means I've had plenty of time to—how do you say it?—sow my oats."

"Hmph."

"Trust me. When I started hanging with Christina's girl gang, I was all about staying single and partying my way through the NHL with you. Nicole is special. She is the yin to my yang. I honestly don't feel like I'm missing anything being with her. You'll see one day."

"I hope not, or at least for a decade. There are too many beautiful women out there for me to pick only one."

I smile. He'll learn one day. "Want another beer?"

"I'm good for now, thanks."

As I turn to leave, Lauren says behind me, "They're falling like flies, aren't they?"

Jack answers, "Yeah. But I'm not worried. It's not contagious."

"Not like what you likely have," Lauren parries.

I snort. Jack's man-whorish ways are well known by everyone, it seems.

Greg clinks his glass with a knife and calls us in for cake.

During a raucous rendition of "Happy Birthday," I notice Scottie swaying, and not in time with the song. Dammit. Is that guy already drunk? We have an early practice tomorrow.

I catch Buzz's eye and gesture with a tip of my head

before starting over to deal with Scottie.

Buzz waves me off, saying, "Go hang with your girl. I've got this."

Chapter Thirty-Nine

Nicole

There were no gifts allowed at the party, but Cam must have given Christina his already, because she comes over and thanks us for our help.

"It was all Cam," I say politely.

Christina slants me a disbelieving look but doesn't pursue it.

As she walks away, Mattie turns to me, looking unusually serious. He lowers his gaze before meeting my eyes. "I get it now, you know."

"Get what?" I have no idea where he's going with this.

"His concern over getting the perfect gift for the woman he loves. We've established that I suck at this, but I'll always try my best for you—gifts and otherwise, mon petit chou."

Is he—does he—? He used the word "love" but not directly about me.

He gulps a swallow and continues, "So when I mess up, please remember I love you more than anything or anyone in the world."

My mouth goes dry. *Ohmygodohmygodohmygod. Mattie du Près loves me.*

But unlike my astonishment when he was first in my

bedroom, it's not about the hot hockey player. It's about the man he is and the one he tries to be. For me.

"Mattie…" I need to pause so I don't start bawling.

He reaches for my hand and squeezes it.

Inhaling a long breath, I say, "First, I am so glad to hear that, because I am completely, deeply in love with you, too. Second, you've already established your superior gift-giving skills, so no need to worry on that count. All of them were wonderful, not only the dress. But third, how dare you almost make me cry in public?"

I frown at him with a mock pout, but they're ruined by the tears that have escaped and are trickling down my face.

"Oh, good girl, I'm sorry. I couldn't wait any longer. Here, come outside for a minute." He leads me through the French doors to the pool patio, drags me off to one side. Wiping my tears off my cheeks, he pulls me close and lays one of his signature hotter-than-hell kisses on me.

My insides liquify, and I cling to his muscled shoulders.

He raises his head. and with his signature panty-melting grin, says, "You're the only one I want to net, pucks, and chill with. Ever."

Epilogue

Nicole

After I gave Mattie context on Anna's comments at the breakfast table, telling him about our conversation at the game, he was quiet. It will take him some time to adjust to this new understanding of his parents' knowledge and motivation. But I'm confident that he'll begin seeing himself as an equal partner.

In the meantime, I guess I have to work on myself in that regard.

I book the boudoir shoot, debating whether I tell Mattie about it or not. In the end, I do. It's not a game day, and he gets a pass from the coach to leave practice an hour early to drive me there. Hopefully, he didn't give specifics on why. He says he has a reservation at another new place for us, for after.

The photographer introduces herself as Kim. She's super chill and tries to put me at ease, walking me through the various rooms she has set up for the shoot. There's a chaise longue—I thought only Christina and old English manor homes had those—a king size bed with plain white sheets, and a longer comfy-looking couch.

She reviews the clothes I brought, fingering the jersey and snorting at the nightshirt as I tell her why Mattie gave me the various pieces.

"This is all great," she says. "I say we start with the jersey. That's for him, and that idea is top of mind for you right now. It'll give you time to loosen up and decide what *you* want. And we'll do the nightshirt near the end because it's playful, and I am almost sure you'll be in a fun mood by then."

Damn. She read me like an open book. I'm glad Mattie paid attention to reviews from women when he chose her.

We start with the jersey, a thong underneath. I kneel up on the bed, facing away from the camera and looking back at it, with the neckline hanging off that shoulder. It feels sexy but stilted. Then again, six months ago, I'd never have dared any of this. The new me is getting braver by the minute.

Next, I lay on my stomach facing the camera at the foot of the bed, feet in the air and crossed, the neckline gaping over my non-existent cleavage. We follow that with a couple more typical magazine-style poses.

When she shows me the images, I'm surprised at how good she made me look. *No, Mattie would be annoyed at me thinking that.* I'm pleased with how sexy I look. But I have a deer-in-the-headlights expression.

"Okay, we'll come back to the jersey later if you want, but for now, let's swap it out for the strappy satin negligee."

First, I lie on my side on the couch. Then I move to recline on the chaise, one hand slipping just under the hem of lace at my upper thigh. Next, I stand facing a cheval mirror. Kim manages to capture my front and my back without getting herself in the shots.

Mattie will love that one with the strappy lowcut cut showing my back. But as I stare at my reflection, I forget him and focus on the girl in the mirror. I think of a few poses of my own. Running my fingers along the neckline. Slipping a strap off a shoulder, raising the front of it so the dark shadow where my thighs meet my pussy is almost visible. I glance up and discover a playful grin on my face. Damn, this is actually fun.

When Kim says, "Told you," I realize I said that out loud.

Feeling more daring, I change into the barely-there bra and panty set and get on all fours on the bed without being asked. Then she has me sit on the couch, on my toes with my legs wide, my hands planted in front of my pussy, which has the added bonus of pushing my breasts together.

It suddenly doesn't matter if no one ever sees these photos. This experience alone has shown me that I can be sexy. I'll never be overt like some of the model-types Mattie attracts, but I can hold my own. Just like Christina, Maria, and Lauren all have their own unique features that make them stand out and look special, so do I.

It kills me that Mattie could ever think he wasn't as smart as me. I wouldn't have figured this out on my own. And I need to tell him that.

We wrap with me in front of the mirror, the magical designer dress on, but unzipped. I'm holding it to my front admiring it with one hand while the other toys with the zipper beneath my bare back. It's clear I'm not wearing a bra, but unclear whether I'm about to pull the zipper up or have just pulled it down.

Kim helps me zip up so I can leave. Mattie meets me outside, but I have a secret. The rough cut of that particular photo is on my phone.

I wait until we're more than halfway through our meal to show it to him and to tell him I'm not wearing anything under the dress at all.

He doesn't even ask if I want dessert, gobbling the rest of his meal down and gesturing for the check while I laugh.

My leftovers get packaged up because I'm so wound up from the photo shoot and him that I haven't eaten much, but I don't care. I need to unwrap my real gift, Mattie, as soon as possible.

Sneak peek at Book 3

Drew

It's Christina Donovan's birthday. Thankfully, her brother specified no gifts because what do you get your boss's boss's boss, one of the owners of your NHL team, who is a billionaire besides?

As we sing *Happy Birthday*, Mattie catches my eye and nods at a swaying Kyle Scott, a defender in our top six. Dammit. Several of us have noticed his increased drinking recently, but to do it at the owners' place is downright stupid. And we have an early practice tomorrow.

Saint—our captain Gabriel St. John—isn't around. Which has also been happening more recently. So as alternate captain, it's up to me to deal with this. I sidle closer and drag the younger man back a few steps toward a doorway. Giving him a chin nod, I try for casual. "What's up, man?"

"Nothin'." Said in the surliest tone I've ever heard from the guy.

"Got something on your mind?" I ask quietly.

Kyle skids a furtive glance toward Coach Steele and shakes his head.

"I'll get you out of here. Don't worry about Coach seeing you."

He grimaces, then shakes his head again.

I herd him through the doorway and the short hallway into the grand entryway. "I'm concerned about you. You seem"—*frequently drunk*—"unhappy."

"Nah. We're living the high life. Players and playas. Let's fucking go and all that." He waves a hand and nearly falls over.

"Yep. Not everyone could be hanging at a party like this one and making millions to play a game the next night. Speaking of, we have an early skate tomorrow, and I was going to get on the road. Why don't I drop you home on my way?"

"Nah, man. I have my car."

"I'm not sure it's a good idea for you to drive right now."

"I need my car to get to practice," he says with a set jaw and a wobbly arm fold. Great, he's going to be an ornery drunk.

I glance back at the party, afraid to leave him alone for long enough to find someone to drive him and his car home with me following.

On cue, Saylet walks through from the kitchen. She takes us in at a glance. "What do you need?"

Anyone else offering to help would have been preferable. Okay, well maybe not Coach. But no. FML, it had to be Saylet Young.

That tiny, tight package of dark-haired sexiness otherwise known as our PR Director is my biggest weakness. She also runs circles around all of us players, like a Corgi nipping at our ankles keeping us in line.

I sigh, giving in to fate. Peeking behind her to ensure no one else followed her, I summarize the situation. "Kyle and I were heading out. He's not quite in driving shape, but he'll need to get to early practice tomorrow."

"I can drive his car, and you follow?" she asks.

Why Kyle, who we call Scottie, was drunk at an owner's birthday party, I have no idea. Saylet probably won't get that out of him, so I'll ask him when he's sober.

Right now, I have bigger things to worry about, like how to avoid popping wood when she climbs into my car with her unique scent. Whatever it is, shampoo, perfume, or other, it's a lovely mix of sweet and spicy, with a touch of floral. Not that I could name a flower smell other than a rose to save my life. Her, I could pick out of a room of a hundred people blindfolded. Dammit, I'm already fucking hard thinking about it.

When we get to his house, I jump out to help him in. He was irate when we wouldn't let him drive home, but now, he's heading into the weepy drunk stage, and I do not have time for this. I need to get Saylet to her car and then go rub one out. Possibly in my car with her fragrance lingering, since today is the first and last time she'll be in it.

But first, as alternate captain, I have responsibilities. She heads to the kitchen for a glass of water, and I lean against the wall of his bedroom as he pulls his shoes off. He tosses them in the general direction of the closet and drops his head in his hands.

"Sorry, Buzz," he mumbles to the floor.

"It's okay, buddy. I just wish I knew what was wrong, so I could help."

"Nah, you don't." His head shakes side to side once.

"Hey, that's not fair. I said I did, and I meant it. Try me."

"I can't. You don't. Trust me."

I sigh. "Okay. I'll be here when you're ready. Judgment-free zone."

Saylet is back and chimes in, "It better be. If it's not, they'll answer to me."

He flinches.

I sigh again. She means well, but her in-your-face brand of defending her players is not what he needs right now.

"Set your alarm, man. Then make sure you've eaten enough to absorb what you drank so you're not puking on the ice. No one wants that."

He nods and reaches for his phone.

I brace myself, hold my breath, and take Saylet's arm to gently guide her out of the room.

As we reach the living room, I inhale a deep breath as though relieved to have Kyle home, but instead I'm wishing I could roll around in her sugar and spice.

She turns to me. "Perhaps I should stay with him and take a ride share back to my car."

I shake my head. "Would you want anyone beyond a close friend to see you drunk? Worse, to babysit?"

She twists her lips. "I see your point."

"Now imagine being a 'macho'"—I put the word in quotes with a half smile—"hockey player."

"Okay. He's a big boy. And I'm sure it's not the first or the last time he'll be in this state." She throws up her hands and walks toward the door.

I hustle around her to open it for her, twisting the lock behind me. Then I speed walk to beat her to the car and open the passenger door. Mostly, so I can smell her again, but also, my grams raised me right.

Sliding into the driver's seat, I say, "Okay, back to the Donovans'."

"Actually, I rideshared there. Lucky for you, I live on the east side of town like you. Unless you were planning to return to the party for a while?"

"No, I don't know how much longer it went on after we left." But holy hell, now I'm imagining her inviting me in. I shift in my seat, my cock plumping, pressing against the seam of my shorts uncomfortably. I usually reserve puck bunny hookups for road games, preferring to keep the drama to a minimum and out of my hometown, but I might have to bend that rule to release some of this tension. Because there's no way in hell I'm messing around with someone within the Tornadoes organization, particularly someone who has my public image in her hands. And I'm not risking my hockey career for anything beyond a booty call.

"Why was Kyle drunk, at Christina's and Greg's house, no less?" Saylet asks.

The Donovans, along with their other sister Amy, are the owners of our team. They're young, and Christina and Cam Hill, our goalie, are in love, so we spend more time with them than most teams do with their owners. But no one other than Cam should forget that a business relationship exists.

"I was hoping you got that information during the drive to his house," I reply.

"Yeah, no. He went from annoyed muttering to weepy mumbling. But nothing coherent, and he wasn't answering questions." She twists in her seat to face me more. "At least it was a private event, and we got him out of there before any damage was done."

I'd have preferred to handle it without alerting her to the situation, keeping it to the team, but I guess it's better that she's prepared, in case he blows himself up. All signs are leading to that probability. Saint and I will do what we can, as will the whole team, to ensure that doesn't happen, but we can't babysit him.

"All right, I'll see what I can get out of him when he's sober. Right now, your guess is as good as mine."

"Maybe it's sexist, but if he was a woman, I'd guess man troubles."

I tilt my head. "Could be. He's young. For the first half of the season, he was chasing skirts with Jack after every game, but now that I think about it, that hasn't happened for a while."

Saylet's tone is bitter when she says, "Don't you mean letting the bunnies chase him? None of you have to work for it."

I scoff and reply without thinking. "It's not like you do, either. You could have any man you want."

There's a deafening silence in the car. I'm pretty sure neither of us is breathing. When I slide a quick glance to her, she's staring at me with her mouth hanging open, and damn if that doesn't make me think about what I'd like to put in it.

I concentrate hard on parking in a visitor spot for her apartment building.

When I glance back, she's looking forward again and says with a hair toss, "Yeah, well, maybe my standards are high."

With that she is out of the car before I can open her door and racing into the building.

I watch her until she is safely behind the locked front door, cursing my idiot big mouth for making things awkward. Now, I'd feel weird jerking off to thoughts of her, despite sniffing the last whiff of her fragrance.

* * *

Preorder **Spicy as Puck** now for $0.99

Want more hockey romance?
Get Emil Bergstrom's second chance love story when you sign up for my newsletter at
https://bookhip.com/TFJRZCH
Future Texas Tornado books will feature (in no particular order):
Jack
Saint
Greg
Kyle
and others

(tell me which you want next when you sign up for my newsletter!)

Acknowledgements

First, a reiterated heartfelt thanks to my two most valuable resources, Stephen Meserve and Milly Bellegris.

Stephen, I love that we've now moved to sharing Google docs and phone numbers, and I look forward to another season of the Texas Stars with you.

Milly, I don't have the right words to thank you for your fantastic and snarky editing. <wondering – is it bad manners to ask you to edit this? LOL>

Both of you made this book far better than I could have.

Two people who helped with Ottawa details are Lis Angus (author of *Not Your Child*, an edge-of-your-seat thriller set in Ottawa) and Jacqueline Lee (romance writer and reader living in Ottawa).

Milly and Corinne LaBalme (author of the *Paris Ghost Writer Chronicles* series) corrected and/or weighed in on my French. Who knew there were multiple French verbs that equate to "to swallow"!

And Jennifer Britt (author of the *Lincoln Falls* series of small town romances) is the person to thank for the scene in which Mattie screws up and is super late to help Nicole.

Last, but not least, Sharon and Rick Hightower, thank you for spending time thinking of hockey pun titles. You gave me a fantastic, long list of ideas, so I better keep writing!

A lifelong romance reader, I cut my teeth on Johanna Lindsey, Jude Deveraux, and Kathleen Woodiwiss, along with Silhouette and Harlequin for palate cleansers.

Opting for a career that provided both a food and travel budget, I earned a BA, CPA, and MBA, and spent far too long being a corporate drone, then consulting other corporate drones.

Along the way, I was one of the few 1990s NBA season ticket holders never to see Michael Jordan play ('93-'94). I also attended a few NFL games, the Belmont Stakes, the NHL playoffs, the World Series, and managed to see more than twenty MLB parks, several of which have since been demolished. More recently, I've enjoyed the Texas Stars, the AHL affiliate of the Dallas Stars.

I have published a number of spicy Regency romances under the pen name Maggie Sims (www.maggiesims.com), along with hot hockey romances set in Austin as Debbie Charles, where I now live with my husband and a varying number of furbabies.